*"I think you'*

Gwen frowned                                    ace
but her body la                                 as
telling the truth. Her leg, she realized. It was
bobbing and he could see it out of the corner of his
eye.

"Big talk," she said aloud, consciously trying to relax.

Tonight Del wore black jeans and a white shirt,
the sleeves rolled up to his elbows. Little things
impinged on her consciousness: the clean scent of
him, the way his jaw was just a bit dark with a day's
growth of beard.

She remembered how he'd looked with nothing on.

"It looks like you're pretty good," he observed,
nodding at her pile of poker chips and tossing down
the table's ten-dollar minimum. "I didn't expect to
see you here tonight."

Gwen immediately raised him twenty. "I figured I
needed to get warmed up for the tournament," she
explained.

"And here I thought you were pretty hot already...."

# Blaze™

Dear Reader,

I'm a firm believer that you've got to try new things in order to stay fresh, both as a person and (for me) as a writer. Gwen's book marks my first dip into romantic mystery/suspense. I've watched other people do it for a long time and was itching to try my hand at the genre. I'm an avid mystery reader, so building a suspenseful story of my own was a fun challenge—layering in the mystery and suspense while keeping the focus on the emotional development and the trademark Blaze heat took some doing, but in the end I think it worked.

I hope you'll write me at Kristin@kristinhardy.com and tell me how I did, and whether you'd like to see more books of this type from me in future. Look for the story of Gwen's sister Joss coming in August. And don't worry, we haven't forgotten about SEX & THE SUPPER CLUB—look for the stories of Paige, Thea and Delaney to come. To keep track, sign up for my newsletter at www.kristinhardy.com for contests, recipes and updates on my recent and upcoming releases.

Have fun,

*Kristin Hardy*

## Books by Kristin Hardy

HARLEQUIN BLAZE

44—MY SEXIEST MISTAKE
78—SCORING*
86—AS BAD AS CAN BE*
94—SLIPPERY WHEN WET*
148—TURN ME ON**
156—CUTTING LOOSE**
164—NOTHING BUT THE BEST**

*Under the Covers
**Sex & the Supper Club

# KRISTIN HARDY

## CERTIFIED MALE

# HARLEQUIN®

TORONTO • NEW YORK • LONDON
AMSTERDAM • PARIS • SYDNEY • HAMBURG
STOCKHOLM • ATHENS • TOKYO • MILAN • MADRID
PRAGUE • WARSAW • BUDAPEST • AUCKLAND

This book would not have been possible without the generous help
of Tyra Bell-Bloom of the Venetian Resort, David Brandon of Brandon
Galleries, Gini Horn of the American Philatelic Society, Chris Johns
of the Las Vegas Police Department, Bill Welch, retired editor
of the *American Philatelist* magazine, and, of course, Stephen,
the Hardy part of Kristin Hardy. All errors are mine.

ISBN 0-373-79191-7

CERTIFIED MALE

# *Prologue*

GWEN CHASTAIN CHEWED HER LIP and studied her cards. "D'you have any jacks?" she asked, one leg curled up under her on the kitchen chair.

The man across the table from her scratched at his salt-and-pepper hair and frowned. "Well, now, I can't say for sure, here. Is that the one wearing a crown?"

"No, the one wearing a crown is a king."

"Ah." He nodded thoughtfully. "Is it the lady?"

She giggled and swung her free foot back and forth at the knee. "You know a jack's not a lady, Grampa. No fair trying to fool me."

"Well, then, I'd better just say go fish."

Gwen reached for the cards just as the kitchen door opened and her mother swept in wearing a swirl of bright color, her hair covered with a red-and-orange patterned turban. "Gwennie, why aren't you ready? We have to leave for the library now."

Gwen swung her foot harder. "Can I stay here with Grampa instead?" She didn't want to go stand in front of a room full of kids and tell what it was like to live in Africa. She knew she ought to feel lucky to be able to do it, her mother told her all the time. She didn't feel lucky, though. She just felt weird. They always looked at her like a zoo exhibit.

Her big sister Joss bounded into the room. Joss was

nine, a whole year older than Gwen, and never felt weird about anything. Joss loved being the center of attention. She could make even Gwen think living in Africa was a cool thing. But then Gwen would remember that Africa was more than zebras and elephants.

Africa was heat and flies. Africa was longing for the cool blue San Francisco Bay that glittered now outside the window. Africa was driving into a dusty village with her physician parents to be surrounded and stared at, unfamiliar hands plucking at her sun-bleached hair, touching her white skin.

Africa was always being different.

"Let the girl stay with me, Glynnis," her grandfather said. "You're going back too soon as it is. We'll play cards until Mark gets home and then we'll all come meet you at the library."

"Well…"

Gwen knew she ought to change and go with her mother and Joss, but she didn't want to. Sometimes when she and Grampa were alone they'd play poker and drink cola from frosty mugs and he'd let her win all his pocket change. She crossed her fingers.

"Come on, Mom," Joss said, bouncing impatiently.

"All right, she can stay." Glynnis ran a fond hand over Gwen's hair and Gwen felt a surge of warmth swamped by guilt. Then she turned to give her mother a kiss and wished, as she always did, that she could put the bad feelings away. She knew what her parents did in Africa was important. She just wished, oh, she wished as the door closed behind Joss and her mother, that it could be someone else's parents doing it.

The tablecloth was a cheerful blue patterned in dancing teapots. Gwen rubbed one of the spouts. In Mozambique they didn't have kitchen chairs, just stools, and the oiled wood of their low, round table was only covered with a brightly dyed tablecloth on special occasions. Some of the Physicians Without Frontiers workers lived in a special compound, but Gwen's parents liked living out among the people they were there to help. It was a priceless education that they were getting, her mother insisted. It would make them like nobody else.

But Gwen didn't want to be like nobody else. All Gwen had ever wanted was to be ordinary.

# 1

"YOU HAD SEX *WHERE?*" GWEN CHASTAIN stared at her sister, Joss, who leaned nonchalantly against the counter of the stamp shop's kitchenette.

Joss adjusted the strap of her splashy red sundress. It was too provocative for the business of selling rarities, but Gwen knew better than to tell her. "In the elevator of the Hyatt Regency. Loosen up a little bit, Gwen, it's not like we got caught."

"Normal people don't have sex in glass elevators."

Joss rolled her eyes. "If you'd ever stop dating boring men, maybe you'd find out. You need to date a guy who's not afraid to mess you up a little. You need to have sex on elevators, let your hair down a little while you're still able. You act like you're sixty already."

"And you act like you're sixteen. It's a good thing Mom and Dad are in Africa," Gwen muttered, pouring herself a mug of coffee, careful not to splash any on her tidy taupe suit. A faint hint of makeup accentuated her blue eyes, framed by stylishly discreet glasses that made her look older than her twenty-four years.

Joss snorted. "Are you kidding? Honey bunch, your mother's done wilder things than that."

"Way more information than I needed to know," Gwen told her, doctoring her coffee with soy milk.

"Haven't you ever talked with her about when she was young?"

Gwen gave her a queasy look. "This is not a conversation I want to have. I haven't even had breakfast yet."

"Shoot, when Mom and Dad were dating, they—"

Gwen stuck her fingers in her ears. "La-la-la, I can't hear you," she sang out.

"Oh, c'mon, you can't say you've never been curious."

"Not about the sleeping together parts, no. I suppose you asked her all about them."

"Of course." Joss grinned at her and turned to open the little refrigerator. "So how can we be sisters when you get so freaked out about everything that Mom and I do?" she asked as she fished out a can of Coke.

"Are you kidding? Sometimes I wonder if I'm even from the same family." How else could a person who prized normalcy as much as Gwen explain her free-spirit mother happily taking her doctor husband, her young daughters and her six years of medical training into a life in the African bush? Gwen looked at Joss, vivid and curvy, her dark hair tumbling down her back in a gypsy mane, so unlike Gwen's quiet not-quite-brown, not-quite-blond French twist. Joss had turned positively wild after Gwen had moved back to the States at fourteen. Joss had stayed in Africa while Gwen had settled into her grandparents' San Francisco home and a college prep course with a sigh of relief.

And wished her mother's wild streak good riddance. Gwen was all about discreet, down to her understated loveliness that was only apparent to those who looked. Her straight nose tipped just a bit at the end. Her chin was just strong enough to hint at a stubborn streak. Only her mouth spoiled the picture, a little too generous, a little too promising. Dusky pink lipstick accented it only faintly. Anything more, she knew, would only attract attention. It was hardly what she wanted during work hours.

"You just got the Chastain conservative gene," Joss said, cracking open her Coke. "It skips a generation. God knows Daddy didn't get it."

"And you have no idea how that pains Grampa." Gwen turned to leave the kitchen, passing through the door to the main showroom.

"Not nearly as much as it pains him that Daddy married a woman who was raised in a commune." Joss grinned, trailing after her.

"I'm serious, Joss," Gwen protested.

"I know, I know, he wants to leave him the stamp empire." She snorted. "Giving up sunrise on the veld for little squares of colored paper."

"Some of those squares of colored paper are worth half that veld." Gwen punched in the multipart code that deactivated the sophisticated alarm system on the front door; as always, she left the back door armed unless they were using it.

"Okay, so Grampa plays in the big leagues. Dad would still be miserable doing it. Grampa should leave it to you. He's practically handed it over to you already as it is."

"He's not leaving it to anyone." Gwen set her coffee on the top of a crimson-lined display case containing stamp tongs and mounts. "He'll take it apart as soon as he and Grandma get back from their trip. It just takes time." She pulled out her keys and walked to the front door, stooping to undo the floor lock. "He's had some of these clients for decades. You don't break that up overnight." Opening the door, she stepped outside to unlock the sliding steel gates that protected the little storefront. Beyond her, traffic whizzed back and forth on Clement Street in San Francisco's Richmond district.

"Sure you do." Joss took one side of the gates, pushing it back to the wall. "Tell 'em you're going out of business and to find a new advisor. I'm sure Grampa could recommend a bunch of people."

"That's not the point. Some of these guys might just want to get out of investment stamps period if Grampa's retiring. They trust him. He's got a couple of accounts he's liquidating already." Gwen finished tucking her side of the gate back into its hidey-hole and turned to the shop door. Glancing at her slim gold watch, she frowned. "I see Jerry's late again. Nice that he's dependable."

"Oh, lay off Jerry. He's okay," Joss countered, following her back inside.

"Jerry's hot for you. Of course you think he's okay."

Joss rolled her eyes. "Please. Don't tell me you're jealous."

"Of Jerry? Hardly." The truth was, Jerry gave Gwen a faint case of the creeps for no good reason she could name. On the surface he seemed fine, and if he was maybe a little too slick, a little too accommodating, that was her own problem. His references had checked out over the phone. Coins, granted, not stamps, but at least he had experience with fine collectibles. She had a few too many degrees of separation from the dealer in Reno to get a personal verification, but there had been nothing to confirm the small stirring of uneasiness she felt about Jerry. And the truth was, if he hadn't been on board and trained, Gwen couldn't have gone to the estate sale in Chicago two days earlier.

She didn't know where the restlessness had come from. Maybe from watching her grandparents leave for a three-month tour of the South Pacific. Maybe it was just the time of year. She'd had an undeniable urge to get out, stretch her wings. Vying with some of the top dealers in the world to come away with best properties did nicely. "Jerry's just not my type."

"Well, you don't have to love everyone who works for you," Joss threw back.

The original plan had been for Gwen to hire someone to help run the store during her grandparents' long-planned trip. Then Joss had shown up broke and in need of a job. Gwen ought to have been impressed that it had taken almost two weeks before Joss was so bored she'd suggested hiring another clerk. Too bad Gwen had let herself be talked into Jerry.

"I've got no reason to think Jerry isn't fine. I'm just a little uncomfortable around him," she said irritably, punching her code into the cash register to start it booting.

"He's noticed. I think it hurts his feelings the way you hang out in the back room and never talk with him."

"You talk with him just fine. That was the deal, remember? You work the store, I work the investment accounts." And avoid Jerry.

"The front of the store's important, too," Joss reminded her. "We made some money while you were gone. Jerry's good at selling."

"I don't doubt it." Gwen picked up her coffee mug. "Call me if you get a sudden run and need help. I've got to log in the new acquisitions and get them into the safe."

GWEN STUDIED THE TEAL-BLUE stamp through the magnifying glass. Across it a stylized steam train chugged—left to right instead of the right to left as it was supposed to. She checked the perforations and used tongs to turn the stamp so she could study the back. Inspect, confirm, log. This was the part of an acquisition she relished—poking through to get a firsthand look at all the new treasures, finding the hidden surprises.

And in this collection there had been more than a few. She rolled her shoulders to loosen the muscles, then adjusted the headset she wore to keep her hands free during phone calls. For a minute she allowed herself to just sit in the blessed quiet of the back office. She'd always loved the store, from the time she'd begun helping out her grandfather at fourteen. After college it just hadn't seemed right to move on—working the business had engaged her mind fully, and her econ and accounting degrees had made her more valuable to her grandfather than ever.

The place didn't feel the same without him, even though he was only on an extended vacation. "Practice retirement," Hugh Chastain had laughingly labeled his wife's cherished four-month trip to New Zealand, Australia and Polynesia. So what if the process of shutting down the business hadn't proceeded on schedule? There would be time to close things down properly when they returned.

Gwen tried not to mourn it.

Even though she had a nagging sense that she ought to be out fighting her way up thc corporate ladder, she didn't regret a minute of the three years she'd spent since graduation learning the investment ropes, polishing her expertise. Stamps fascinated her—the colors, the sometimes crude art, the shocking jumps in value of some of the rarities. The clients who chose investment philately over, or in addition to, the more traditional stock market were driven by a certain streak of romanticism, she suspected. There was no beauty or history to an online stock account. You couldn't pick up a mutual fund with tongs.

Not that they kept any of the investment accounts in the store, of course. A safe-deposit box was the place for holdings whose values could reach into the hundreds of thousands or even millions.

Or it ought to be, she thought, glancing at the wall safe with her usual twinge of discomfort.

She put her grandfather's stubbornness out of her mind

and resumed the process of inspecting and logging the new collection. The auction catalog had focused on the plums, the Columbian Exposition issues and the 1915 Pan Pacifics. She'd never expected to find a mint block of four early Cayman Islands stamps, and the profit from their sale would more than pay for the trip. She already had plans for the Argentinian and Brazilian issues.

Thoughtfully she set down her stamp tongs and reached for the Scott catalog just as the phone rang. She punched a button and a man's voice greeted her.

"Gwen, how've you been? It's Ray Halliday."

"Hi, Ray." It was amazing how quickly word got around about who was and wasn't at an auction, she reflected. Suddenly people you hardly knew became your best friend.

"Did you go to the Cavanaugh sale?"

He knew the answer to that already or he wouldn't be on the phone to her. "It seemed worth the trip."

"How'd you make out?"

He undoubtedly knew the answer to that, too. "I'm looking it over right now."

"Anything interesting?"

"Maybe." She turned back a page or two and lifted a quartet of stamps from their mount to inspect them. "Don't you have a client who specializes in Caribbean issues?"

"Yeah, why?"

"I've got a nice little block of four early Cayman Islands. Very fine, by the looks of it."

"I didn't see that listed in the catalog."

Gwen grinned. "Pays to actually get out and do some legwork, Ray."

"I suppose this is going to cost me," he grumbled.

"I've got to get something for my time and travel," she said reasonably. "The question is, what's it worth to you?"

The dickering over price didn't take as long as she'd expected. After eleven years in the business, they'd finally realized she was no pushover. Her grandfather had taught her well.

"Anything else I might care about?"

"Just some South American issues that already have a home."

"Stewart Oakes, no doubt," he said sourly.

"Now, Ray, what kind of businesswoman would I be if I told you all my secrets?"

"A wealthier one. I'll pay you more than he will."

"If I need the money, you'll be the first to know."

She was still chuckling as she depressed the button on the phone. Might as well call Stewart while she was thinking of it. She hit a speed-dial number.

"Stewart Oakes."

"You missed out at the Cavanaugh sale."

"Gwennie." The pleasure was warm in his voice. Only her family were allowed to call her by that nickname—her family and the man who'd helped her understand life in the U.S. back in the early days when she'd first arrived from Africa. Stewart Oakes had been her grandfather's employee and protégé, but at thirty-five, he'd also been young enough and hip enough to introduce a shy fourteen-year-old to grunge music, Thai food and a culture she'd been separated from since she'd been a toddler.

"Got some goodies for you, Stewie."

"Always nice to know you're thinking of me."

"Well, you're going to love these."

"I bet."

"Careful, now, I thought you were giving that up."

"Hey, I moved to L.A. and left behind my home poker game, didn't I?"

"And we miss you every week."

"Nice to know I'm appreciated."

"And we miss the money we used to win from you."

"Cheap shot, Chastain."

She laughed and reached for another catalog even as the intercom buzzed. "Hold on a second, Stewart." She pushed the button for the intercom. "What do you need, Joss?"

"I've got too many people out here. Can you come out?"

"Where's Jerry?"

"He still hasn't shown up."

Gwen gave herself a moment to steam. "Okay, I'll be right out." She took Oakes off hold. "Stewart? I've got to run help Joss at the front of the store. Can I call you back?"

"I'll be here."

Gwen gathered the stamp albums together and slipped them into one of her desk drawers, locking it carefully. Even so, it nagged at her a bit that some one hundred thousand dollars in stamps was protected only by a desk lock that any self-respecting toddler could pick. A hundred grand of the most liquid, easily portable wealth known.

In countries with unstable stock markets—or none at all—stamps provided a relatively safe investment. Gold coins were heavy, they took up space. Mounted properly, a stamp worth thousands or tens of thousands of dollars could be slipped into a square of cardboard, tucked into a wallet or the inside pocket of a suit, walked over international borders and converted into cold, hard cash in virtually any major city in the world.

SHE WAS BACK IN HER OFFICE when four o'clock hit. A muted "hallelujah" from the front, followed by the rattle of the steel security gates, told her that Joss was closing up. It had been a good day, all in all, Gwen thought in satisfaction as she stacked up the stamp albums. She'd logged three quarters of the collection, had set aside the cream for important clients and found stamp dealers only too happy to take on the rest. They'd make money out of the deal. It was a small triumph for her.

Joss stuck her head into the room. "The front is all locked up, nice and tight."

Gwen swung back the white board that concealed the wall safe. She inserted her key and spun the dial of the combination lock. "First thing tomorrow I'm firing Jerry," she told Joss. "Then I'm going to put an ad in the help-wanted section." The dial moved smoothly under her fingers.

"You can't just fire someone out of the blue, can you?" Joss asked. As the day had gone on, her defense of Jerry had ebbed. "Can't he take it to the employment board? What if something came up?"

"And what, he couldn't even call? Joss, he's been late to one degree or another for seventeen of the twenty days he's worked for us."

Joss raised her eyebrows. "You kept track?"

"Of course I kept track. I'm an employer, that's what you have to do. If he wants to protest, I can show cause." Gwen spun the dial to its final position and opened the door.

And stared in alarm.

# 2

"DID YOU OPEN THE SAFE WHILE I was gone?" Gwen's voice sounded unnaturally loud in her ears.

"No." Joss crowded up behind her to look at the stack of stamp albums in the safe. "What are you talking about?"

"The books have been moved. I always put them in the same way every time. Joss, you swear you haven't touched anything?"

"Cross my heart."

*Stay calm,* Gwen ordered herself. Maybe she'd been careless the last time she'd unlocked the safe door. Maybe she hadn't put things back the usual way. In her gut, though, she knew.

Someone had been in the safe.

She spilled the albums onto the desk, opened them with shaking fingers. There was no point in bothering with the blue books that held the store inventory or the green book that held some of her own acquisitions. They didn't matter. Not now. She focused solely on the burgundy albums that held her grandfather's collection—the books that held his treasures, his pride and joy, bits of his childhood.

The books that held his retirement.

Holding her breath, she opened one and flipped through to the back, made herself look.

And her mouth went dry as dust. "They're gone."

"What's gone?"

Gwen battled the wave of nausea that threatened to swamp her. "Grampa's best stamps. The Blue Mauritius. The one-penny Mauritius. The British Guiana one-cent. And maybe more." *Definitely more,* the voice of certainty whispered to her. She'd seen at least two other blank spots as she'd flipped through.

Gwen squeezed her eyes tight shut and then opened them to stare at the empty squares. Why had her grandfather insisted on keeping his collection close at hand instead of safely in a bank vault? She knew his reasons, knew the joy he got from regularly looking at his holdings, but they didn't outweigh the risk.

And now her worst fears had come to pass.

Joss stared at her. "Those were his big stamps, right? My god, what are we talking about—forty, fifty thousand?"

"Not even close." Gwen's lips felt stiff and cold. "The last Blue Mauritius auctioned went for nearly a million dollars."

HALF AN HOUR LATER, GWEN stretched to ease the iron pincers of tension. She'd gone through every one of the books meticulously, recording what was missing.

It was worse than she'd imagined.

The four most important issues of her grandfather's collection were gone: four nearly unique single stamps and one block of twenty, in aggregate worth some four and a half million dollars. The inventory books were missing another thirty to forty thousand dollars in more common, lower-value issues.

"Grampa has other investments, right? This is just a part of what he's got." Joss didn't ask but stated it a little desperately, as though saying it would make it so.

Gwen shook her head. "He says he trusts his judgment when it comes to stamps, that he doesn't know anything else as well."

"This is it? This is all he has for retirement?"

"Had," Gwen said aridly. "There's maybe a million left at this point."

Joss spun and reached for the phone. "I'm calling the cops."

"No!" Gwen's tone of command was so absolute, it stopped her dead. "That's the one thing we absolutely can't do right now."

"What are you talking about? There's millions of dollars in property missing. We've got to do something."

"But not that," Gwen emphasized.

"Why not?" Joss glared at her, inches away.

"All an investment dealer like Grampa has is his reputation. He's still got about twenty-five live accounts right now waiting to be closed out, some of them with millions in holdings. And every one of them has a clause in their contract that if he sells their stamps below current catalog price, he'll have to make up the difference."

"So?"

"So, if they hear about the theft and decide they don't trust him anymore, they may want out immediately. If he has to sell in a rush instead of at the right time, and if buyers know he's hurting, he'll definitely have to sell below catalog." Gwen swallowed. "And there goes the other million."

Gone. All gone. It made her shiver. They were his pride and joy, part of what made the philately business vibrant to him. The loss was unimaginable.

She leafed through one of the store inventory albums, staring at the empty squares. A fifteen-cent stamp showing Columbus's landing, worth maybe three thousand dollars. An 1847 Benjamin Franklin stamp worth six. Why bother, she wondered suddenly. The store inventory stamps were chump change compared to the major issues. Gwen chewed on the inside of her lip. Then again, the important stamps would be difficult to unload immediately; there would be questions. The inventory stamps would provide a thief with money in the meantime.

A thief who knew how the world of fine collectibles worked.

"Jerry," Gwen said aloud.

"Jerry?"

"It couldn't have been anybody else. The alarms weren't tampered with, the security company doesn't have any record of the slightest glitch. It had to be him." Gwen rose to inspect the safe. "Nobody appears to have messed with this, but then I doubt he was an expert safecracker. Somehow I see Jerry as taking an easier route." She turned to lean against the bookshelf full of reference catalogs. "Tell me he didn't cook up some reason to get you to give him the key and combination."

Joss's eyes flashed. "Give me a break. I left them right here, safe and sound."

"Here?" She resisted the urge to rant at Joss's carelessness. "I told you to keep them safe. Where did you put them?"

"In the desk drawer." Joss raised her chin. "I locked it."

A lock any self-respecting toddler could break.

"I didn't want to lose them. I figured this would be the only place I'd need them so I might as well leave them close by." She stared at Gwen. "You don't know it was Jerry."

It wasn't Jerry Joss was defending, Gwen knew. Joss didn't want to think it was Jerry because she didn't want to think she was at fault for the theft. But she wasn't at fault. Gwen, in the final analysis, had made the decision to hire him. Gwen had been the one in such a hurry to get out of town that she'd left Joss in charge of the store and the safe.

If anyone was at fault, it was she.

The key and combination lay in the paper-clip compartment of the drawer, Gwen saw, but it didn't mean a thing if Jerry were as quick as she thought. "Was he ever alone in the shop?"

"Of course not," Joss snapped. "I was here to open every morning and here to close down and set the alarm at night. Things were always locked up. I checked."

"Was he ever alone here at all?"

"Never." Joss paused, then stiffened slightly. "Except..."

"Except when?"

Joss closed her eyes briefly. "Yesterday. Lunch. He offered to buy, but the deli was shorthanded and not delivering. He said he'd pay if I went to get them." She hesitated. "I was broke."

"How long were you gone?" It wouldn't have taken much time, Gwen thought, not if he'd been prepared.

Not if he'd known what he was looking for.

"Fifteen minutes, maybe twenty," Joss told her. "There was a line and they'd missed our order."

"Convenient."

"How was I supposed to know?" Joss flared. "We'd hired him. I thought that meant we were supposed to trust him. There's an explanation," she muttered, grabbing the phone and punching in a number. She waited and an odd look came over her face.

"What?" Gwen asked.

"Jerry's cell phone. It's shut off." She set down the receiver.

Gwen swallowed. "Why change the number on a cell phone unless you don't want to be found." On impulse she turned to her keyboard. It took only a minute to send a quick e-mail out to a stamp dealers' loop she belonged to, asking if they'd recently acquired the five-cent Ben Franklin or the Columbian landing stamp. If they popped up somewhere, it might give her an indication of where Jerry was fencing them. It might give her a place to start from.

Mostly it was a way to keep busy. Activity kept her from screaming. She had to get them back, pure and simple.

"That son of a bitch," Joss muttered suddenly. Taking two steps to a cabinet on the wall, she yanked out her purse. "Give me your car keys."

"Where are you going?" Gwen demanded, rising.

"To find Jerry."

"I DON'T THINK THIS IS A GOOD idea."

"It's your chance to live on the edge," Joss snapped, driving so quickly that Gwen's silver Camry bottomed out at the base of the hill.

Gwen winced. "So how do you know where he lives?"

"We went out to see a band while you were gone. He invited me back for a drink."

Gwen looked at her in horror. "You didn't…"

"Of course not," Joss told her impatiently, following the streets into the Mission district. "I saw his building and thought I could probably live without seeing the inside."

Gwen nodded. "I thought you were sure he didn't do it. So why are you flying off the handle?"

"I want to find out." Joss scanned the street for an opening and started to whip into a space to park.

"Why don't you get out and let me do it?" Gwen couldn't bear Joss's Braille-style approach to parallel parking. Still, even with her experience, it took several tries to get the car in place. "Okay, it's probably smart to see if he's around," she said aloud as she got out of the car. "If there's a reasonable explanation, maybe we'll find it out and then we'll know to look somewhere else." Where else, she had no idea, but she knew in her gut that it came down to tracking the stamps stolen from the store inventory.

They stood on cracked sidewalk looking up at a sagging Victorian that had seen better days. "He might have been a snappy dresser, but he sure lived in a pit," Gwen commented, studying the peeling gray paint on the shingled building.

"Now you know why I decided not to go in."

It was a residence hotel, the kind of place that catered to the transient trade. Gwen's stomach began to gnaw on itself. She'd never bothered to check to see how long he'd been living at the address he'd given. Then again, at a place like this, twenty dollars to the front desk clerk would pretty much get the person to say whatever he wanted.

And, with luck, twenty dollars would get them into his room.

It took forty. "Why do you want him?" An unsmiling dark-eyed woman, her hair skinned back from her face, stared at them from behind the desk.

"He's got something of ours," Gwen told her.

"Yeah, well, he's got something of ours, too," the woman said sourly. "He skipped on the rent." She studied the folded twenties Gwen had slipped her and the line between her brows lessened. Abruptly she jerked a thumb at the hall. "I'm cleaning out his room right now. Wait for me at the top of the stairs."

The dim stairwell held the musty smell of a building that had seen too many anonymous people pass through. The paper on the walls might have been flocked forty or fifty years before. Now it was dingy and scarred. At the end of the hall a parallelogram of light from an open door slanted across a cleaning cart sitting on the bare pine floorboards.

Gwen glanced at Joss. Footsteps sounded on the stairs behind them. "Over here," the woman said briskly, walking past them toward the open door.

It was less grim than the hallway only because of the weak late-afternoon sunlight that streamed in through the single window onto the dirty beige carpet. What little of it that wasn't covered by the bed and bureau and uncomfortable-looking chair that constituted the main furnishings, anyway.

"I ask him for his rent and he says tomorrow." The woman stood nearby. "Always 'tomorrow' with him."

Empty drawers gaped open in the scarred bureau. No clothes hung on the open steel rack in the corner that served as a closet. Gwen drifted to the window. She itched to pull out the drawers, look underneath them and on the ends for hidden envelopes, to check under the mattress, but she didn't think the forty dollars would get her that far. Instead she poked her head into the tiny bathroom.

"You have a lot of business?" Joss asked, squinting into the cloudy square of mirror fastened to the wall.

The woman shrugged. "Hey, I'm just the desk clerk. Trust me, if I owned this dump, it would look a lot nicer."

"No idea where he went?" Gwen asked, walking over to stare out the window across to the neighboring building.

"Nope. We don't exactly get a lot of forwarding addresses around here." The woman dragged a vacuum cleaner in from the cleaning cart.

"Mind if I look in this?" Gwen asked, gesturing at the trash can.

"As long as you've had your shots." She jerked her head toward it. "A real pig, this guy. Nothing in the trash can if it could go on the floor."

Gwen poked gingerly through the refuse. Cigarette cartons, an empty toothbrush wrapper, a screwed-up McDonald's bag that still held the scent of stale grease. Then her eyes widened. In the bottom of the bin were scraps of cardboard, the thin type that came on the back of a pad of paper.

The type that could be used to make a stiff pocket for a stamp.

She pulled some out of the waste bin, staring at Joss. In her eyes Gwen saw knowledge and acceptance.

And a bright flare of anger.

The woman picked up the bin. "Okay, you guys had your chance to look around. I got to get back to work."

Gwen nodded slowly. "So do we," she said and turned toward the door. Her foot scuffed against something. An open matchbook. Clement Street Liquors, it said—the business next door to the stamp shop. She leaned down to pick it up.

And glimpsed writing on the inside. Excitement pumped through her. Maybe it was nothing but maybe, just maybe...

"What's that?" the woman asked.

"Matches." Gwen held them up. "I could use some. All right with you?"

"Sure, whatever."

"Thanks for letting us look around," Gwen told her, already walking out. She didn't say a word to Joss about it until they were outside, waited in fact until they were in the car. Hope formed a lump in her throat.

"Jerry buys his cigarettes at Clement Street Liquors," Joss told her.

"Bought. Jerry's long gone."

"The question is where?"

Gwen opened up the matchbook and showed Joss the writing. "Maybe Rennie will know." It was just a name and a phone number, but maybe it would lead them to a guy who'd know where to find Jerry. She dialed the number on her cell phone, her heart thudding.

"Thank you for calling the Versailles Resort and Casino, can I help you?"

Gwen blinked. "I'm looking for a guest named Rennie," she said and spelled it out.

"Last name?"

Gwen hesitated. "I'm not sure. Try it as the last name."

Keys clicked in the background. "We have no guest under that name."

"Can you search under first names?"

The operator's voice turned cool. "No, ma'am."

"Okay, thank you." Disappointment spread through Gwen, thick and heavy, as she hung up.

Joss looked at her questioningly.

"A hotel. They don't have him listed."

"So much for our lead. What do we do now?"

Gwen started the car. "We go home and call Stewart."

"YOU'RE MISSING *WHAT?*"

Saying the words aloud made them more real. "The Blue Mauritius. The red-orange one-penny Mauritius. More." Her stomach muscles clenched.

"Does Hugh know?"

"Not yet. They're on their trip for another twelve weeks. I don't know what to do, Stewart." The words spilled out, and for the first time since she'd opened the safe, tears threatened. "He could wind up losing everything, *everything,* and it's all my fault." It was a relief to let the panic out. Stewart would know what to do. Stewart would help her.

If anyone could.

"It's okay, Gwennie. It's going to be okay," he soothed. "Hugh has them insured, so even if we can't get them back, he'll get replacement value."

"But he doesn't," she blurted.

*"What?"* His cool disappeared.

"The premiums went too high. He let the insurance lapse last year except the basic policy on the store. He put all the money into the business." And his granddaughters were the weak link.

Stewart cursed pungently. "Dammit, what was he thinking? Why the hell didn't he have them in a safe-deposit box?"

"You worked with him for ten years, Stewart. You know how stubborn he is."

"That's no excuse for not having them protected, though. That was the first thing he taught me—protect the clients' holdings and protect your own."

"It wasn't just financial with him. He was a collector at heart."

Stewart let out a sigh. "I know. Come on, it's still going to be okay. We're talking about world-famous issues. They're not going to be easy to unload, especially if your thief is someone who doesn't know the stamp world."

"Oh, I have a good idea who the thief is," she said grimly. "We hired on a new clerk, Jerry Messner, about a month ago. As near as I can tell, he's bolted."

"Coincidence?"

Gwen laughed without humor. "He had motive, he had opportunity. Security wasn't compromised from the outside. You tell me."

"You called the police?"

"Not yet."

"Good. Keep it that way for now. The last thing you need on this is publicity."

Gwen nodded. "That was my thinking. I'm hoping we can get them back before we have to tell anyone."

"Any ideas?"

"Maybe. The prize issues aren't the only stamps missing. There's another twenty or thirty thousand in value gone from the store inventory. Common issues he can unload pretty easily, get himself some money to tide him over."

"Well, isn't he a greedy little bastard," Stewart said, an edge of helpless anger in his voice.

"I put out a few feelers on the loop, asking if there's any

action out there with the low-cost issues. I'm keeping quiet on the high-value ones for now."

"Smart thinking."

"If it is, it's the first smart thing I've done since Grampa left."

He sighed. "Don't beat yourself up, Gwen. There's no point. The thing to focus on is getting them back. I'll tell you what, e-mail me a list of everything that's gone. I'll make a couple of quiet phone calls to a few people I trust, just to see if they've heard any word of some of the issues coming on the market."

"As soon as we hang up," she promised, reaching over to switch on her computer. "And Stewart?"

"Yeah?"

"Thanks. I feel a lot better knowing we've got some help."

"It's going to be okay, Gwen. Trust me on this."

And for a moment, as Gwen hung up the phone, she felt as if it actually would be.

Joss stared at her as Gwen logged on to the Internet. "So, what did he say?"

"He's going to ask around, see if anything's surfacing." Gwen sent Stewart the file she and Joss had compiled earlier.

"Is he going to tell people why he's asking?"

"Stewart understands the situation. He'll keep the theft quiet."

Joss rose to pace around the office. "You know, I'm surprised. I would have picked you for the first one to run to the cops."

"Normally I would have been," Gwen told her, clicking on her e-mail in-box. "These are different circumstances." She scanned the contents of the messages that popped up in her preview pane. "I just don't want to blow—" The thought evaporated from her brain as she stared at the words on-screen.

Joss crowded up behind her. "Did you get something?"

It took her a couple of tries to speak. "It's a dealer. He just bought a Ben Franklin, same perf, very good condition. It sounds like one of ours."

"Well, call him."

"I am." Gwen scrolled down, searching for the contact signature at the bottom of the e-mail. And then suddenly she was yanking open the desk drawer and pulling out her purse.

"What? Where is he?"

"Las Vegas." The blood roared in Gwen's ears as she pulled out the matchbook and compared it to the numbers on-screen. "It's the same area code as where Rennie is."

Joss's gaze took on a particular stillness. "Call it," she ordered, her voice barely audible.

Hands shaking, Gwen dialed the number and listened to the tones of a phone ringing hundreds of miles away.

"Versailles Resort and Casino," an operator answered crisply.

Gwen resisted the urge to cross her fingers. It couldn't just be coincidence the stamp had surfaced there, it couldn't. "Jerry Messner, please." She crossed her fingers. All she needed was a chance.

There was a clicking noise in the background. "How was that spelled, please?"

Gwen told her.

The keys clicked some more. "One moment, I'll connect you."

And the line began to ring. Gwen banged down the handset hastily and stared at Joss. "He's there."

# 3

LIGHT, COLOR, NOISE. SLOT machines chattered and jingled in the background as Gwen walked through the extravagance that was the Versailles Resort and Casino.

"You want to tell me what I'm doing here again?" she asked Joss over her cell phone as she walked across the plush carpet patterned with mauve, teal and golden medallions. Ornate marble pillars soared to the ceiling overhead, where enormous crystal chandeliers glittered. Waitresses dressed in low-cut bodices and not much else hustled by carrying drinks trays. The casino had the sense of opulence, a decadent playground for the wealthy, though it was open to all comers.

Under the luxury, though, was the reality of gambling. The air freshener pumped into the cavernous main room of the casino didn't quite dispel the lingering staleness of cigarette smoke. The faces of the gamblers held a fixed intensity as they hoped for the big score. Or hoped just to break even. She couldn't have found anyplace more unlike herself if she'd tried.

Then again, she couldn't have looked more unlike herself if she'd tried.

"You know why you're there," Joss said. "You've got to find Jerry."

A balding man in his thirties glanced up from his computer poker machine as Gwen walked by. "Hey, baby," he said, toasting her with a plastic glass that held one of the free drinks handed out by casino waitresses. After a lifetime of wanting to be unremarkable, Gwen had gone the other way completely. Exit Gwen and enter Nina, the bombshell.

"I look like a tart," she hissed, tugging at her tight, low slung jeans and her scrap of a red top.

"You don't look like a tart. You just look like a woman who's not afraid to flaunt what she's got."

"Yeah, well, the flaunting part's working." A bellhop walking by tripped over his own feet and stumbled up with a grin. "Joss, this is not my style. This should be your job."

"It had to be you," Joss told her. "Jerry knows me too well. He'd recognize me in a second."

"Like he's not going to recognize me?"

"All Jerry's going to register is blond, tight and built. I doubt he's going to think much beyond his gonads. Anyway, you were always in the back room. He hardly saw you. And no way would he expect you to look like this. You're different head to toe."

"Tell me about it," Gwen muttered, resisting the urge to pull up her neckline. "And don't think I didn't notice you took my regular clothes out of my suitcase."

"I didn't want you to be tempted to backslide," Joss said smoothly. "You've got to be Nina through and through."

Joss had effected quite a transformation, Gwen thought, catching sight of herself in one of the enormous gold-framed mirrors that hung on the wall. Gwen—tidy, understated Gwen—was gone. In her place was Nina, whose Wonderbra-induced cleavage alone was likely to distract Jerry from recognizing the person underneath. How Joss had managed to get her into a good salon without notice, Gwen had no idea, but her brownish hair was a thing of the past. Now it had the same streaky, sun-bleached blond look it had had in Africa, only better. The makeup artist had made her eyes more vivid, her smile more bright, somehow without making her look as if she'd troweled on the makeup. She was undercover and, she had to grudgingly admit, she looked good.

Just not like herself. Still, the sooner she got the job done, the sooner she could turn back into Gwen. "All right, well, I'm in the casino, so it's time to get to work," she said briskly.

"What's the plan?"

"Haven't a clue. Wander around and get the lay of the land. Watch for our friend. I'll figure something out and call you tomorrow."

"Have fun," Joss said a little enviously. "Put a five spot on red for me. I've always liked red."

"Right."

Gwen switched off the phone and tucked it into her pocket. She was here. She was incognito. Now she just had to find Jerry, cozy up to him, figure out where the stamps were and spirit them away from him, all without being recognized.

Piece of cake.

Gwen drifted steadily through the ranks of slot machines and computer poker games, scanning the players. No Jerry in sight, but then he didn't strike her as the type for a sucker's game. He'd want cards, where he could influence the outcome.

She resisted the urge to yawn. Between the shopping, the styling, the packing and the flight to Vegas, it was nearly eleven—about the time she usually clocked out for the night. Since it was a weeknight, the ranks of the players had thinned out some. Maybe Jerry had gone to bed, too.

Yeah, right. She snorted at herself as she passed the croupiers at the craps tables. Jerry was more likely to stay up all night, sure in the knowledge he was going to hit it big, throwing away her grandfather's money all the while.

As she crossed the broad carpeted avenue that separated the slots floor from the green tables of the real games, the suffocating crowd and noise lessened, replaced by a steadily rising sense of purpose. The people playing at these tables still relied on chance, but they knew their games, and the knowledge gave them a sense of confidence.

Gwen ambled casually down the aisles between tables, as though she couldn't quite decide where to stop. No point in telegraphing to everyone that she was on the hunt. A tall, ebony-skinned dealer smiled at her. "Baccarat, lovely lady?"

Gwen shook her head, a faint flush tinting her cheekbones.

A burst of giggles rose from the blackjack tables behind her. "Oh, come on, Rennie, you know you're a winner," said a woman's voice.

Gwen whipped her head around to see two female dealers laughing with the player sitting at their table. A single male player.

Rennie.

What were the chances that two guys named Rennie would be at the same hotel as Jerry? Coincidence? Maybe, but Gwen didn't much like coincidence. She was a bigger fan of probabilities. Odds were that Rennie might very well know Jerry, and if he did, he could just lead her to him. And that was enough to make him her new best friend, she decided as the dealer going off shift walked away.

Gwen sat down next to Rennie and slid some twenties across to the dealer.

"Change a hundred," announced the current dealer, an ample redhead with laugh lines liberally marking her middle-aged face. She slid a stack of chips across the table and used the paddle to push Gwen's money into the bill slot.

Gwen studied Rennie out of the corner of her eye. His brown hair was a bit long on top, disordered, she imagined, by a long night at the tables. Even as she watched him, he ran a hand through it again, pushing it out of his eyes. He didn't hunch tensely like the gamblers she'd seen at other tables or sprawl with exaggerated confidence. He just sat loose and relaxed, a glass of what looked like whiskey at his elbow, next to the stacks of chips that attested to a combination of luck and skill. He wore jeans and a pine-green shirt patterned in faded burgundy and gold. Clearly he'd chosen more for comfort than style.

Then he turned toward her, and she understood why the dealers had been giggling with him.

He looked as though his habitual expression was one of wry amusement. A startling green, his eyes held a glint of devilry that invited her to join in. His sideburns were just a bit long, making him look a bit like some nineteenth-century rake. A day's worth of beard darkened his jaw.

And his mouth…

Adrenaline skittered through her veins.

"Welcome to the fun house," he said.

The dealer shuffled the decks and refilled the shoe.

*Flirt,* Gwen thought feverishly. *Keep him talking.* Nina wouldn't be struck dumb by his looks. Nina would be enjoying herself. "You looked like you could use a little company."

"What I could use is luck. Did you bring any with you?" He looked her over.

Gwen glanced at his stacks of chips. "You don't look like you're having any problems with Lady Luck to me." Lady Luck probably fell for that killer grin just like every other woman he met. She couldn't be thinking about that now, though. She had to strike up a relationship with Rennie—and fast. If she let him walk away, she gave up her link to Jerry.

"Can I get you something to drink?" A waitress stood at Gwen's elbow, tray in hand.

*What to choose,* Gwen wondered. She'd prefer white wine, but that didn't really fit with her profile. A martini, maybe? Or… "A cosmopolitan, please." At the expectant look of the dealer, Gwen pushed out two five-dollar chips. Her natural leaning was to bet a dollar at a time. Nina, though, wouldn't do anything by halves. Nina would take chances.

With brisk efficiency the dealer laid the cards out. Gwen worked to concentrate. It wouldn't do her any good to have found Rennie if she wound up broke and leaving the table in fifteen minutes. And she wasn't about to put up another hundred. She'd already dipped into her savings account to finance the trip; she was going to make it last.

Her hand held an ace and a two, for a soft thirteen. The dealer had a seven showing and Rennie had a four. He took a sip of his whiskey and tapped his cards to indicate a hit. Gwen couldn't tell if the three he got satisfied him or not, but he didn't bust. He took a sip of whiskey and glanced over at her with interest. "Waitin' on you, darlin'."

Gwen tapped her cards, embarrassed to have been caught watching him. The seven she drew made her forget all about it, though. The dealer drew a nine and flipped over her hole card to show eighteen. Gwen's surge of triumph was probably completely out of proportion to the fifteen dollars she'd won, but it was a good way to start.

Rennie turned over his cards to show a four and a nine and gave her that devilish smile again. This time it sent a pulse of adrenaline through her system that had nothing to do with nerves. "Looks like you brought me that luck."

"Maybe I'll stick around," she said carelessly, picking up the chips the dealer slid her way.

"Maybe you should." He had a way of looking at her as

though she were the only thing in his field of view that interested him, as though the game were irrelevant now that she'd arrived.

Her cosmopolitan appeared at her elbow.

He raised an eyebrow. "Girlie drinks?"

"A woman's got to do what a woman's got to do."

"And I'm sure you do it well." He lifted his whiskey and touched it to her glass.

Cool and sweet, the drink slid down her throat easily.

The dealer coughed. "Bets, please."

Gwen studied her bet circle. Aggressive but not foolish. She slid six five-dollar chips into the circle.

Rennie gave her that look again, the one that said he knew exactly what she was thinking and it amused him. "Living large?"

"Feeling lucky."

And her feeling was borne out when the dealer busted, leaving them both ahead.

"So, you out here for business or pleasure?" she asked casually.

"Business, but no reason it has to be all work. How about you?"

"Pleasure. I was supposed to meet a friend named Jerry, but he had to bail." This, of course, was his lead-in to talk about his own friend named Jerry, but he didn't bite.

Instead he just raised an eyebrow and pushed out a couple of chips. "A friend friend or just a friend?"

Gwen flushed. "Just a buddy."

"His loss is my gain." Rennie shifted in the chair. He had broad shoulders on what looked like a rangy build. That was all right—she liked leanly built men. He gave her a slow smile that had her stomach turning cartwheels.

Gwen blinked. Wait a minute. Back up. This was not part of the program. It was one thing to flirt and convince him she was interested. It was another thing to do it so well she convinced herself. He was the enemy. She needed to remember that. Get close, sure, but keep her distance.

The dealer flipped them a new hand with quick, economical motions. Gwen checked her hole card and tapped for another. Rennie did, too, but he took it too far and busted.

"Bummer," Gwen said, stacking her chips.

"I thought I had enough breathing room."

"You know what Penn and Teller say—Las Vegas is powered by the Hoover Dam and bad mathematics."

He studied her and took a swallow of whiskey. "That's a pretty cynical opinion for a player."

"I look at it as a challenge." She tipped her glass to take a drink and found to her surprise that it was nearly empty.

"And you like challenges?"

"I think they make life a little more interesting."

"You don't look much like the type who likes to be bored." He pushed a short stack of chips into his betting circle.

"How about you?"

He gave her that smile again and her pulse bumped a bit. "I'm all for excitement." He considered. "Then again, there's something to be said for just hanging."

Gwen checked her cards. "Just you and your buddies. You know, whoever you're here with?"

"Not necessarily," he answered, tapping the table for another hit. "My buddies can fend for themselves."

"Are they around?"

He gave her an amused look as she moved to hold. "You seem awfully interested in my friends. A guy could take it kind of personally."

"I don't think you should do that," she said quickly, pleased to see she'd won another round. "I was just curious."

"I'm much more interesting than my friends."

The look he gave her this time sent a shiver right down to her toes. The cocktail waitress set another cosmopolitan by her elbow, and Gwen fell on it as though it were salvation.

CHIPS SAT STACKED IN COLORED towers in front of her. She had no idea what the hour was—in a Vegas casino there were no clocks, no windows. High noon looked like midnight when you were at the tables. Time was irrelevant. The only thing that mattered was the flip of the cards, the spin of the wheel, the roll of the dice.

She felt no fatigue—far from it. She was wired, playing on house money. Her luck had been solid so far, but it was beginning to flag. Gwen drew a queen to a hand that was already twelve and busted.

Rennie looked at her. "We got a bad trend going here," he observed, gesturing at his own busted hand. "I'm thinking it's time to knock off while I'm ahead." He pushed his chips to the dealer, asking for a consolidation.

Panic seized Gwen. He couldn't leave—how would she find him again? She knew almost nothing about him, aside from the fact that he had a sexy smile and a weakness for banter.

And maybe a weakness for her.

Nina, of course, wouldn't be shy about putting her looks to work for her. No way would she just let the guy walk away. If Nina were trying to follow the trail of millions of dollars, she'd do whatever was necessary to persuade him to stick around. Gwen sent him a look from under her lashes as she collected her consolidated chips from the dealer. "So, how about a drink?"

# 4

Was it her imagination or was there more devilry in his smile? "Sure." He slid his handful of hundred-dollar chips into the pocket of his jeans.

Cosmopolitans, Gwen discovered as she rose from the table, had more of a kick than white wine. Her heel caught in the carpet as she slid off the stool.

"Whoa." Rennie caught her as she stumbled. "Here, why don't you grab my arm?"

"That's very gallant of you." His bicep was a solid swell under her fingers. The contact shivered through her. He wasn't built lightly at all, she realized as he tucked her hand against his body. The guy had some very real muscle. Her imagination instantly conjured up images of washboard abs and cannonball shoulders.

"Just call me Sir Galahad," he said. "So, where do you want to go?"

"Let's find a nightcap."

"You sure? We've been drinking for the last two hours. Have you had dinner?"

Gwen thought back but couldn't remember. "Something on the plane, maybe." He was an inch or two taller than she was, even in her spike heels, she realized. There was something alarmingly cozy about him standing there holding her hand against him protectively.

He looked down at her a moment and considered. "How

about if we go to the Reef Bar. Maybe we can get some food there. Trust me, you'll be happier tomorrow."

The bar was dark and yet lit with an aqua luminescence from the aquarium that took up one wall. Tropical fish made bright flashes of color amid rocks and waving green fronds. Music played in the background, but there was no crowd and no dance floor.

Quiet and dark was perfect for her purposes, Gwen thought as they took seats off in a corner. Or maybe not. The tabletop was about the size of a dinner plate, she realized. By the time she'd scooted onto her high stool, she found herself much, much closer to him than she'd anticipated. Close enough to find herself staring at that enticing mouth. Close enough to find herself noticing the way the aqua light reflected off his cheekbones. He really was gorgeous, she realized, not to mention sexy as hell.

Okay, reality check. Getting distracted was not good. She was here only to try to track down Jerry. Recreation with Rennie—one of the bad guys—was out of the question.

On the other hand, she'd do what was necessary to accomplish her purpose.

A waitress appeared, dressed in the bikini top and sarong uniform of the bar. "What'll it be, folks?"

Rennie studied the drinks card that sat on the table. "An Anchor Steam for me," he said. "And an order of potato skins."

"Sorry, guys, kitchen's closed. If you want food, you'll have to go to the coffee shop."

"Let's stick here," Gwen said quickly. No way did she want to go to a bright and noisy coffee shop. Anyway, Nina would probably sniff at coffee. She'd want a real drink. "How about a Courvoisier?" She wasn't exactly sure what Courvoisier tasted like, but she liked the idea of swirling a brandy glass.

His eyes were very dark in the dim light as he studied her. "My name is Del, by the way."

Gwen leaned closer to him. "What?"

"My name. It's not Galahad, it's Del."

"Del?" All the fun evaporated in an instant. She stared at him. "Wait a minute. You're joking, right? I thought your name was Rennie."

He shook his head. "'Fraid not."

*Disaster,* Gwen thought. *It was a disaster.* This was supposed to be Rennie, her conduit, the one who was going to lead her to Jerry. If he wasn't, then she was back to square one, no better off than she'd been when she'd walked into the casino. Worse, because Rennie had been around there somewhere. Now where was she? No lead, no closer to finding the stamps. Instead she was stuck here with him while the true Rennie was still out in the casino somewhere. She struggled to master her disappointment.

And ignore the small, sneaky sense of relief that lurked underneath.

"So, where'd you get the idea I was—who was it—Ronnie?"

"Rennie. That's what the dealer called you."

He looked at her, mystified.

"Before I sat down," Gwen clarified. "I thought the dealer said something like 'You always win, Rennie.'"

She watched the answer dawn. "Ah. She was joking around with the other dealer."

"Which other dealer?"

"The one who left when you came up."

"Was that her name?"

He shrugged. "I don't know. It sounded like a nickname."

"What did she look like?" Gwen asked sharply, thinking back. But she'd fastened so quickly and completely on him that everyone else was a cipher. She cursed under her breath. "I can't picture her at all."

"Does it matter?"

He was looking at her attentively—way too attentively. Relax, she told herself. "No, it's no big deal. I was just surprised." So how willing would the staffers be to help her find Rennie? And would she be back on shift the next evening? Maybe a quick conversation with the other dealer would help. Then again, Gwen didn't want to make Rennie suspicious.

"Boy, you've got some serious wheels turning in that head of yours," Del commented. "Not that it's not an entirely gorgeous head, but if I were Rennie, I'd be a little scared."

He'd leaned back to watch her, the frank curiosity on his face more than a little alarming. She needed to defray that, pronto. *Flirt, Nina, flirt.*

Gwen traced a pattern on the tabletop with one fingertip and sent him a look of promise. "Who cares about Rennie or whoever? You're here and I'm here, that's all that matters."

The amusement was back in his smile as he leaned forward and propped his elbows on the table, putting him disconcertingly near. "I suppose. You're holding out on me, though," he added conversationally.

Alarm surged through her. "What—what do you mean?"

A beat went by. "Your name. You know mine, I don't know yours."

"Oh." She almost sighed with relief. "Nina."

"Nice name. So what brings you to Vegas, Nina?"

"A couple days off. I wanted to get out of town."

He watched her for a moment, his mouth curving in a way that suggested he could see more than she wanted. "Searching for people named Rennie?"

Gwen flushed. "No. I just wanted a break."

"From what?"

"Oh, life." That much was true. She thought of the restlessness that had plagued her of late. "You know, you get tired of being stuck at home."

"Where's home?"

"San Francisco."

Genuine pleasure slid over his features. "No kidding? That's my stomping grounds."

"Really? Small world. What are you here for?"

"I'm doing a series on poker. I'm a sportswriter for the *Globe*."

"You're a journalist?" Gwen asked faintly. That was all she needed—a curious reporter around.

Again he gave her that look. "I don't think I'd dignify it with that word necessarily. Let's just say I can bang out twenty column inches on the Giants versus the Dodgers by deadline."

"You don't sound thrilled with it." The waitress set their drinks down in front of them.

Del shrugged. "It's a living. What about you?"

Gwen swirled her brandy glass to buy time. Lying wasn't in her nature. Then again, the last thing she wanted to do was give any personal details to a reporter, especially to a reporter who was entirely too interested in her earlier gaffes already. Even if he was a sportswriter. "I'm an accountant," she told him. It wasn't really a lie. She did the books at Chastain Philatelic Investments. She just did a whole lot more.

"Seriously?" He grinned, sending a little flutter through her midsection. He was so close, she realized suddenly. Close enough to whisper. Close enough to kiss.

Gwen blinked. "Yes, seriously. Why, what did you think I did?"

"I don't know. But I could have guessed a couple dozen possible occupations for you and none of them would have included accounting."

She could just imagine. "So, what occupations were in your couple dozen?"

"Oh, I don't know," he said offhandedly, "neurosurgeon, astrophysicist, president of the World Bank…"

"You know, if you'd have said lingerie model, I'd have had to belt you." She reached out a hand to mime slapping him. He caught it in his and held it to his face.

Heat bloomed through her. Sensation piled on sensation, the rough stubble of his day's growth of beard, the strength of his fingers on hers, the slight calluses on his palm.

It lasted only a second or two and drove every thought out of her head except the desire for more.

Del released her hand, changing his hold to bring her fingers to his lips. Warm and soft enough to make her melt. "Whatever you do, I'm sure you're very, very good," he murmured.

Eyes wide, Gwen sat stock-still, forcing herself to breathe. "I…excuse me for a minute," she managed to say and stood up on knees that trembled only a little.

DEL SAT WATCHING HER WALK away and waiting for the drumming in his head to stop. He hadn't been able to resist the impulse to touch her. The sudden urge to have her had surprised him, though. He considered himself a civilized man, but there was nothing civilized about this overwhelming need to drive himself into her deep and hard.

Colorful fish circled lazily in the aquarium beyond. He'd sat down at the blackjack table for a change of pace, to kill a couple of hours, not to hook up with a woman. Then Nina had sat down, fragrant, silky and looking hot enough to melt wax.

It wasn't completely outside his experience to have a woman hit on him, but it certainly wasn't his normal style to bite. He'd learned from personal experience—in his relationships and in his professional life—that the easy pickings were generally not the way to satisfaction, they were just...easy.

There was something about her, though, more than the looks. The combination of the promise in that wide mouth and the sharp intelligence in those eyes had captured his attention utterly. But something else was going on, something more than blackjack, more than sexual jousting. What about the consternation over his name? And why had she pumped him so hard about his friends?

And how was it that he didn't really give a damn about any of it, so long as he could have her?

He watched her cross the room toward him again, in her low-cut jeans and skimpy, fire-engine-red T-shirt. The confidence was back in her swagger, in the toss of her head. For a moment earlier she'd seemed like a high school girl, completely undone by his move. It seemed incongruous for a woman who looked the way Nina did, a woman who'd probably been romanced every way possible.

"Welcome back," he said as she sat.

"Thanks. I'm happy to be here."

He grinned and raised his beer. "Well, here's to being here." Her eyes watched him over the rim of her glass, the deep aqua of the Caribbean. Her scent drifted across to him, something that whispered of dark nights and forbidden passion. "So, how'd you get so good at blackjack?" he asked.

"My grandfather's got a weekly game. Blackjack, poker, whatever. I usually sit in with them."

"Win much?"

She shrugged. "I walk away with my share of pots."

"That's because you've got a genetic advantage." He propped his chin in his hand. "They probably can't concentrate a lick with someone who looks like you at the table, and on top of that you're smart."

He couldn't be sure in the dim bar, but he'd swear she flushed. "I've known most of them since I was about ten. I'm sure they can ignore it."

"You underestimate yourself. I don't think any man who sees you can ignore it."

She gave him a smoky look and propped her arms on the table herself. "Really?"

"Really."

"And would that include you?"

He felt the stirring in his belly. "What do you think?"

HIS MOUTH. SHE COULDN'T STOP staring at his mouth. She couldn't stop wondering how he tasted. The table had shrunk, or maybe she'd inadvertently moved her stool closer to him when she'd returned, because when he reached out to tangle his fingers in hers, it was only a small movement.

This time there was no shock, just the hot and sexy snap of connection. All the way to the bathroom and back— merely an excuse to get away and think for a minute— she'd thought about what it might be like with him. It wasn't the sort of thing Gwen would do, but she wasn't Gwen, was she? She was Nina. Nina wouldn't just sit and wonder what it would be like to kiss this man. She wouldn't wait for him to make the move. Nina would satisfy herself. Nina would just do it.

His eyes seemed darker, deeper as she leaned closer. She flicked a glance at his mouth and her tongue darted out to lick her own lips. She wanted this, she thought, tipping her head slightly. For tonight Jerry and the stamps could take a backseat. For tonight she just wanted.

And then their mouths came together and she didn't have to want anymore.

Her fingers were still curled in his but she didn't feel it.

All her awareness was concentrated in the feel of his mouth on hers. He didn't just kiss, he savored, feasting on her as though she were some rare delicacy. A shift, a nip, a quick slick of tongue. There was a sumptuousness in the slide of lip against lip, temptation in the taste. Her system began to buzz.

When his hand slid to cup her neck and pull her closer, Gwen went willingly. When his mouth opened against hers, she made a little sound of pleasure in her throat. It didn't matter that she hardly knew him, that he was just a pair of teasing eyes and a devilish smile. Something about him tempted her to take a risk. Something about him sent desire surging through her with an intensity she couldn't recall feeling before.

In the casino a cacophony indicated that someone had won a big jackpot, but neither of them even registered the noise. All that mattered was this moment, this place, this feeling.

If he'd felt the need to take before, now Del fought the urge to plunder. Up close, her scent wove around his senses, making him imagine her naked, hot and urgent against him. Her mouth was warm and alive. She tasted of Courvoisier and arousal, he thought hazily. Driven by the slide of her tongue over his, the nip of her teeth, he only wanted more.

And so he took the kiss deeper.

The teasing swirl of her tongue around his had desire coiling in his belly. She might have been an enigma, but her trembling response didn't lie. Throughout the night she'd been an odd mix of uncertainty and confidence. There was nothing tentative here now, though, only a heated certainty that sent urgency thudding through his system.

Finally Del broke away. He sat for a moment, waiting

for his system to level. It was going to take a while, he realized. "You pack quite a punch," he told her.

"So do you." It took her two tries to get the words out. Gwen stared back at him, breathing hard. She wanted, oh, she wanted. If he could take her this far with just a kiss, how much more was waiting for her? Her lips still felt as though they were vibrating, she realized. And she wanted more. She leaned toward him again, but he stopped her.

"Maybe we should go somewhere else," he said, staring at her. "Someplace less…public."

She nodded, not in answer to the words he'd said but to the question in his eyes. "I think you're right."

"Oh, yeah?"

Gwen leaned forward to press a kiss on him. "Oh, yeah," she breathed. Del tossed a twenty on the table and rose, catching her hand.

And a bubble of exhilaration began to swell in her chest.

It wasn't her usual style. Gwen dated clean-cut, serious men who took her to a few weeks of movies, concerts and dinners before they segued into decorous sex. That part usually lasted until she was bored mindless with them. She certainly didn't pick up the kind of men who hung out in casinos. She definitely didn't kiss them in bars the first night she'd met them, even if they did have perfectly delicious mouths.

And she absolutely didn't wind up in bed with them.

Maybe it was being in Vegas, maybe it was the cosmopolitans, but suddenly it didn't matter. Suddenly what she wanted was this moment with this man. She could go back to being careful and deliberate Gwen tomorrow.

Nina was taking over.

# 5

THE ELEVATOR WAS A BLUR, THE walk down the hall a desperate trek broken up by pauses to just stand fused together, desperate to get their hands on one another. Finally they stood at a door, Del fumbling for his passkey.

Gwen had never known anything like this before. Certainly sex had involved some excitement, but all to a manageable level. Getting swept up in passion was what Joss did, not Gwen. Gwen kept things tidy and controlled.

But now she was Nina, and Nina wanted no truck with tidy and controlled. Nina wanted hot. Nina wanted the rough feel of a man's hands, the pumping urgency of his body.

Nina wanted it all.

Gwen leaned against him, up on tiptoe. "I want you naked," she whispered over his shoulder. "Now."

And the door latch clicked open.

Inside the room Del groped for a light switch, and a recessed light in the entryway came on. It was as though Gwen had a fever in her blood. She was hot, light-headed with wanting. Del turned to her and she flowed into his arms.

She'd never been kissed like this. She'd never had a hot mouth and a pair of hands fling her into arousal so quickly. As he pressed her against the wall and took the kiss deeper, she could taste a faint hint of the bourbon he'd been drinking. The stroke of tongue against tongue sent desire arrowing through her. He was hard, she could feel it, and she shivered a little with anticipation as she shifted her hips in response.

He groaned. With an exultant laugh Gwen broke the kiss and let herself nuzzle his throat, the skin taut under her lips. She could feel his hard-muscled body under the shirt and made a noise of impatience.

"More," she breathed. "I want more." Her mouth still on his, she stepped back enough to push his shirt away from his shoulders, and he shrugged it off.

And she caught a breath of delight. His was a body made for movement, the arms hard and sculpted, the belly corrugated with muscle. She traced her fingers down over the ripples of his abs. When he sucked in a breath, she dipped lower to trace over the swell of his hard-on under his jeans.

She wanted the feel of his skin against hers. Gwen reached for the hem of her own top, but Del caught at her hands. "Oh, no, that's for me to do," he murmured. He slipped his hands around her waist, sliding over the bare skin and up under the stretchy crop top she wore. His fingers trailed up her back, and the immediacy of the contact made her shiver, and shiver again when he slid them around to the front to fill his hands with the curves of her breasts. The fabric diminished the sensation, and she strained against him with a noise of frustration. She wanted his touch on her naked breasts. Instead he slid his hands up her sides and along her arms, until the rolled-up shirt was just a memory tossed across the room.

"God, you're gorgeous," Del said hoarsely as he stepped back and just looked at her in her sheer black bra. She flushed and glanced down, pulling her arms in toward her in what seemed like a reflex action. Catching her wrists, he pulled them gently aside. "Let me look at you. You're such a turn-on."

She was delicious, all soft and curvy. He wanted more, though. One minute she was all confidence, the next minute self-conscious. There was something about the way she met his eyes, suddenly hesitant. He wanted it gone. He wanted her wet and abandoned, twisting against him. He wanted to hear her cry out. He wanted to taste her. Reaching down, he unzipped her jeans. "These come off. Now."

Slipping the denim down, he savored the feel of her silky skin against his palms, then pressed her back onto the ridiculously high sleigh bed that mirrored the decadence of the rest of the hotel. One at a time he pulled off her spike-heeled shoes. Her jeans followed and he tossed them aside.

She sat up. "I want to…"

"No." He pressed her down. "Let me." He started at her instep, kissing the tender skin, then tracing the inside of her calves with his tongue. Working his way up her thighs, he pleased himself by teasing her, licking close to the silky lace at the vee between her legs, going just under the edge before moving away. Because he had plans and he was nothing if not a patient man.

Rising, he stripped off his own jeans and leaned over the bed. Her breathing became more ragged and she shuddered a little as he moved up over her flat belly, along the sides of her waist. With a snap he unfastened the front clasp of her bra and peeled back the cups.

Dry-mouthed with anticipation, Gwen stared up at him. The touch, when it came, wasn't the cupping of a hand or the brush of fingers but the stroke of a tongue, wet and warm against her. She licked her lips and waited for more. When he bent to her breasts again, he took his time, until the suction and rub of his tongue over her swollen nipples started an answering resonance down where she was wet and fevered.

Tension tightened her and she twined her fingers in his

hair, drawing him up to her so that she could press a hard, openmouthed kiss on him. She curved her arms around him, mad for him to lie alongside her, but he kept away. "Later," he promised and moved back down her body.

This time he focused on her breasts, kneading them, rolling the nipples with light pressure as he kissed his way down her body. The brush of the hair on his forearms against her body made her shudder, the warmth of his lips made her toss and turn. When she felt him slip off her lacy underwear, she slid her fingers into his hair. "Oh, god," she breathed.

The mattress gave just a bit as he settled himself between her legs. She felt the brush of his hair against her inner thigh, felt the warmth of his breath. Every atom of her being was tensed in anticipation. Her hips moved just a bit, involuntarily. He gave a chuckle deep in his throat and settled himself between her legs. "Not until you're begging."

Lightly, maddeningly lightly, his tongue brushed the lips that enfolded her clitoris. When he separated them, she gave a hum of satisfaction and expectation, but he ignored the hard bud where she ached to be touched. Instead he licked at her folds, dipped inside her, touched her everywhere but the point that would give her release.

She clawed at his shoulders, pulled him toward her. "Please," she managed. "Oh, please."

And then his mouth was on her, sending her gasping and flinging her head back into the pillow. Hard and relentless, he drove her, tongue tracing maddening patterns that sent her flailing upward toward some crest, some climax, some pinnacle of ultimate release.

Yet just as she was trembling at the edge, he backed off again, leaving her achingly unfulfilled while he teased her with other touches, his hands on her breasts, his mouth against her thigh. She dragged at him, hands on his head as she urged him to take her over.

And he did, his mouth driving her up, sending her gasping, hips jolting against him, seeking that final touch. But just when he had her shuddering, crying out mindlessly, just when she could feel the climax looming, he moved away.

"Don't stop," she cried raggedly, the pressure of the unrealized orgasm pounding through her.

"I'm not. I'm just changing gears." Breathing hard, Del slid off to stand beside the high bed. She felt a little thrill as he pulled her to the edge, stepping close enough to stretch her legs up the length of his torso, her ankles hooked over his shoulders. Stiff and hard, his cock jerked just a little with arousal as he sheathed it. Then he took the head of it and slid it into the slick cleft between her legs, running it up and down a few times, each brush of the smooth skin against her engorged clitoris making her gasp.

"Oh, like that," she rasped, but he shook his head.

"I think you're resourceful enough to do it for yourself," he murmured and in that instant pumped his hips to slide into her up to the root.

Thick, hard, solid, it dragged a cry from her. Moving against him, she savored every bit of friction as his cock slid in and out, in and out. She trembled on the edge of orgasm.

But she didn't quite go over. It was taunting to feel so much, to have his hands sliding up and down her legs and still have her desire remain unslaked.

She had to do something or she'd go mad. She needed hands on her breasts, needed something to ease the throb. One hand crept closer to the vee between her legs. When her finger slid into the warm wetness, when she felt the slide of it over the hard knob of her clitoris, she gasped.

"Oh, yeah, touch yourself," Del said softly, and Gwen swore he got harder. "Show me what you like." He caught her ankles and moved them apart a little, watching her avidly, watching himself move in and out of her.

Any vestige of self-consciousness was gone. Gwen circled her finger over her clit, each touch tightening the tension that strung her taut, each touch in time with the hard, swift strokes of his cock. She was almost delirious with the sensation that battered her from all directions. Close to the edge, she was so close she didn't think but raised her free hand to her breast, brushing the tender skin, squeezing the nipple.

"Oh, man," Del cried out raggedly, even as the bolt of sensation flung her over the edge to orgasm. It was hard, jolting, tearing staccato cries from her as the pleasure battered her over and over again. And even as she was still shuddering with pleasure, he groaned and spilled himself.

SOFTNESS. WARMTH. DEL REDMOND woke to find his face pressed against a fragrant spill of hair, his arms full of silky, curvy woman. It wasn't an experience he'd had very much of since his divorce two years before. Or very much the year or so before his divorce, come to think of it. He liked it, the way Nina fit in his arms, spooned against him. He liked it a lot.

As to the night before, well, it had been mind-blowing, pure and simple. The way she'd touched him, the way she'd moved, had brought him astonishing release. The two of them might not know each other from Adam outside of bed, but in it they were incredibly compatible.

Of course, he was in Vegas to work, not to have a fling with a woman. Then again, so long as he got the job done, who was to care? And this wasn't just any woman. This was a woman who attracted him, who aroused him.

Who intrigued him.

A low whine had him glancing at the nightstand to see

his muted cell phone flashing. Recognizing the number, he gave a quiet curse and slipped his arm out from under Nina. She rolled over with a sleepy murmur, dragging the covers with her.

Del rose and headed to the bathroom. "Redmond here," he said, closing the door and sitting down on the edge of the tub.

"It's ten-thirty in the morning. Where's your copy, Redmond?"

"Morning, Perry, how are you?" Del could picture Ed Perry, the *Globe*'s comfortably paunchy sports editor, his balding head counterbalanced by a neat Vandyke.

"How am I? Not nearly as good as you, I'm sure. So where's my column on the poker life, champ? What are you doing—drinking, chasing after women?"

Del glanced uneasily at the door. "I wrote a story yesterday. I'll get it filed this morning."

"You know, I send you to Vegas, plum assignment. This is not what I expect in thanks."

"Hey, this was your bright idea, not mine." Walking to the counter, Del pulled his electric shaver out of his leather toilet kit.

"Who was the one bitching about another year covering the All-Star game?"

"Me," Del admitted.

"Is that a razor I hear? Are you shaving?" Perry demanded. "You really *have* spent the day in bed."

"You're the one who's always telling me to multitask," Del reminded him. "I'm not a gambler, Perry. The last time I was in Vegas was when I played here in college."

"Not a gambler, huh?" the editor grunted. "So how was it again you fleeced me for forty bucks in last week's poker game?"

Del moved the razor in circles over one cheek, then the

other. "Look, a friendly poker game with the guys to drink beer and shoot the shit is one thing. Out here you're talking hard core. These people are up all night. Everything I own reeks of cigarette smoke." He ran the razor along his jaw.

"Switch that thing the hell off, will you? It's buzzing in my ear like a mosquito."

"Bitch, bitch, bitch."

"Me? What about you? Anyway, you were getting stale. I figured something different would shake you up."

Del snorted. "Hardly. You just wanted to distract me from the newsroom job."

"Newsroom job?" Perry repeated innocently.

"Don't give me that. You know I want to apply for that opening in the metro section."

Perry sighed. "Del, you've got a good gig here in sports. Why do you want to gum up the works going after an entry-level reporter's job?"

"You just don't want to have to break in a new writer."

"I just don't want to see you get shot down."

"Why would I be?" Del scowled. "I've worked on the sports section for nearly eight years, since I washed out of the pros."

"Yeah, and the whole time there's been a crew of bright-eyed kids over in the newsroom busy building their contacts so they can get half a dozen city hall staffers on the phone for a story. You can get Felipe Alou. You can't compete, Del."

"Let them tell me that," he snapped. "I want stories that take work. I want to dig, not just interview a bunch of genetically gifted millionaires."

"You've got a gift for interviewing genetically gifted millionaires."

Del sat back down and leaned his elbows on his knees. "I've got a little bit of one for investigation, too. What about that series I did on the BALCO scandal?"

"Some good work there," Perry admitted reluctantly.

"I want to do more."

"Fine. The doping scandal's still going. Follow it up."

"It's not enough, Perry."

"What is this, an early midlife crisis? Is this about the divorce?"

"No. Maybe. I don't know." Del rose and scrubbed a hand through his hair. "I just know I took the easy way out for way too long and it didn't get me anywhere I wanted to be. I want to make something happen, not just take what comes my way."

"Sports not good enough for you?" A hard note entered Perry's voice.

"You know better. I just want to do something that didn't fall in my lap, you know?"

"Life's so tough when you're a golden boy." The sarcasm was rich in Perry's voice.

"It's not that," Del said simply. "I feel like I let myself down by not trying. And I let everybody else down, too."

There was a silence and then a long sigh. "Okay, fine. You really want me to forward your application to the news desk, I'll do it. But I'm making no guarantees."

"I'll make my own."

AT THE SOUND OF THE CLOSING bathroom door, Gwen's eyes opened and she breathed a silent sigh of relief. He was out of the room. She might have had a momentary brain lapse the night before, but now she could get up, get dressed and get on with it. Time was a-wasting and Jerry was out on the loose with four and a half million in stamps. She didn't have time to lie around. She moved to the edge of the bed, wincing at the slight soreness between her legs.

And winced again at the thought of the night before. From the day she'd started having sex—at a respectable nineteen—she'd vowed no one-night stands. None of those cheap, tawdry scenes of waking up the morning after with a total stranger. And now, fueled by too many cosmos and too much Nina, she'd popped her one-night-stand cherry. It was just the sort of fiasco Joss would get involved in, coming to town for a serious purpose and getting distracted by sexy eyes and clever hands.

Gwen paused and a slow smile stretched unbidden across her face. And what clever hands they were, not to mention the rest of the machinery that went with them. She wasn't a novice when it came to having sex, but her interludes tended to be moderate, dignified. Not for her, wild monkey sex where the positions changed by the minute and the lovers clawed and gasped.

At least, not until now.

Yawning, she rose and began to sort her clothes out of the tangle on the floor. Then again, sex—however amazing—was her last priority right now. One night? Okay, she'd been restless lately. She could give herself one night. It was over, though. Today was for Jerry-hunting and she couldn't lose focus. The stamps were the only things that mattered.

Gwen slipped into her black lace underwear and hunted around for her bra. The ideal thing to do would be dress and beat a hot retreat—if only she weren't dying to use the bathroom. How would Nina play it? At ease and in control, of course. Say good morning, go in and powder her nose and be on her way with a swagger. Not self-conscious, not in a million years. Nina ran the show.

At the sound of the bathroom door opening behind her, Gwen clutched her clothing to herself in reflex action. *Relax,* she told herself, willing her arms to loosen up. Nina was totally comfortable being naked and would act that way.

"Good morning," she said and gave him a bold look.

Del stared. "Um…"

Gwen's confident smile wavered. "What?" She touched her nose.

"Your eye, it's a little…"

She whirled to inspect herself in the mirror over the bar. Everything was fine around her nose, but the white of one eye had a brilliant turquoise circle on it. One of the damned colored contacts that Joss had insisted she wear had moved while she'd slept. "Oh, for god's sake," Gwen muttered and went into the bathroom without a word.

It was just as well, she figured as she pulled out the contacts and dressed. Forget about awkward segues, now she'd just be ready to roll. Hand on the doorknob, she took a deep breath and walked out into the room.

Del had pulled on his jeans but hadn't bothered to fasten the top button. His waistband hung tantalizingly open below the rock-hard ripples of his belly. She remembered the way the muscles had felt under her hand, with their light dusting of springy hair.

Before she could speak, he walked over and pressed a kiss on her. "Good morning. Sorry for getting distracted before."

It didn't matter that they'd spent the night together, it didn't matter that they'd done much, much more, the kiss had her lips buzzing. Taken off balance, she faltered. "They were probably a bad idea. Something new." *Stupid,* she thought immediately. And certainly never should have admitted to doing anything goofy.

"If it matters, I like the real color better," he remarked and slid the fingers of one hand along her jaw, curling them around her neck. She read his intentions in the darkening of his eyes and stepped back hastily even as she felt the first fizz of desire begin to bubble in her system.

"Well, got to get the day started," she said briskly. "I should get rolling."

"Why?" He moved toward her again. "You're here for pleasure. I can help you with that."

"I've got business that can't wait." Although if she didn't get away from him soon, it would have to.

"Business?" He lowered his hands, interest flickering in his eyes. "I thought this was a vacation for you."

Gwen coughed. "Oh, yeah, well, you know, business and pleasure, better together."

"Is this about Rennie?"

That stopped her for a moment. "Where'd you get that?"

"That's who you were looking for when you sat down last night, wasn't it? Rennie?" Del backed up to lean a hip against the bureau.

She flushed. "I don't think that's any of your business."

"You're right," he agreed, "but it's kind of an odd thing. Makes me wonder."

The last thing she needed was a curious reporter on her hands. "There's nothing to wonder about," Gwen snapped, checking her jeans pocket for her room key. "Last night was last night and this is today. And I've got things to get done."

"So I see. Doesn't mean we still can't spend some time together."

Had she thought he had devilish eyes? Now they were just way too perceptive and persistent for her own comfort. She needed to cut this off—now. "You seemed like a nice guy last night. Don't turn into one of those jerks who can't take no for an answer. It was a one-nighter. Deal with it."

The look in his eyes hardened. "I don't have any problems with the word no. I just don't take bullshit very well."

"What's that supposed to mean?"

"You tell me. You're kind of a moving target."

"And you're kind of an asshole." She shook her head like a dog shaking off water. "Why are we even having this conversation? I am out of here. Have a nice life."

"Give my love to Rennie."

She answered with a rude word. Unfortunately the pneumatic closer prevented the door from slamming, so she had to listen to his laughter all the way down the hall.

# 6

GWEN STOOD ON THE SIDEWALK near the corner of Sahara and Decatur, squinting in the late morning sunlight. Away from the Strip, Las Vegas was anonymous and pedestrian—computer stores nestled up against muffler shops, fast-food joints and video stores filling up the minimalls. It was like any city in America.

Except for the temperature.

Not even dark glasses blocked the merciless desert sun. Baking heat shimmered up in waves from the sidewalk. It was a good thing she'd worn something skimpy when she'd left the air-conditioned comfort of the hotel, not that Nina's wardrobe held anything else. Of course, Gwen would have chosen a sleeveless top and shorts rather than Nina's clingy lime tank dress. It was right for Nina, though. She'd wear an attention-getter.

And get attention it had, from the elevator, through the casino, to the front door. It had certainly brought the door-man on the run, and the cabbie had been ready to throw aside his day job to show her around. Instead she'd had him take her out to the boulevard of strip malls and drop her at LV Rarities.

A low chime sounded as she pushed open the door. Inside the shop provided a cool, dark contrast to the sun-baked outdoors. In the quiet confines of the store, it felt as if the air never moved; spotlights just shone down endlessly and timelessly on the glimmering coins and stamps and antique jewelry in the display cases.

"Can I help you?" A man with salt-and-pepper hair combed discreetly over a thinning patch appeared from the back.

"Hello," Gwen said coolly. He was about her height. From the way he held himself, she was pretty sure he was sucking in a paunch.

"Hot enough for you today?"

"Oh, a little warm, maybe. Nice and cold in here, though."

"Only the temperature. Our merchandise is hot."

Gwen raised an eyebrow. "You sell stolen goods?"

"No, no," he said hastily. "I meant top-of-the-line."

"I'm sure." Never hurt to have him on the defensive if what she suspected was true, Gwen thought and walked slowly around the U of display cases, bending over occasionally for a closer look at the precious goods inside. "So, what are your specialties?"

"Whatever you're looking for, we've got." He smoothed his hair. "What's your name?"

"Vera." Another character was called for, she'd decided on the way over. She was trying to hunt down Jerry as Nina. The last thing she wanted was for him to find out that someone named Nina was asking questions about him. "My—" she paused "—friend has just won big at the casino and he wants me to pick out something nice."

"We've got some gemstones or some gold wafer jewelry that would look fine on you."

Gwen waved a dismissive hand. "I've already been jewelry shopping. I'm interested in owning something with a little more distinction. You carry rare stamps, right?"

"Oh, I could set you up with some interesting pieces for a few hundred each."

She flicked him a glance. "I want valuable stuff. Don't you have anything really rare? What do they cost?" She wandered back and stopped in front of him.

"How much money are you looking to invest?" he countered, unable to entirely disguise the hint of eagerness in his voice.

Gwen traced a pattern on the glass of the display case. "Oh, we don't need to get specific just yet. What could I do with, say, three to five thousand?"

"Looks like someone brought luck to the table."

"I do my best." She didn't flirt, but she gave him a smile of vague promise. "So, what's your best?"

His eyes brightened. "I might do better showing than telling."

*In another lifetime, bub.* "Bring them out, then. If I like what I see, I might be back later this week."

She watched his nostrils flare as he took a breath. "Give me just a minute." He stepped in the back and came out with a plush catalog. "We have the German 1864 one-schilling or the Great Britain 1882 one-pound." He opened the pages to show her each.

Gwen nibbled her lip, watching him watch her. "Do you have anything more colorful? You know, Pony Express stamps or something with airplanes?"

He laughed indulgently. "It'd take a little more than five thousand to get you a Pony Express stamp, but I've just picked up a nice 1847 Benjamin Franklin stamp that might suit you."

"Yeah, I bet in a town like Vegas you pick up nice pieces all the time."

He shrugged. "It's a business. They need money, I need stock."

She looked at the stamp in its clear holder and felt a thrill of excitement. She recognized the perforation pattern, the width of the border around the stamp—characteristics that were as sure identifiers as fingerprints to a person. The stamp was from her grandfather's inventory. "So, how do you know it's for real? You have a certificate or something?"

He cleared his throat. "This is a recent acquisition. I don't have paperwork for it yet, but I hope to."

"Then how do you know it's authentic?" she asked casually, flipping the pages of the catalog to spy another stamp from the store collection. And another. "Do you know where they got it?"

"I don't ask those questions."

*I'm sure you don't,* Gwen thought. "How much?" she said aloud.

He looked at her and looked at the stamp, considering. "Oh, normally I'd ask six thousand, but since you look like you might be interested in long-term collecting, I'll take five to get you started."

Outrage flooded through her. Five? The catalog value of the stamp was thirty-five hundred.

"Of course," he said silkily, brushing his fingers over the back of her hand, "that price includes personal advice on the investment value of rare stamps, perhaps in a more… conducive setting. Who knows, you might even get me to drop the price even further."

It made her skin crawl but she took care not to show it. "Well, you can start by telling me more about this stamp. I guess every one of them has a story. Tell me—" she looked at him speculatively "—did the guy who sold it to you say where he got it?"

"I make my business buying and selling, not asking."

"How do you know it was his to sell?"

The dealer moved his hand away. "The appraisal takes care of all of that," he said briskly, seeming to realize that he'd already said too much. "Are you interested?"

"Let me think it over." She gave him an intimate smile, but she'd let her moment slip away, she understood. He wasn't going to tell her any more. "Can you set the stamp aside? I need to talk with my friend. I'm sure he'll want an appraisal."

"For you, anything." His hand drifted south of his belt. "And think about what I said. I can teach you a lot about stamps and maybe throw in a tour of the city. I've lived in Vegas for twenty years. I can show you all the sights."

"I'll bet you can," Gwen told him. "I'll just bet you can."

BACK IN HER ROOM, SHE DIALED Stewart's cell phone. "I've found him," she said without preamble.

"Huh? What?" She could practically see him trying to catch up. "Where?"

"Vegas, of all places."

"Vegas! How'd you find him?"

"I tracked the 1847 Benjamin Franklin. A guy from out here answered that posting I put on the loop."

"What do you mean, out here? You didn't go carting off to Vegas to find him, did you? For god sakes, Gwennie, use some sense. Your thief could be dangerous."

"Stewart, I've got to get those stamps back."

"So, what, you're going to grab him and pound him until he tells you where they are? Point a gun at him and make him sweat? This isn't a movie."

"I know," she said, her excitement dissipating. No, it wasn't a movie, but the whole thing certainly felt unreal. "And I don't know where he is exactly, anyway. I just know he's been here. The dealer's got three of our stamps."

"You sure he bought them from your guy?"

"They're ours, that much I know. Where he bought them, I can't be sure. He's giving me the runaround." Gwen rose and began pacing, the cordless phone in her hand. "He had to get it from Jerry, though. It's too soon for them to have changed hands more than once."

"I'm surprised he'd bother messing with you."

His confidence warmed her. "I didn't tell him who I was or why I was asking. I couldn't take the chance of it getting back to Jerry."

"Even if you didn't tell the dealer your name, I can't imagine anyone trying to get around someone like you. You mean business and it shows."

Outside on the Strip, a giant video screen showed a phalanx of dancers gyrating through a dance from the latest hit show. "I'm kind of in disguise."

"What does that mean?"

"Well, I didn't want Jerry recognizing me before I figured out what was going on. Joss fixed me up…." She stopped helplessly as Stewart began laughing, a deep belly laugh that went on and on. "Well, it's not that funny," she said frostily.

"Little Gwennie undercover." Amusement was rich in his tone. "Sorry, I'm sure you look great."

"Actually I'm a total babe," she informed him, flopping down in one of the dark red upholstered chairs by the window. "The cab driver volunteered to take the day off and give me a personal tour of Vegas."

"I'm sure he did," he said more soberly.

"So did the stamp dealer, but what he didn't give me was anything on Jerry I could use."

"Assuming it's this Jerry in the first place."

"It's Jerry, all right. Anyway, I wonder if you know the guy here. Tom Horton of LV Rarities?"

Stewart considered. "I've met him once or twice."

"You think you could give him a call, see what you can find out?" For now, Horton was her only link to Jerry and Jerry was her only link to the stamps.

"I'll do better. I'll come out and do it in person."

Half of her was relieved, half of her felt like a kid whose parents were taking over. "You don't have to do that, Stewart. I've got it under control for now."

"You're only three hours away, Gwennie. I can be there tonight."

"You've got a business to run," she protested.

"So what? This is Hugh's future we're talking about."

"I want to do it myself," she burst out, knowing as she said it that it was true. There was silence on the line. "I'm sorry, I didn't mean it to come out that way. Look," she tried, "it was my fault the stamps got taken. I need to do this, to at least try to make it right. Can you understand that?"

"I suppose." His tone was guarded.

"I need your advice and I need your connections. I just don't need you here right now. You're still helping me, though."

"Not enough."

"More than enough," she countered. "If you can get anything out of Horton, that would be huge. I'll call if I need you out here."

"Promise?"

"I swear. You're always first on my list, you know that."

"Oh, I bet you say that to all the middle-aged guys you know." The tone was a little too hearty, but he sounded mollified.

"Only you." Relieved to have the difficult moment past, Gwen smiled. "Were you able to find out anything on the other stamps?"

"Big goose egg, which is good news for you. As near as I can tell, no one out there is putting out feelers on the Post Office Mauritius stamps or the inverted Jennys. I'm still waiting to hear on the two-penny."

There wasn't a name for the level of relief she felt. "Maybe he's lying low."

"Probably," Stewart agreed. "You don't have a lot of time to waste, though. Swear you'll call me if you need help?"

"I do. I'll keep hunting and let you know what I find out."

"Same goes. And Gwennie?"

"Yeah, Stewie?"

"Be careful."

DEL CAME OUT OF THE CASINO office and stopped, surveying the room with the same amazement he always did. Noise, motion and color as far as the eye could see. Day or night, it was all the same, with the same nameless faces and bodies lined up at the slot machines and the craps tables in a sort of numb gambling daze, mechanically placing the next bet, the one that was going to win them big.

To one side of him lay the hotel registration counter. In an ordinary hotel it would be immediately inside the front door. In a Vegas hotel getting to the registration desk required a Sherpa guide and provisions. The hotel designers knew where the cash money part of the business came from and they put it right up front. Del remembered a reporter in town to cover a UNLV football game losing three hundred dollars at blackjack before he ever even got checked into his hotel.

A curvy blonde walked by and gave him a smile of promise. And all he could think was that she didn't hold a candle to Nina. Not the sleekly sexy Nina of the night before, but the Nina of this morning, with her hair tousled and her eyes shining their natural blue-gray. Underneath the glossy packaging was an unstudied, intriguing woman who stayed on a man's mind—at least, on his.

*Get over it,* he told himself, remembering her words. The strange thing was, he didn't seem to be able to. Del shook his head, wondering about himself. He'd been involved with plenty of women in his life and he'd been interested in plenty of others who didn't return the favor. It wasn't a problem. If a woman didn't want him, there were bound to be others who did. He wasn't hung up on challenges or afraid of rejection. He was a pragmatist.

Certainly he'd had more than his share of experience with golden girls, genus California, species beach babe. He'd even gone so far as to marry one—and discovered that underneath the polish and packaging there wasn't a whole lot else.

Maybe that was why Nina stuck with him, because the more of her package and polish he got under, the more levels to her there were—clever, funny, smart, subtle, stubborn. That and the fact that there was something going on with her that wasn't quite kosher. There was probably an easy explanation for it, but if so, why didn't she just say something? Maybe it was simple, maybe it was innocent.

And maybe she was out of her depth.

Not his problem, he reminded himself. *Get over it.*

But it was hard to get over it when he looked up to see her walking by, leggy and curvy in all the right places, with a loose-limbed stride that made his mouth go dry. Her bright hair swished around her shoulders. Those legs, those legs were nothing short of stupendous. But it was her eyes that got to him, those eyes that couldn't disguise the hard-headed intelligence within.

And then she saw him and stopped. Her gaze flicked in his direction, then out at the casino, then back at him, as if she were debating something. Then like a kid sent to do an unpleasant errand, her feet all but dragging, she approached.

"Hello," she said, not sounding at all happy about it.

"Hey, there." He admired her. "So, were your errands a success?"

She blinked and flapped her hand vaguely. "Sort of."

"Sort of," he repeated and crossed his arms, watching her with interest. He wasn't about to push. If she had something to say, the play was all hers.

Gwen squared her shoulders with a hint of defiance. "Don't get any ideas because I stopped."

"I wouldn't dream of it."

"I came over here…" She hesitated and suddenly looked very young. "I came over here to apologize for this morning. I shouldn't have called you an—"

"Asshole?" he supplied helpfully. "I believe that's what you said."

Her face flamed. "Yes. I'm sorry. I'm not usually a name caller. I'm just a little stressed out right now."

"Those must be some errands."

Something flickered in her eyes. Caution? Fear? Whatever it was, it shut her down. "It'll be fine."

"And how's Rennie?" He couldn't resist poking a little.

"Get off the whole Rennie thing, already, will you?" she snapped. "It's nothing."

"I guess you are kind of stressed."

Her eyes flashed with temper.

"Look," she began. And stopped abruptly, staring at something or someone behind him. He turned to see. The door to the casino offices had just closed behind a guy with dark blond hair and a casino staffer. Del couldn't hear much of what they were saying above the chatter of the slot machines, but the blond guy was sounding persuasive.

Then again, he looked like the kind of guy who spent most of his time trying to talk someone into something. The whole package was just a little too slick, a little too pretty. His hair was disarranged and gleamed just a bit with gel, his shirt and jacket were tailored just a little too sharply.

He put his hand on the staffer's shoulder as if he was his best buddy.

*Operator* was the word that sprang to mind.

Nina was riveted.

# 7

SHE COULDN'T SEE WHERE HE'D come from. One moment she'd been standing there, fumbling her way through an apology and avoiding Del's eyes. The next Jerry had been there talking with someone who wore the dark blue jacket of the casino management.

Her heart jumped into her throat. This was the telling moment. Would her disguise hold? Jerry glanced across at her, looked away and glanced more deliberately this time, even as he continued his conversation. Had he recognized her? No, the look wasn't one of identification, she realized. It was the same look a glutton might give to a plate of gooey cream puffs set in front of him.

Only she wasn't a cream puff, and Jerry was going to find that out the hard way.

The shock of locating him was fading as her mind started racing through the possibilities. She'd found him, sure, but at this point keeping contact with him was like trying to grasp water. He could walk any minute, and she'd be in the same spot she'd been in five minutes before.

Establishing some kind of connection with him, even for a moment, was imperative. Right now she didn't even know his room number, and the hotel desk clerks resolutely refused to budge on that matter. Cultivating a staffer might help, but who knew how quickly that would pay off? She needed to get to Jerry now.

The two men moved toward the archway that led to the bank of elevators. Gwen's decision was instantaneous.

"I have to run for a minute," she said to Del without taking her eyes off Jerry.

"But we were having such a good time." He followed her gaze. "Ah. I see. Find your man?"

She glanced back at Del quickly. His look told her she wasn't fooling him even a little. It was something she couldn't afford to think about, though. She hurried toward the bank of elevators, turning the corner just as Jerry disappeared inside a car.

"Hold the elevator," she called out desperately.

She saw him move toward the control panel of the empty car, but the door was already closing. Gwen could only stand and watch in helpless defeat as it went. And then she looked at the sign above the car. Express elevator to concierge level. Penthouse suites. Either he was visiting someone or that was where he was staying.

Seething with suppressed fury, she walked back into the casino. The little creep had cashed in her grandfather's stamps so that he could roll around in a five-hundred-dollar-a-night suite. She gritted her teeth. She'd get the rest of the stamps back somehow, some way.

And she'd get Jerry while she was at it.

"You run well in heels," someone said. She turned to see Del.

She flushed—she could feel it. A more accommodating guy would have taken the hint, but no, he just hung around. Until she could convince him that nothing was going on, she'd have him keeping an eye on her—surveillance she could ill afford. "I thought I left my phone in my room," she lied.

He gave her a skeptical look. Embarrassed, Gwen moved her gaze to the wall behind him. And then she

saw it, the sign that stood by the door to the casino office. Circle of Champions Poker Tournament, it read.
Enter Now. "There's a poker tournament?" she asked
blankly.

"Yeah." Del watched her. "Texas Hold 'em. It starts
Saturday. What do you think I'm doing here?"

"You told me you were writing a story on poker," she
said, resisting the urge to shout. The casino suddenly felt
stifling, as though there wasn't enough air.

"Exactly. I'm playing in the tournament and writing a
first-person series on what it's like."

Gwen stared at the sign. Oh, it fit. It was exactly the way
a slick little operator like Jerry would think—use the stolen
money as a stake to win even more. Or lose it, but guys like
Jerry never thought of that. They always looked for the easy
way. And if she wanted to keep an eye on him… "Are they
still taking entries? Do you think I could get into it?"

"Got ambitions of winning a bundle?"

"You have no idea," she said grimly and opened the
glass door.

GWEN STOOD IN LINE BEHIND half a dozen people, waiting
her turn at the registration counter. A slender auburn-haired
woman in low-cut white pants and a lace-up leather vest
walked into the office and stared at the tableau. "You have
got to be kidding," she said in disgust as the men all stared
at her. "I so do not have time for this." She got in line behind Gwen and tapped her foot impatiently.

"You could come back later," Gwen pointed out.

The woman shook her head, what looked like real diamonds glittering in her ears. "Too close to the limit as it is."

"There's a limit?"

"Uh-huh. Seven hundred and twenty players, period.
World Series of Poker lets in anyone who can pay the fee.

Unlike some casinos that don't want to let us make any money." She raised her voice.

"You talk foul, Roxy, you're not gonna get in," called the gray-haired clerk at the counter.

"Do my registration for me, Tommy, and I'll make it worth your while when I win," she tossed back.

Tommy just snorted.

Roxy jiggled on the balls of her feet, then turned her attention to Gwen. "So, I haven't seen you at one of these before." She looked at her assessingly.

Gwen shook her head. "I just happened to be in town and figured I'd give it a try."

"Gotta get your kicks while you can, right? You play a lot?"

"I've got a weekly home game."

"Watch out, honey bunch, 'cause this is a whole different ballgame. You might think twice about that ten K you're about to cough up."

Gwen glanced at her with pursed lips. "This wouldn't by any chance be a move to get me to drop out of line, would it?"

"Shoot, that obvious?" Roxy asked in disgust. "I'd better brush up before the playing starts." She grinned, sticking out her hand. "Roxanne Steele, last year's champion."

"Nina Chatham." Gwen shook. "So, you won last year, huh?"

Roxy nodded. "Finished just out of the money in the World Series main event, too. That's right, boys," she said more loudly, "the chicks are moving in."

"I got a place you can move into, Roxy," said the man at the front of the line as he walked away from the counter.

"In your dreams, Buchanan." She slapped hands with him as he walked by and turned back to Gwen. "So, a weekly home game, that's it?"

"Well, one of the players who used to be in the game was a high-stakes regular in Reno, so we got it second-hand." Roxy's pitying look got Gwen's back up. "Another guy competed in last year's World Series. He pushed us all into studying up so we'd be better to practice against."

"How'd he do?"

"Not great. Fifty-fourth."

Roxy whistled. "Fifty-fourth out of twenty-seven hundred some-odd players is pretty damned good. You ever beat him?"

"Took a couple of pots from him in our last game," Gwen said with enjoyment. "One of them was a bluff on a pair of treys."

"Nice," Roxy said admiringly. "You might just have the chops for it. Maybe I'll see you around. After all, we chicks got to stick together."

"Don't we just," Gwen murmured.

DEL STOOD, MIND BUZZING. HE knew what she'd be doing inside—filling out paperwork, handing over the ten-thousand-dollar stake money, getting her number. What he couldn't figure out was why. Nina didn't strike him as the tournament type. Then again, he didn't know quite how to categorize her. One minute she was giving him an awkward apology, all but scraping her toe on the pavement. The next she was practically vibrating with excitement at the sight of the little hustler. Not like a woman who was intrigued or turned on, though. She'd had more of the quivering intensity of a hunting dog pointing at its quarry.

Maybe she was right. Maybe he was so hung up on investigating stories that he *was* imagining things. Maybe it was all in his head.

Then again, maybe it wasn't.

He waited for her to come out and fell in alongside her

as she walked, her hands full of rule sheets and tournament information.

"So, I guess you made it in." He gestured at her paperwork.

"I don't have time to talk with you right now."

"Do you know anything about how the tournament works? You don't have a lot of time to find out." She stopped impatiently and turned to face him, mouth open to say something. Del held up his hands. "I'm not trying to bug you," he promised. "Have lunch with me, I can help you out."

She gave him an indecisive glance.

"I'll keep it to poker, I swear."

"All right," she said reluctantly.

He steered her into a café and held up two fingers to the hostess. "You're in the second half?"

Gwen nodded. "It starts Sunday night."

"Saving the best for last."

The hostess led them to a table and seated them. Del opened his menu. "So, you know what you're doing?"

"Why does everybody keep asking me?" she snapped. "I'm going to do just fine in this tournament. I might just surprise you."

"She said with steely determination in her eyes."

Gwen glowered at him. "Don't mock me."

"Sorry. Bad habit. I've seen you play blackjack. Granted, it's not Texas Hold 'em, but you look like you can handle yourself okay."

The waitress stopped for their drink order.

"Thanks for the vote of confidence," Gwen said when they were done. "I'm just glad I got in."

"I'm impressed. You make a decision and you go for it. Gotta love a woman who walks around with a spare ten grand in her purse for emergencies."

"That's what cash advances are for," Gwen said breezily, though the reminder of the stake money required for tournament play made her stomach clench. She dearly hoped all those years of playing poker with her grandfather were going to pay off, because otherwise she'd just tossed away a huge chunk of her future. "Sign and smile."

"And think about the bills later?"

"I'm too busy worrying about how I'm going to spend the other nine hundred and ninety thousand of the prize money."

"An optimist, I see."

"Remind me to gloat at you when I accept my check."

A mural of the Strip covered one wall, showing casino after casino, from the Venetian down to the glossy black pyramid of the Luxor. "God, what a weird town this is," Gwen said, shaking her head.

"How so?" Del took his beer from the waitress.

"Well, look at it." Gwen gestured, waving at the Eiffel Tower of Paris, the pyramid of the Luxor, the pumped-up Manhattan skyline of New York, New York. "It's like Disneyland on steroids. You've got all this kid-friendly stuff, you've got the roller coasters and the wave pool at Mandalay Bay and Circus Circus and then you've got taxicabs advertising strip clubs, complete with photos and call girls in the hotel lobbies."

"Call girls? Here?" He looked around hopefully. "No one told me."

She fought a grin. "I just think it's a strange mix."

"So if you feel that way, why are you here?" The look, she saw, was back. "I mean, you came for a getaway, not the tournament. Why here? Why not San Diego or Mexico?"

Gwen busied herself taking the wrapper off her straw. Her and her big mouth. That had been Gwen talking, not Nina, who probably loved the luxe decadence of Vegas. Then again, Nina never apologized or explained about anything. *Brazen it out,* she reminded herself. "Anyplace that's going to let me turn fifty bucks into two hundred is okay with me. Anyway, the tournament's worth it all."

"That's right, you're planning on winning the million."

"Just watch me."

# 8

PRACTICE, GWEN THOUGHT AS SHE walked through the casino. If she was going to be even remotely competitive against a field of more than seven hundred in the Texas Hold 'em tournament, she needed practice. As much as she cringed at the idea of sacrificing another few hundred dollars to the Las Vegas gods, Gwen knew it was a necessary evil.

As were the tight, low-rise turquoise pants she wore. The fact that her devotion to aerobics and Pilates meant she could fit into them and still breathe did little to make her comfortable with the admiring stares she earned as she walked into the poker room. She'd find a table with both men and women and play a few hands just to get limbered up, she figured.

She walked up to the entrance to check out the rules posted and then stopped. "Oh, yes," she whispered, staring at the table across the way where Jerry was sitting. What better way to strike up an acquaintance than over a friendly game of poker? She fluffed her hair and licked her lips. Who knew, maybe they'd hit it off.

She'd make sure of it.

A squadron of butterflies skittered around in her stomach as she neared the table. What if Joss were wrong and he recognized her? Stewart had laughed at the idea of her undercover. Maybe it was ludicrous. What if all she accomplished was to tip him off that he was known? What if he wouldn't talk to her at all?

And what if he did?

Okay, so what if he did? She squared her shoulders and took a deep breath. Nina could handle him. Nina knew how to have guys eating out of her palm and she'd have Jerry, too. Gwen remembered the way he'd looked at her that afternoon. *Like taking candy from a baby,* she told herself.

And tried to believe it.

Besides, she had experience now striking up an acquaintance with someone she thought could give her information. She'd done it the night before and it hadn't been a disaster.

Outside of finding herself the next morning with one very inquisitive man, of course.

*That didn't count, though,* she told herself hastily. She had zero intention of winding up anywhere near a bed with Jerry. The very idea of his hands on her raised the hackles on the back of her neck.

Jerry turned to look at her as she stopped. "Well, hello, there."

"Hello, there, yourself." Gwen pulled out a chair. The sign said the limit on bets was ten dollars minimum and twenty dollars maximum. It would fit in her budget so long as the cards went her way. "Room for another player here?"

"This seat here is the lucky one," he said, patting the chair to his right.

"I'm sure it is, but I'll take my chances," Gwen said, sitting on his left, where she'd generally bet after him. The later, the better was her motto. It wouldn't hurt her a bit to take some of Jerry's money.

"I see you know the game."

She gave him a provocative smile. "Sugar, I know every game there is."

To her left sat a couple of guys she figured for conventioneers out for the night. They were like Mutt and Jeff— one tall and narrow, one short and plump.

To Jerry's right sat a middle-aged couple wearing wedding rings. A horseshoe dangled from a silver chain around the woman's neck. From their accents, Gwen pegged them as from Arkansas, maybe, or Oklahoma. From the fumbling way they finished out the hand, she pegged them as beginners. The conventioneers, she'd reserve judgment on. Jerry, she figured, was a player—or at least fancied himself as one.

Gwen passed a handful of twenties to the dealer.

"New player, change a hundred," the dealer said briskly and pushed a stack of five-dollar chips toward Gwen.

"Sorry I couldn't hold the elevator for you this afternoon," Jerry said to her as the dealer swabbed the deck around on the table in front of him, then gathered it together for the more conventional shuffle.

"I'm flattered you remembered me."

"Oh, I'm good at the important stuff—cards and women. Shoot, I almost stopped and came back down for you."

"What a prince."

"Yeah, that's me."

The dealer gathered the deck together and tamped it a few times on the table. "Blinds?" he called.

"That's you, Fred." The woman nudged her husband. She sat in front of the white plastic disk, or button. Fred was to her left, which meant that he bet first throughout the hand, starting with the small blind, a required bet of half the minimum—in this case, five dollars.

"I guess that makes me the big blind," Jerry, next to Fred, said with a leer that Gwen ignored. Carelessly he flicked out the table's minimum bet required for the big blind; the two five-dollar chips clicked as they hit Fred's.

With a flick of the wrist the dealer dealt them their pairs of facedown pocket cards. Gwen pulled up the corner of her cards to discover a pair of queens. She allowed herself the luxury of a small frown. "I thought you promised me luck," she complained to Jerry.

"I can't guarantee the cards, doll, I can only guarantee me."

"Big talk," she scoffed.

"I'll show you how big, if you want."

Gwen resisted the urge to groan and instead ordered a martini from the waitress who stopped by. Maybe it would help her ignore the fact that he was a cretin. Judging by the sound of Jerry's voice, he'd already knocked back a few himself.

Fred folded without laying a bet down, frowning at the five-dollar chip he'd sacrificed to the small blind. Jerry seemed to like what he had, tossing out a ten-dollar chip. Gwen nibbled her lip. He might have something, but then again, her pair of queens made her competitive right off the bat. With a made hand, she could afford a little risk. More importantly, she needed to drive players away from the table and get Jerry to herself. Quickly she doubled Jerry's bet.

The conventioneers matched her with confidence perhaps fueled by the beers at their elbows. Fred's wife turned a chip over and over again in her hand before nervously tossing it out.

The dealer turned over the flop—the first three of the community cards—to reveal an ace and two nines. Two pair for Gwen, though given that everybody at the table could count a pair of nines from the flop, it didn't really mean much. The queens, though, they gave her a nice, warm feeling.

The betting came around to Jerry. "You going to bring luck to me?"

"Probably as much luck as you bring me," Gwen returned.

"You sit here long enough, I can guarantee you'll get lucky."

Gwen didn't cringe. She congratulated herself for that. Nina wouldn't. Nina wouldn't care how classless his innuendoes were, so long as she achieved her goal. Gwen raised and watched the betting continue. Fred's wife folded before the next community card—the turn card—which was a queen. Gwen gave a mental hallelujah. If all went well, she'd make a little money on the deal.

When the betting came back to her, she raised—and substantially. It was time to see just what the conventioneers were made of.

Mutt didn't hold on to see what the dealer would turn over for the river card, the last of the five community cards. Instead he folded. *Conservative,* Gwen diagnosed. He'd be hard to break but might be easy to push away from the table with a series of high bets, assuming her luck held. Jeff checked, playing wait and see and also giving the scent of blood in the water. Jerry raised.

"You gonna keep up with me?" he asked with a wink.

Gwen smiled and called, matching his twenty dollars in chips and adding twenty of her own. "I'll leave you in the dust." She flicked her gaze to the side as she said it, though, adding a bit of false bravado to her voice. He had something, she figured, maybe two pair, maybe the start of a straight, but probably not enough to beat a full house.

She nodded to the dealer for the river card. He turned it over to show a two. Jeff folded, leaving only Jerry and Gwen. The betting went around again, with each of them raising. Finally Jerry checked.

Gwen gave him a smile like a cat at a dish of cream. "Full house," she said, flipping over her pocket pair.

Jerry blinked. "Well, hell," he said feelingly, not bothering to turn up his cards.

Gwen raked in the chips. "Looks like I brought that luck, sugar, just not for you."

DEL WALKED UP TO THE POKER room, tuning out the familiar hubbub of the casino. With the tournament due to start in just a couple of days, he was itching to log some time at the tables. Granted, he was writing about an average guy's experience at the tournament, but he had a couple of ten spots riding with various hecklers at the paper who were betting he wouldn't last the first day of play.

Practice made perfect —so said his mother and every coach he'd ever had. A couple of hours at the tables, he figured, couldn't hurt.

He looked over the room, searching out a table that seemed favorable. And saw Nina curled up at the table with the hustler, giving every appearance of being charmed. Del watched for a moment, felt the clutch in his gut that was becoming familiar.

Okay, so why did he care? Maybe she was the type who liked variety. With looks like hers, he couldn't blame her. And yet for every minute she was the man crusher, there was an instant when she looked like an uncertain teenager playing dress-up. Like the contact lens that morning, he thought with a smile.

Only idiots got hung up on women who didn't want them, he reminded himself. Then his eyes narrowed as the little hustler brushed a hand over her shoulders. She tensed for a moment, almost flinched. It was small, but Del saw it, just as he saw her take a breath and then, he swore consciously, lean closer to click her glass with the hustler's. Like a woman who was pretending to have a good time.

And suspicion rolled back over him.

It was none of his business—hadn't she told him that just that morning? He'd do well to listen to advice and leave well enough alone. Del Do-Right, his sisters had always called him in amusement. Always ready to help the maiden in distress. She wasn't his to save, though she might just need saving.

He watched her flinch again at the hustler's touch and consciously loosened his jaw. It wasn't his problem. Then again, he'd come downstairs for some poker practice. Why not be congenial, play at a table where he knew someone?

And he walked over.

FRED AND HIS WIFE were long gone. Mutt had taken a look at his dwindling supply of chips and decided to call it a night. Jeff had followed, leaving the table to Jerry and Gwen.

"Want to move to another table?" the dealer asked.

"No, this is perfect," Gwen told him, admiring her own stack of chips.

"Looks like it's down to you and me," Jerry said, leaning toward her.

Just what she'd been hoping for.

"Not exactly," said a voice over Gwen's shoulder, and Del Redmond sat down beside her. "Evening." He handed a pair of hundred-dollar bills to the dealer.

"You want a bigger game, pal." Jerry threw him a look of sulky dislike.

"This one suits me fine," he said pleasantly and reached out for his chips.

The waitress came by to take a drink order from Jerry. Gwen took a swallow of her martini and leaned toward Del. "What are you doing here?" she hissed.

He gave her a bland smile. "Just getting in a practice game before the tournament starts." He leaned forward to look across her. "You playing in the tournament?" he asked Jerry.

"Yeah."

"Me, too. Del Redmond." He reached out to shake hands.

"Jerry Messner."

"I'm doing a story for the *San Francisco Globe* on the experience. Maybe I can interview you later."

The dealer cleared his throat. "The game, gentlemen?"

This time the chemistry was totally different. There were no amateurs at the table, and Hold 'em was a game designed to encourage big bets. Del took a stack of chips between the fingers of one hand, splitting it into two stacks and riffling them together like cards. She remembered how those hands had felt on her body, the way they'd made her feel.

And wasn't that just the last thing she needed to be thinking about? *Pay attention to the game,* she scolded herself. Nina wouldn't let it get to her. Nina would put it in a box and set it aside. Nina wouldn't be so blown away by chemistry because Nina would be used to it. Nina would be in control.

Gwen only hoped she could be.

This hand, Jerry was the small blind. Gwen tossed out her bet for the big blind and turned to see Del watching her with that look that said he knew a joke and she and Jerry were the punch line.

She wondered if he was as good at Hold 'em as he was at everything else.

Her pocket held a ten and a king, both clubs. Potential for a straight or a flush, but not one she was going to bank on unless the flop turned up something. Then again, attacking might throw both men off balance. Jerry bet twenty dollars in chips. She raised him twenty. Del merely lifted an eyebrow and kept up.

Then the dealer turned over the flop to reveal a three of clubs and a ten and a five of spades. The pair of tens gave her something, but she was going to put her faith in the turn card and the river card. *In the meantime bluff,* she figured and did what she usually did when she had a good hand.

"Now, don't you go doing that again, babe," Jerry told

her at her frown, tossing down a pair of ten-dollar chips. "Last time you did that, you were sitting on a pair of ladies."

She raised him. "You figure I got something sweet?"

"I don't," Del said. "I think you're bluffing."

Now she did frown for real. Trust him to read not only her face but her body language, whatever part of her that was telling the truth. Her leg, she realized. It was bobbing, and he could see it out of the corner of his eye. "Big talk," she said aloud, consciously trying to relax.

Tonight Del wore black jeans and a white shirt, the sleeves rolled up to his elbows. The little things impinged on her consciousness: the clean scent of him, the way his jaw was just a bit dark with the day's growth of beard, the look of his lean wrists as he reached down and tilted up the corner of his pocket pair for a look.

She remembered how he'd looked with nothing on.

"Your bet."

Gwen jumped and glanced to see Del grinning at her. Jerry had put down twenty on the flop. She doubled it. When Del raised on that, she nibbled the inside of her lip. The turn was a jack of clubs.

When she had her chance, she raised, then raised again.

The dealer turned over the river card to reveal a club. She could have kissed him. With a disgusted noise Jerry folded. It was down to Gwen and Del.

"It looks like you're pretty good at Hold 'em," he observed, nodding to her pile of chips and tossing down the ten-dollar minimum. "I didn't expect to see you down here tonight."

Gwen immediately raised him twenty. "I figured I needed to get warmed up," she told him.

"I thought you were pretty hot already." He called and looked at her.

She paused for effect, checking her pocket cards and tapping her finger against them. It was worth seeing if she could draw him into another raise. She began bobbing her leg again.

Del raised her. Gwen smiled and checked. She flipped her cards over. "Wall-to-wall clubs." She gave him a challenging stare. "Don't know me as well as you thought you did."

"Oh, yeah, I do." He turned up his pocket cards to show a full house.

She uttered a sharp, pithy curse.

He raised his eyebrows. "Pretty spicy language there."

"I don't like being played."

"You'd better go home now, then," he told her.

It reminded her of why she was there in the first place and she turned her attention back to Jerry as the dealer shuffled. "So, when's your first round in the tournament?"

"Tomorrow." He sounded petulant, out of sorts at being ignored.

"Well, here's to luck, then." She raised her glass to his and licked her lips.

"Maybe I'll get lucky."

"Maybe you will."

Gwen played the next hand more conservatively. Her pile of chips was down after the big loss to Del and she needed to recharge. The flop turned the single king in her pocket into a pair, and the river made it a trio. Del, to her disgust, folded early, but she was able to lure Jerry into betting enough that she had a solid take when they finished the hand.

"You better leave me with some of my money, babydoll," he complained, "or I won't have any of it to spend on you."

"You got plans to spend money on me?" She turned away from Del, deliberately ignoring him. It made her more conscious of him than ever. When Jerry reached out to brush his fingers through her hair, he caught her unawares and she jerked back just a bit.

"Take you out for a drink after. They got that fancy revolving bar at the top of the hotel. How about if we play a few more hands, then go on up, have a nice time?"

She gave him a warm smile of promise. "I can't think of anything else I'd rather do."

"That sounds good," Del said from behind her. "Why don't you let me buy you two a drink? I can interview you both about the tournament."

She could have spit. He was nothing but trouble. He'd already figured out she wanted to get Jerry to herself and seemed hell-bent on sabotaging her. "Oh, I think three's a crowd. He and I have plans to—"

"Can I have a fake name?" Jerry cut in suddenly, as though not tracking the conversation too well. The tequila sunrises he'd been sucking down all night seemed to finally have begun blurring his words. "I mean, I don't want to show up as me."

Del's expression was harmlessly affable. "Sure, we can give you a pseudonym. People just want the story." He signaled to the dealer to consolidate his chips. "Why don't we call it a night here and go chase down some liquor?"

Anger vibrated through her as they walked from the poker room to the bank of elevators. She didn't know what he thought he was up to, but as soon as she got a chance, she was going to find out. Better yet, she'd jump down his throat first, ask questions later. The casual brush of his fingertips in the small of her back as they passed through a crowd of people had her tensing. She could feel his touch through her shirt like four small coins of heat. "Hands off," she snapped.

"You say something, babe?" Jerry asked, knocking obliviously into a woman passing on his other side.

"Not at all. I'm looking forward to the view."

A large party of conventioneers milled about at the express elevator that led to the revolving bar. When the doors opened, Jerry crowded in with them. Del gripped Gwen's arm and held her back. "We'll catch the next one," he explained, waving at Jerry as the doors closed.

As soon as the car was gone, Gwen whirled to him. "What in the hell do you think you're doing?" she snapped. "You are *not* invited to this little jamboree."

"It's been a long night. I figure I could use a drink."

"I need to talk with him."

He shrugged. "So talk with him."

"In *private*. Is it that hard for you to believe that I'm interested in someone else?"

His stare was direct. "It's hard for me to believe that you want him."

"Everything was going perfectly until you came along," she muttered, stomping onto the express elevator as soon as the doors opened. "I was having a good time."

The door closed, leaving just her and Del inside. "Really?" He punched the button for the restaurant. "You didn't look like you were having much fun at all."

Suddenly the space felt very small. Gwen leaned against the brass railing that encircled the glass arc of the elevator and swallowed. "What's it your business?"

Del stepped closer to her. "That's what I keep asking myself. There's no real reason I should care, but I watched you flinch every time he touched you and I didn't like it."

"I didn't flinch."

"Sure you did—just a hint, before you caught yourself." He ran his thumb across her cheek and sent heat singing through her. "You might have convinced him because he's too drunk to see it, but it didn't fool me."

Suddenly she felt a little dizzy. "And who made you the expert?"

"I know how you act when you want to be touched," he said, leaning in toward her. "Remember?"

"You're jealous," she managed, feeling his lips a hair's breadth away from hers.

And then his mouth came down on her. All day she'd been pushing him back, setting up defenses, trying for distance. In one swift move he stripped them all away. In one swift move he showed her how desire could slice through it all. She thought of herself as strong; he made her weak. She thought of herself as calm; he made her wild. She thought of herself as controlled; he brought out the frenzy.

And, oh, it felt right. She knew she should be worrying about Jerry, she knew she should be worrying about the stamps, but all she could think about was the soft, driving heat of Del's mouth, his body against hers. It felt so right, washing away the creeping unease Jerry's frequent touches had built. She felt clean and right and ready. She wanted more. With a soft sound Gwen pulled herself closer.

He didn't know what drove him. It wasn't her challenges, though she'd thrown them out with abandon. It wasn't the way she looked, drenched with sexuality. It was the bright spark of her, the riddle, the complexity, that drew him in. Knowing that she wanted him, knowing that she didn't want to, knowing that she would yield to him in spite of herself.

Knowing that they weren't finished with each other yet, not by a long shot.

The elevator slowed and Gwen jerked away, breathing hard. "This is my time with Jerry and I don't want you here," she said intensely, turning away as the car shuddered to a stop.

"Maybe you can ask him about Rennie."

Quick as a flash she rounded on him. "Don't you dare mention that name," she said urgently, gripping his forearm with surprising strength. "This is not a game, Del. I don't know what you think you're doing, but you have no idea what's at stake."

Del shook his head. "What's going on, Gwen?"

"It's none of your affair."

"It's pretty hard to walk away from. You're pretty hard to walk away from. Show me what you're holding."

She shook her head, eyes turbulent, mistrustful. "They're my pocket cards, Del, and they'll stay down." And as the doors opened, she turned away.

# 9

"HELLO?" THE VOICE WAS FROGGY with sleep.

"Joss." Gwen held her cell phone, her hands-free cord connecting it to her ear as she walked down Flamingo Road, away from the Strip.

"What time is it?" Joss croaked. Something thudded to the floor in the background.

Gwen gave a half smile. "Seven." The morning air was cool, the casinos out of sight and out of mind behind her. The constant atmosphere of the gambling had begun to stifle her. Out here she could almost breathe.

"Great. You have all day and night yesterday to call me and you pick the crack of dawn today instead." Gwen heard the sound of a jaw-creaking yawn. "Your timing is perfect."

"I wanted to catch you before you got busy."

"I was busy. Sleeping."

"Sorry."

"Well, I'm up now, so talk. Why didn't you call me yesterday? What's going on?"

"I found Jerry."

Joss choked.

"Are you okay?" Gwen asked in concern.

"Yeah. Just took me by surprise there. You do get a kick out of springing things on a person, don't you?" She coughed again. "So, what happened? Did he recognize you?"

Gwen studied her reflection in the window of a video

store. "Hadn't a clue. Although he was pretty well oiled at the time, so that might have had something to do with it. He's quite a drinker, our Jerry."

"What about Rennie? Did you find out anything there?"

"Not exactly. I found a guy I thought was Rennie," she said, her mind drifting to Del. Absently she found herself touching her mouth with the fingers of one hand.

"And?"

"And nothing." She dropped her hand. "It was a mistake." Exaggeration of the year. She frowned. "I don't want to talk about it."

"Why'd you bring it up?"

"No reason."

Joss made a sound halfway between a snort and a laugh. "I've known you pretty much since the first day you could talk and you've never said anything for no reason. Who's the guy? What's his story?"

A palm tree planted during some long-ago urban-renewal project curved up from a niche in the sidewalk, its fronds making a basket-weave pattern of shadows on the pavement. Looking down the street, Gwen could see reddish-purple mountains rising in the distance. "I'm not sure."

"You're dying to tell me, I can hear it in your voice."

"I'm not—"

"Never argue with your older sister."

Joss was right, she was dying to tell someone. And before she knew it, the whole story came tumbling out.

When she'd finished, she could hear Joss clapping. "Honey bunch, your first one-night stand. You've grown up."

"Don't be smart. I could have screwed up everything."

"Oh, don't be such a drama queen," Joss said impatiently. "Did you have fun?"

*Fun* didn't quite describe it. "It was pretty amazing."

"Amazing enough for a rematch?"

"Joss, let me just worry about Jerry."

"I don't see how the two have anything to do with one another."

"Because Del's a reporter, remember? He's decided something's up and he won't let it go."

"Well, something *is* up."

"And he's the last person who needs to know that. We've got enough to worry about right now without winding up on the front page."

"Do you really think he'd do that?"

*Why not?* Gwen wondered. He didn't know her and she certainly didn't know anything about him. "I don't know. I just know I'm trying to work Jerry and he keeps getting in the way and I can't get rid of him."

"Do you really want to?"

"What I want to do is get back the stamps and I can't do it if he shows up every time I try to get Jerry to give me something I can use," she said impatiently.

"What's your plan?"

"I've got to find out if Jerry's got the stamps with him and the only way I'm going to do that is to get into his room." Simple enough, as plans went. Only the execution was tricky.

"So bribe a maid."

Gwen turned so that she was cruising along Paradise Road, parallel to the Strip. "Oh, yeah, I'm sure they help with break-ins all the time. Besides, I think he's on concierge level."

"So?"

"So that means getting into a special elevator that requires a passkey and past the host up there and then getting into the room. It's not going to be easy."

"It's four and a half million, Gwen. Easy is too much to expect."

"Yeah. There's an upside, too, though."

"Yeah?"

"Jerry's fenced three of the store inventory stamps that I can tell, but according to Stewart's sources, no one's making noises on the market about the really valuable ones. That gives us some time." Gwen only hoped it would be enough.

"Want me to come out? I could stay out of sight."

"No. You've got to watch the store. Besides, someone's got to be around in case Grampa calls."

"Yeah, I know." Joss blew out a breath. "So, back to this Del. What do you want to do about him?"

What did she want? Gwen sighed.

"Hey," Joss laughed. "You sound like your dog just died. Has this guy actually gotten under your skin?"

"I don't know. Every time I get within ten feet of him I get this incredible urge to either strangle him or to rip his clothes off and boff his brains out."

"Well, at least you're clear about things."

Gwen rolled her shoulders. "I can't think about him right now. I just can't. I've got more important things to worry about." Four-point-five million, she couldn't forget.

Not even for Del Redmond.

In the enormous ballroom the mass of people at the tournament reception ebbed and flowed like some giant amoeba. Chandeliers glimmered overhead. In the corner a band played a Jimmy Buffett tune, the music only slightly louder than the hubbub of several hundred voices talking all at once. It was the sort of scene Gwen avoided like the plague.

These weren't normal times, though, and if there was even a chance of running into Jerry, she had to take it. So she'd forced herself to put on the magenta slip dress, pin on her competitor's ribbon and make an appearance. She'd scout around, she told herself, see if she could find Jerry and lure him to dinner. Liquored up a bit and bathed in the warmth of wide-eyed female fascination, who knew what he'd say? It should have been a piece of cake.

She'd never expected to walk into party central.

Standing just inside the doorway, she gave herself a silent pep talk. Taking a deep breath, Gwen prepared to dive in.

"Coming to meet the players?" asked a voice behind her.

She turned to see Del. He wore a pewter silk shirt and black jeans. His eyes were very green. No matter what words had passed between them the night before, he was a familiar face, and Gwen found herself smiling at him in relief. "Where did this mob come from?"

He shrugged. "Well, they've been telling everyone who walked into the casino for the past week to come tonight and meet the players. Appears everyone took them up on it."

"Came for the food and open bar, more like it," Gwen said.

"Same difference. The point is to get 'em here, get 'em all loose and excited about playing. When they're ready to leave, the only way out is that nifty little escalator outside that goes down to the casino."

"Convenient."

"And no accident. I'm sure the cost of this is a drop in the bucket compared to what they'll haul in from all the little stops their guests make on the way out."

"Cynical."

He shook his head and gestured for her to walk ahead of him. "Realistic."

They wove their way farther into the room, past the various gambling tables that had been set up around the perimeter, from roulette to blackjack. They stopped in a little clearing where the craps table was located.

"I guess they're trying to give us a little variety." Gwen nodded at the croupiers.

"Maybe the craps tournament is next week."

"Now there's an id—"

"Hey, poker chick," a voice called from behind her. "How ya doing?"

Gwen turned to find Roxy, resplendent in a pair of black leather pants and a silver halter top. Laughing, she carried two bottles of beer in each hand.

Gwen nodded at the bottles. "Planning ahead?"

"Nah. I'm here with a couple of the guys and I lost a bet. Loser had to go to the bar." Adroitly she managed to drink from one of the bottles without spilling. "So, who's your good-looking friend?"

Gwen turned. "Roxy, this is Del Redmond. Del, this is Roxy Steele. Roxy won the tournament last year."

"Congratulations. You planning to do an encore?"

"Maybe." Roxy winked at him. "Are you a player or just her rooting section?"

Del's lips twitched. "A player, but I'm pretty good at rooting, too."

"Tall one, aren't you?" Roxy stared up at him.

"Guilty as charged."

"So, when are you up, stretch?"

"First wave," he told her.

"Great. I'll give Nina here a list of the guys I want you to bust out of the tournament for me, okay?"

"Consider it done."

Someone shouted Roxy's name from down the way. "Okay, I'm being paged. Hey, nice to meet you. I'll see you at the final table." She raised one hand with bottles in jaunty salute and walked off.

"So that's Roxy," Gwen told him with a laugh.

"And the world of poker will never be the same."

Gwen gave Del a thoughtful look. "She's right, you are a tall one."

"One of my many fine qualities. It's particularly helpful in getting the attention of the bartender. Can I get you a drink?"

"Sure. How about a cosmopolitan?" Gwen told him.

"More girlie drinks?"

"I am a girl, in case you hadn't noticed."

He looked her up and down. "Oh, I've definitely noticed."

He was as close to her as he'd been in the elevator. He'd kissed her, she remembered, pressing her back against the glass, his mouth hot on hers. System suddenly humming, she stared at him.

And a drunken partygoer pushed them apart, en route to the craps table.

It was enough to break the spell.

"I'll go get those drinks," Del told her, backing away.

Gwen nodded and watched him walk off, lean and rangy in his black jeans. She didn't want to think about the moment that had just passed. She didn't want to think about the night before. She didn't want to think about him. Instead she cast about for a distraction.

A shout from the craps table behind her caught her attention and she took a few steps over to watch. At her end of the table a bearded man in a polo shirt blew on the dice in his hand and tossed them to the far end. When he frowned disgustedly, she figured he hadn't gotten the results he'd hoped for. The croupier hooked the dice with his stick and handed them back.

Taking the dice, the bearded guy glanced around and stopped when he saw Gwen behind him. He tossed the dice a bit in his palm and held them out. "A kiss for luck?"

Gwen grinned and pressed her lips to the red cubes. He threw them out and a cheer erupted.

"So, can I get you to give me a kiss for luck before the tournament starts tomorrow?"

She turned to see Jerry at her elbow. Involuntarily she tensed, then consciously forced herself to relax and give him a slow smile. "Well, I don't know. If I give you luck, then I won't have any for myself."

"Just stick around me." He smirked. "I guarantee you'll get lucky."

"So you've told me." Gwen surveyed the reception crowd. "You ever been in a tournament before?"

"First time," he admitted, taking a swig of the beer he held. "I figure I'm a natural, though. I've been doing pretty well in the poker room all week."

"Except last night," she pointed out.

"You had an unfair advantage."

"What was that?"

His eyes shifted, his gaze skating somewhere below her clavicles. "I was being a gentleman."

"Careful. Real winners focus," she reminded him.

"Oh, I'm focused all right," he said with a lascivious smile, "and I'm already a winner."

"Really?"

"A big winner. I don't even need to win this tournament. This is just for fun."

"Really?" Ignoring the rush of excitement, she moistened her lips and leaned closer. "Tell me more."

Jerry puffed up like a peacock in his bright blue shirt. "Well, I—" He stopped, frowning, and reached in his pocket for his cell phone. With a glance at the display, he flipped it open. "What do you want?"

The cockiness became, if anything, more pronounced, but his eyes narrowed with purpose. This wasn't a social call, she thought, this was business.

"Look," Jerry said, "you get what you pay for. And if

you don't pay, there's a penalty. Deal with it." He glanced over at Gwen. "Just a second," he said into the phone. "Hey, babe," he said to Gwen, "I've got to take this. Give me five minutes, I'll be right back and we can pick up where we left off." He sauntered back toward the door.

Gwen watched him go. Just what kind of deals did a guy like Jerry have in play, she wondered? A deal that involved the Post Office Mauritius, possibly? Could she afford not to find out? She drifted after him, trying to ignore the twinge of guilt she felt at abandoning Del. It had just been a funny little moment. It still didn't make any sense to be involved with him. She was here to get a job done.

Glancing out in the hall, Gwen spied Jerry behind a seven-foot-tall ficus in a waist-high terra-cotta planter. He leaned against the wall, his back to her as he spoke into his phone. She crept nearer.

"Hey, I agreed to do a job for a reasonable price. Then you sit there telling me you can't come up with it. That's a problem." He paused. "Price jump? Think of it as a late fee, my man. You increased my cost of doing business. It's the law of supply and demand in action. I've still got what you'd call a supply, and you've got the demand."

Gwen could hear the squawk of protest from the phone. "Oh, give me a break. We went over this already," Jerry said impatiently. "You're lucky I'm still talking to you. Come up with the rest of the money and we'll do business. Otherwise, leave me alone, I'm busy."

He was silent again, then laughed a bit. "Sure, sure, you wanna go with the installment plan, fine. You give me your installments and I'll give you mine. That's more like it. I knew you had it in you." Suddenly he straightened. "Here? What are you doing here?" He began to pace back and forth a few steps, tension vibrating in his voice. "I told you I'd come to you. Where the hell do you get off…okay, okay,

I'll come meet you. But don't get any ideas about getting cute. The merchandise is safe and I've got a couple of guys watching my back who know what's going on. You want to see your goodies, you'll play it clean." He hunched over the phone, now totally absorbed. "All right, all right, fifteen minutes."

Gwen stepped hastily back toward the door as he hung up the phone. Then she stepped outside as though looking for him. Flipping his handset closed and tucking it away, he walked back toward her.

"Hey, baby."

"You ready to party now?"

"I'm ready to do everything," he told her with a wink as he stopped beside her. "But I gotta go meet a guy right now. I'll be back soon, though."

"The party'll be over by then," she said with a pout.

He slid his fingertips up and down her arm. "Maybe we can have ourselves a little party of our own, then."

It made her skin crawl, but she didn't react. She was Nina, and Nina used the power at her disposal to get what she wanted. "Don't be gone too long."

"Half hour," he promised and leaned in. For a kiss, she realized, turning at the last minute enough to deflect it to her cheek.

"Hurry back," she said, standing in the doorway and watching him walk away.

"I got to hand it to you, you don't waste time," Del commented from behind her. There was a little edge to his voice and he stood holding their drinks and watching her steadily. "Strike out?" He stepped out into the hall to stand with Gwen.

"Not exactly," she said without looking at him. She was a little embarrassed, but it was outweighed by equal parts of hope and anticipation. This was her first real chance to find something out and she couldn't afford to let it pass, even if that meant looking like a get-around gal. She flicked him a distracted smile. "Thanks for the drink but I've got to go."

Jerry was just stepping onto the escalator to the ground floor. If she hurried, she could keep him in sight.

# *10*

IT WASN'T HIS BUSINESS, DEL thought as he watched her hurry away, the skirt of her pink dress swishing. Then again, sticking his neck into what wasn't his business was starting to become habit, at least where Nina was concerned. He watched her walk off, bright and leggy and gorgeous. He had to be out of his mind to keeping worrying about her. For a couple of minutes there, it had actually felt as if they'd reconnected. Then, the minute he'd turned his back, she was running after Jerry again.

Why couldn't he let it go? Why couldn't he let *her* go?

The problem, of course, was that he had a pretty good idea it wasn't chemistry that had her chasing Jerry, any more than it had been chemistry the night before. Something was going on.

And wherever a little hustler like Jerry was running off to at a minute's notice, it couldn't be anywhere good.

Del set the drinks on a nearby bussing tray and brushed off his hands. It really couldn't hurt for him to follow along.

JERRY GOT OFF THE ESCALATOR on the ground floor and sauntered through the broad concourse that surrounded the casino for all the world, as if he had nothing on his mind. Maybe he didn't, Gwen thought, trailing him from as far back as she dared, focusing only on keeping his blue shirt in view. The phone call she'd overheard had sure sounded like an assignation between uneasy allies. More to the point, it seemed to involve some sort of property that Jerry was holding. Now, maybe it was perfectly innocent and aboveboard, in which case she had no business being nearby. But maybe, just maybe, it had to do with stamps.

And if so, she couldn't run the risk of missing it.

The horizon was dark and the air was cooling off when she stepped out onto the Strip. Even on the crowded pavement she could see the royal blue of Jerry's shirt bobbing with his stride, moving away from her in the direction of the Venetian. In her magenta dress she'd have been conspicuous anywhere else, but the crowd of tourists and hawkers and working girls on the sidewalk masked her quite effectively.

The gondolas floated serenely through the fake lagoon of the Venetian as Gwen walked by, not hurrying, not dawdling, always watching the back of Jerry's neck. Keep him in sight, that was all she needed to do. Keep him in sight, see where he went and who he met. Hopefully she would learn something.

Hopefully she could figure out what it meant.

A passing pedestrian bumped into Gwen, turning her half-around. She brushed off his apologies and started forward again, then stopped.

Jerry was nowhere in sight.

Panic washed over her. She couldn't lose him now. He could have gone anywhere—into a casino, into the liquor store on the corner, into a passing cab. She hurried the last few steps to the liquor store and peeked around the corner. A block down the street he sauntered along.

Now she faced a problem. On the boulevard she was inconspicuous. On a deserted side street all it would take was one glance back from him and she'd be busted. She wasn't sure he'd buy sexual jealousy as her reason for being there, or if she wanted to deal with the fallout of that particular excuse. Still, he didn't seem to have the least concern about being followed. It was worth taking a chance, she thought as she turned the corner herself, walking past the posters advertising specials on rum and vodka. The Dumpsters in the alley behind the store were overflowing, redolent with the stench of ripe trash.

Suddenly an arm swept around her from behind. Fear sprinted through her. A hand clamped over her mouth before she could scream. "Where do you think you're going?" someone whispered harshly.

She struggled uselessly. He was bulky but strong and dragged her effortlessly back into the alley. The hand on her mouth made it hard to breathe. She struggled against panic. Who was he? A mugger? A rapist?

"You keep being nosy, you're gonna get hurt."

She twisted against him. Then the words he'd whispered penetrated her brain and a new fear arose.

And a new need to escape.

Galvanized, Gwen raked her heel down her attacker's shin, digging in viciously, and stomped the spike into his foot. Her reward was a bellow of pain. She twisted away from the hands that held her, stumbling toward the mouth of the alley, and opened her mouth to scream.

"You bitch, you're going to pay for that. You—"

A form hurtled toward the attacker.

It was Del.

The assailant ducked back so that his reach missed its mark. Del backed up, balanced and surged in with a pair of quick punches, balletic in their form, ferocious in their violence. "Nina, get out of here," he yelled, ducking a right hook from the attacker.

She could only stand frozen, watching their struggle. Del struck again and a fountain of blood erupted from the assailant's nose and mouth. Groaning, he sagged over onto the ground.

Del ran to her. "Come on, let's go."

It was only when they were back among the lights of the Strip that the reaction hit her and she began to tremble. Del stopped once they were in front of the Doge's Palace at the Venetian and safely among the crowd.

"Are you hurt?" he demanded brusquely, his hands on her shoulders.

"No," she said, her voice more unsteady than she'd like. "No," she said again more strongly. "I'm fine."

"Who was he, Nina? What did he want?"

"I don't…a mugger, I guess. I've never seen him before."

Del paced away from her and then turned back.

Her hands began to shake. With an effort she fought it back. She was not going to fall apart.

Del studied her. "Come on, let's get you back to the hotel," he said abruptly.

"I'm fine. I don't need your help."

"I'm doing it for my benefit. I'm not going to be able to relax until I know you're inside and safe."

"I don't need you to take care of me."

"Goddammit, Nina, don't argue. He's long gone. Just admit that you missed it this time out and call yourself lucky. Now come on."

She should have fought. She would have fought, but she was suddenly exhausted. "All right."

DEL SHUT THE DOOR BEHIND THEM and slapped on the dead bolt. He watched Nina make her way to the sofa. The trembling that had worried him became more pronounced until she was shaking hard.

It made him feel helpless. He wished for the Nina who spit and snapped, the Nina who'd toss him out on his ass.

Anything would be better than the terrifying paleness and air of fragility that hung around her. He prayed that she wouldn't cry. That would do him in.

Turning to the armoire, he opened up the door that hid the minibar refrigerator and pulled out a small bottle of vodka. He dumped it unceremoniously into a glass and handed it to her.

"Drink it."

She didn't question, just took an obedient swig. Instantly she broke into a coughing fit. When she'd finished wiping away the tears from choking, she seemed steadier. Though she still held the glass, knuckles showing white, she looked a little more like the Nina he knew, the one who gave as good as she got.

He drew up a chair to face her and sat down. "What's going on, Nina?" he asked flatly.

"What do you mean?"

"No more stories. The door's locked, it's just you and me. Time to stop pretending. I think that guy wanted something and it wasn't your money." He didn't want to think about the sick, cold fear that had clutched his throat when he'd looked into the alley and seen that animal with his hands on her. Instead he concentrated on his frustration.

"I don't know what he wanted."

"Okay, let's do this another way. How about you just tell me why you were out there to begin with?"

"What were you doing there?" she flared.

She was recovering, he noted with relief. "To keep an eye on you."

"I don't need taking care of."

"No?" he asked grimly. "You sure looked like it tonight."

"I didn't need your help," she snapped. "I'd broken free of him."

"Yeah, you could run a long way in those shoes."

"I've taken self-defense courses. I know how to handle myself."

Del rose and began to pace. "Something's up. You're in some kind of a mess—it doesn't take a genius to see it."

"I can take care of my own business."

"Like you did back there? Goddammit, Nina, tell me what's going on."

"Why?"

"I don't know. Maybe because I care what happens to you, although the reasons for that might be escaping me right now." He stopped. "I can help you if you let me."

She stared at him, eyes huge, face pale. It was as though she were trying to see inside of him. As though she were trying to decide whether to trust, even as he was trying to figure out whether she was scamming him. Finally she sighed.

"For starters, my name's not Nina."

As THE VODKA SNAKED ITS WAY into her system, the trembling eased. In the bright lights and comfort of her room, she could forget the way it had felt to be gripped in the darkness, the fear that had choked her. Del crossed back to sit in his chair and she moistened her lips.

How much to tell him was the question. She could trust him, but how far? She took a breath.

"I worked with Jerry in San Francisco. He managed to steal some merchandise, some very valuable merchandise, and I'm trying to get it back." She took another belt of the vodka. It slid down more easily this time.

"Are you an investigator?"

She shook her head. "Just a person."

"What was the merchandise?"

Gwen straightened her spine. "Stamps."

"Stamps," he repeated.

"Rare stamps. Some of the issues he took are one of only a handful that exist in the world."

"Did you call the police?"

"No police," she said quickly.

Suspicion flickered in his eyes. "Why not?"

"I've got my reasons."

"That's not good enough."

"It'll have to be," she flared.

He nodded. "I'll hold on to that for now. Okay, what are they worth?"

She hesitated. "In the low seven figures."

"What!" he said explosively. "I don't care what your reasons are, call the cops."

"No."

He frowned. "You're not being straight with me."

"I am," she protested.

"You're not. Were they stolen property to begin with?"

"No, of course not." His eyes said he didn't entirely believe her. Should she tell him more? Could she trust him with all of it? Caution, innate to her, took over and she remained silent.

"So Jerry worked with you?"

She nodded.

"Then why doesn't he know who you are?" Again the skepticism.

"Well, he was new. I didn't have a whole lot of contact with him. I mostly worked in the investment part of the business. Jerry worked up front, in the store." She glanced down uncomfortably. "Also, I don't usually look like this."

"Like what?"

"You know…" She gave an embarrassed shrug. "Nina. Blond. Tight. My personal style is a little more toned down."

"No wonder you've been so hard to figure out. I thought maybe you just had a split personality. So who's Rennie?"

She closed her eyes. "I'm not sure. It was a name written in a matchbook I found at Jerry's. It had the number of the casino here, so I figured Rennie might know where to find him."

"Which is why you were all over me when you thought I was Rennie."

"It's less important now that I've got an in with Jerry."

Del nodded. "So, what happens now?"

"Get close to Jerry, find out if he's got the stamps with him. Search his room if I can. I think he's too dumb and disorganized to have done anything with most of them. He's sold a few of the more common stamps he boosted, probably for living expenses. A friend of mine confirmed it with the dealer." She set down the vodka now, absorbed. "I think he's working with someone, someone he was going to meet tonight."

"Which was why you were following him."

"Bingo."

"What about the guy who jumped you?"

"I don't know," she said quickly.

"He looked a little too nicely dressed for a mugger."

"Maybe. I'd think it was random except for something he said when he first grabbed me."

"What?"

"I don't remember exactly. Something about where did I think I was going." *You keep being nosy, you're gonna get hurt.*

"A warning, maybe?"

"From who, though?"

"Maybe he's working with someone?"

"I don't know." She tilted her head consideringly. "I thought at first that Jerry had lifted the stamps on his own. Now I wonder. When he was talking on the phone, it was almost like he was ransoming them."

"A commission job, maybe."

"Maybe. Then again, that conversation may have been about something totally different."

Del nodded. "Jerry's still the key, though."

"Absolutely. I keep thinking if I can flatter him enough and get him drinking, maybe he'll talk."

"And maybe he'll expect a little something from you after the talking's done," Del said with an edge to his voice.

"Nina can take care of herself."

"I'm sure she can, but how about Gwen?" He gave her a searching look and took her hands.

"Gwen's doing okay."

"Yeah? Well, maybe you don't have to go peddling your virtue to Jerry to get information. He and I are well on our way to becoming buds."

"You are?"

"Yeah. I'm supposed to interview him tomorrow. Once he gets talking, who knows what he'll say, particularly after a few beers."

"Great minds think alike. I figured I'd drag him out for a drink after play is over. If he's won, he'll be cocky. If he's lost, he'll want to drown his sorrows."

"I don't like the idea of you being alone with him."

"We'll be in public," she reassured him.

"What if I come along?"

"Del, you can't. He won't talk if you're there, not like he will if we're alone."

"I still don't like it," he muttered. "Not after tonight."

Gwen looked up at him. "Why are you doing this?"

He hesitated, staring back at her as if trying to figure it out himself. "Maybe I just can't resist a puzzle. Besides—" he reached out and tucked her hair back behind her ear "—I have a soft spot for Nina."

The sweet, simple gesture rocked her and, illogically,

tears threatened for the first time since the incident. She looked down.

"I'm sorry, you're probably wiped out." Del stood. "I should lay off and leave you alone now."

Mechanically Gwen rose and walked with him to the door.

"I don't know how to thank you for what you did tonight."

He stopped and faced her at the door. "Shucks, ma'am, it warn't nothin'."

"I mean it. That guy could have really hurt me." And the thought of it had marched through her head ever since.

"But he didn't and you're okay. You're tough. You would have had him anyway. Now get some sleep." He leaned in to kiss her on the forehead and turned to open the door.

"Wait." The word hung in the silence. She hadn't known she was going to say it.

Del turned back to look at her inquiringly.

"Stay with me, please," she said in a rusty voice.

"You sure?"

She nodded. "Not to, you know…I just really don't want to be alone right now." Just then the idea was impossible to face.

Del turned and folded her into his arms. "I'll stay with you as long as you want," he murmured, kissing her hair. And he swung her up in his arms and carried her back to the bed, lying down next to her to hold her—just hold her—as the tears and shudders finally came.

# *11*

SO NOW HE HAD A PRETTY PUZZLE on his hands, Del thought the next morning as he sat at his desk and checked voice mail. Gwen needed help, he'd offered it. But she wasn't telling him everything, and for all he knew, she could be conning him. He didn't want to believe it, thinking of how it had felt to hold the warm, fragrant bundle of her against him. The problem was, he just didn't know and he didn't know what to do about it.

He did know what to do about the call from Greg Jessup at the *Globe* city desk, though. It was probably only to set up a phone interview, Del told himself as he dialed Jessup's number. Still, it meant he had an opening, a chance.

The tones rang in his ear, then with a click the line connected.

"Jessup."

"Del Redmond, Greg. You called?"

"Hi, Del. Yeah, Perry over in sports handed along your application for our opening in metro. I wanted to talk with you about it a little if you've got the time."

If he had time? He'd make time. "Sure."

"You've got a track record with the paper and Perry gave you a thumbs-up, so I don't really need to go into the usual who, what, where. I guess what I'm really wondering is why. You've got a solid long-term career on the sports desk. Perry tells me you've got the second highest reader-response rate of all his columnists. Why are you coming after what's practically an entry-level job in metro?"

Jessup was a newsman to the core, Del reflected. No time wasted getting to the point. "I had a chance to do a series last year on the whole doping scandal. Investigative. I dug up sources, wormed my way in where I didn't belong and I came away with information solid enough that the folks running the litigation wanted to talk with me."

"I hope you cited the fifth."

Del grinned. "I told them to do their own jobs. The thing is, it gave me a taste for investigative work. I want to do more of it. Work on real stories, you know?"

"Well, that's just the problem. You understand you wouldn't get to at first, right? And you'd have to take a pay cut."

"Yep."

Jessup was silent for a moment. "I don't know, Redmond. I hear where you're coming from, but I'm just not sure you know what you're in for."

"Who've you been interviewing for this job? What kind of background do they have?"

"They're young," Jessup admitted.

"Doesn't experience count for something?"

"Not when it's all sports columns."

"It's not. Take a look at the BALCO series."

"I did. It was good work," Jessup acknowledged, "but it was still sports. I want to see how you handle something that's not a game."

"Give me an assignment."

"That's just it. If you're a reporter, no one's going to give you an assignment. There's nothing so easy as the nightly game to write up. You've got to be out there digging, fighting for the stories and getting them before the competition does. You've got to constantly be alert."

"I am digging up stories. Hell, I've stumbled into something out here in Vegas that's about as juicy as they come."

"Mob corruption?" Jessup snapped to attention.

"What would you say to a heist, a poker tournament and a couple of the rarest stamps in the world?"

"Sunday-supplement stuff."

"You think? If four and a half million's at stake?"

"That makes it sexier. What do you know about it?"

He'd blurted it out without thinking. Now he backpedaled. "Not a whole lot yet. I'm just giving you an example. The point is, I know how to dig."

"The point is, you're onto a story that we could use. You want me to take a second look at you, you'll hunt down that story."

"I don't know if this particular one—"

"This was a real story, right, Redmond? I mean, you weren't just spinning something out of your ass to impress me, were you?"

Del controlled the surge of irritation. "It's real."

"Good. Then get it on my desk."

And he disconnected with a click.

"NOW SEE, THIS IS THE WAY TO start out a tournament," Roxy told Gwen. The first wave of round one had opened up earlier that afternoon. They watched now from a few rows up on the temporary aluminum bleachers that lined the perimeter of the playing area. From there they could get a good view of the forty tables that crowded the room, supplemented by the view from the wide-screen televisions that hung overhead. "No stress, just a chance to sit back and keep an eye on the ones who are taking the big pots, see who you need to worry about in the next round."

The ballroom had changed from the night before. It was perhaps crowded with as many people, but gone was the social atmosphere. Now a sort of hyperintense circus giddiness had taken hold. Some wore outlandish costumes. Others carried lucky tokens ranging from rabbits' feet and coins to photographs. The players were a mixed bag, from guys barely out of high school who'd probably soaked up their strategy from computer simulators to craggy-looking graybeards with a lifetime of poker experience etched into their features.

"Hey, what about that hunka hunka burnin' love?" Roxy gestured to a sideburned player in a sequined Elvis-style jumpsuit. "I think I want his baby."

"I can see it now. You'll have him in an Elvis pompadour and teething on poker chips."

"Who said anything about having a he?"

Only a bit over ten percent of the three hundred and sixty people who'd opened the first wave would advance to round two, breaking the losers hand by hand. In the end only five percent of the tournament entrants would finish in the money. For now, though, everything was possible.

"I can't believe they're going to cut down all these players to forty in only two days."

"And then do it again for our half of round one," Roxy reminded her.

"I wish they'd let us just start all at once."

"Maybe they don't have enough tables. Last year they had the whole opening round start at the same time. Smaller, I guess. We just played every day until we hit their target."

"How late?"

"Eleven one night, two in the morning the next. The deeper you get, the slower they go. Minimum bets start at a hundred dollars and go up every two hours for the rest of the tournament. This group will winnow down pretty quickly. I'm guessing they'll take it until ten or eleven tonight."

"Makes my behind hurt to think about it."

"They give you breaks and dinner, so it's not so bad." Roxy propped her feet up on the bench below them. "The tough part is the way they're constantly consolidating the tables as people go out. Just about the time you get used to how one group plays, either you're getting tossed to another table with an opening or someone with a whole mess of chips drops into yours."

It made Gwen just a bit queasy to contemplate. "Why don't they just play each table down to one winner."

Roxy shook her head. "Changes the dynamics of the game too much when you drop down below six players. You lose the advantage of being the late bettor."

"On the other hand, lower pocket cards are stronger with a shorthanded table," Gwen reminded her. "You might try using a suited queen eight to beat five players where you wouldn't trust it to beat nine. I think they like to keep the pressure on."

"Keeps things exciting. That's why they let the play go on so long if they need to—when you've been at it for ten or twelve hours and you're brain-dead, that's when you find out what you're made of. Watch and learn, grasshopper. Watch and learn." Roxy stared across the room. "Hey, there's your boy. Now that is what we call in Montana a fine-looking specimen of a man."

Gwen followed her pointing finger and felt the jump of adrenaline in her system. Under the pitiless lighting over the tables, a five-o'clock shadow darkened Del's jaw. A dark gray Alcatraz T-shirt stretched over his shoulders. His hair was a little disordered, as though he'd had his hands in it. From the grandstand she could look her fill at his hollow cheeks, the firm line of his mouth. Only his eyes were hidden, behind mirrored sunglasses. The eyes were the single biggest tell in poker. Expression could be controlled, but the expansion of the pupil at a good hand or contraction at a bad hand was involuntary. Del, apparently, was taking no chances.

"I could turn into a poker groupie for a guy like that. I'm sure I could give him a few Hold 'em lessons."

"Down, girl."

Roxy gave her a sidelong glance. "Didn't you tell me before that you didn't want to get involved with him?"

"I don't," Gwen said firmly.

Roxy studied her and looked out at the tables. "Yeah, maybe I'll hold off. Never been a poacher and I'm not gonna start now."

"There's nothing going on between us."

"Oh, really?" Roxy's eyes were amused. "You've got to bluff a whole lot better than that if you want to make it out of round one, honey."

Gwen glowered at her and turned to watch the games.

Del and Jerry were playing at different tables, though as she'd already seen, that could change at a moment's notice. Still, competition at this point wasn't head-to-head so much as a matter of holding enough chips to stay alive.

"Who's that asshole?" Roxy asked, pointing.

Pointing at Jerry. He wore a baseball cap turned backward and a shiny silver Oakland Raiders warm-up jacket. Compared to his tournament persona, he'd been positively low-key when they'd played a few nights before. He was, in short, a punk. Cocky and hyper, he stood and paced, he talked to himself, he gloated when he won and sulked when he lost. "If he were at my table, I'd have to kill him," Roxy observed.

He was already earning decidedly hostile glances from some of the players at his table. Unfortunately for them, he was more than holding his own. He had that edge of instability that made him impossible to predict and could tip him into either riotous success or disaster at a moment's notice. For now, the cards were with him. His increasing hoard of chips stood haphazardly in uneven, tilted towers that he fiddled with constantly.

Del, by contrast, was a study in calm. Whether he held a made hand with a pair of aces or a hand begging to be folded, he maintained the same focused expression, watching everything, reacting to nothing.

If he was composed, he was also a predator, ruthlessly competitive, able to sniff out the weaknesses of his opponents. Traditionally the player who was the big blind was in a position of vulnerability compared to the rest of the table. Del seemed not to know that. He fearlessly attacked from the blind, throwing his competitors off balance so that at the end of the hand they discovered they'd been expertly fleeced as Del raked in their chips. He relentlessly sought out his competitors' vulnerabilities while presenting a smooth, inscrutable wall to them. His neat stacks of chips rose steadily.

Gwen had seen him play, so she hadn't expected him to be dead money in the first round, but she hadn't been prepared for his lightning attacks and parries. Jerry appeared to carelessly throw out chips on a hunch. Del wagered with an inexorable authority that made it clear he was pushing to do just what he wanted. He'd clearly mastered the other players and was picking off their chips at his leisure.

The hand at Del's table ended, and a skinny, jumpy-looking guy who looked as if he was on break from college raked in the pot. He'd knocked out one player on the hand and taken a surprising amount of chips from the others, including Del. Now the table was down to Del, the young kid and five others.

And raw nerve.

"This should start getting interesting now," Roxy murmured into Gwen's ear. "Looks like your boy's the big blind."

Gwen watched Del push out a stack of thousand-dollar chips as though they were Necco wafers. If he had no visible nerves, though, she was awash with them, her mouth dry as dust. The kid pushed out the small blind and the dealer dealt the pocket cards. With the lazy elegance of a master fencer toying with his opponent Del casually raised without even looking at his cards.

"So, does he have steel ones or are they actual flesh and blood?" Roxy whispered to her.

"They felt like flesh and blood, but they might have changed since I saw them last," Gwen whispered back.

The tension ratcheted up.

The rest of the players at the table folded after a glance at their pocket cards. Del took a quick glance at his and raised, putting pressure on his foe.

The kid rose from his chair, bouncing a little on his toes and muttering to himself. He curved his fingers around his stacks of chips. For a moment he held on, licking his lips. Then he pushed them all forward. A little mutter rippled through the crowd around the table. All in, Gwen thought tensely. It would be up to Del whether to match him or to check, refusing to bet.

The kid stared at his chips with a certain fascinated horror, paced around a little, swinging his hands.

Del sat in his chair, taut and coiled, studying the kid as much as his hand. Seconds ticked by. Nerves twisted in Gwen's stomach. Finally in a smooth, decisive move Del pushed his chips forward to match the kid.

It was like that moment on a roller-coaster ride after the first descent, when the car was racing up the next hill. The tension had eased a fraction, but everyone in the room knew that the stomach-dropping stuff was yet to come.

Both players turned up their pocket cards. It was pointless to hide anything, since no more betting was possible. The kid had a pair of kings. Del had a suited jack and ace. The rest of the hand would play out quickly.

The flop held a jack and a king. Gwen clenched her hands together. Three kings versus two jacks—the kid had him. This was it. There was no possibility of retreat. Folding was meaningless. Everything was at stake.

Two cards still remained in the hand, though, and anything could happen. The dealer flipped over the turn card to reveal another jack. It gave Del three of a kind, but the kid's three kings still outranked Del's hand.

It all came down to the river card.

The dealer laid the card facedown on the green baize. He paused a moment, with innate theatricality. Gwen wanted to scream with the tension. The kid scrubbed his hands through his hair. Del sat, as relaxed as though he were back in his room watching television.

The dealer put his hand on the river card and flipped it over.

And the ace of spades lay on the baize.

Gwen whooped and clapped before she even realized she was doing it. Del had taken the hand with a full house. He'd nearly doubled his chip count in a single hand.

Victory.

He looked up and winked at her.

"Looks like your boy knows how to play Hold 'em," Roxy observed.

"That he does," Gwen said, "that he does."

# 12

PLOTTING TO PLY JERRY WITH drinks and get him drunk enough to tell her something was a good idea in theory but not nearly so entertaining in practice. So far she'd been regaled with a replay of every hand of his round, though the details had been glossed over somewhat in Jerry's favor. He dragged out the description of his final winning hand that bumped him to the next round until she wanted to scream.

"An' then the flop gives me my other ace. I know these other two guys at the table and they're acting like they've got something good but the guy on the end is blinking too much and the guy next to me is beginning to sweat. I figure they're bluffing, so I go all in. Balls to the walls, you know? I figure I'll either win big or I head on up to 5111 and call it a night."

A little leap of excitement went through her. At least she had his room number now. It was a start, anyway. "What would you have done if you hadn't gotten the full house on the flop?" she asked him. "You just coughed up ten thousand to enter the tournament. That's a lot of money."

He snorted. "Chump change. I could go out tomorrow and come back with fifteen, twenty grand, easy."

"Really," she said, with a pretty good idea of just how.

"Oh, I'm set, all right. This time next week I'm gonna

be rollin' in dough. Yo bartender!" He thumped the bar. "'Nother round here. My ladyfren's fallen behin'."

The bartender gave him a glance. "I think you might have had enough, friend."

Jerry straightened up. "I think I know when I've had enough," he said, clearly taking pains to speak distinctly.

The bartender gave a long look at Jerry and a longer one at Gwen. "Buddy, everybody's got a job."

"An' yours is to pour drinks."

"It's also to take care of you. That includes not letting you get drunk and rolled by some pretty lady." He paused. "No offense," he added with a look at Gwen.

"None taken, I'm sure," she said coolly.

"I wanna drink," Jerry said obstinately.

"You go out of here and hurt yourself or somebody else, the law says it's my responsibility," the bartender told him. "You look like you've got a pretty good buzz as it is. Why don't you ride it?"

Jerry fumbled in his pocket and slapped his card key down on the bar. "I'm staying at the hotel, pal, so I ain't gonna get in any car. Now bring me a drink."

The bartender flicked a look at the security camera at the end of the bar, then back at Jerry impassively.

Jerry gave him back a stubborn stare. "Dammit, everybody thinks they know what's good for me." He stood unsteadily and leaned toward Gwen. "Gotta go…you know. Be right back, okay. Make him give us a drink." And he weaved off to the bathrooms.

Gwen sat at the bar, staring at the blue-and-gold plastic wafer of Jerry's passkey out of the corner of her eye. It practically vibrated, sitting there out in plain sight. And yet there was no way to just pick it up, not with the bartender watching her.

"Your friend's had a little too much tonight. I'd hate to

see something bad happen to him." The bartender leaned his hands on the inside of the bar and stood staring down at the key.

Gwen swallowed and pulled her shoulder bag up into her lap. "I know." She pulled out her lipstick and a small mirror and proceeded to outline her mouth.

"The safety of our patrons is our first concern." He lifted her glass and replaced the bar napkin underneath it.

Gwen finished and gave him a brilliant smile, capping her tube of lip color and sliding it back into her purse. And stealthily removing her own passkey.

"You enjoying yourself at the casino?" the bartender persisted.

"Very much." She slung her bag back over the chair back, keeping the key in her other hand and safely out of sight. *Go away,* she telegraphed to the bartender, but he was obviously in no hurry to leave and just as obviously hanging around to keep an eye on Jerry's key.

The seconds slid by and she sipped her martini. The bathrooms might have been out in the lobby, but it wouldn't take forever for Jerry to get there and back. Fighting the urge to lick her lips, Gwen palmed her passkey and rested the elbow of the other arm on the bar. And prayed. On the television monitors overhead, Paul LoDuca hit a homer over the wall in Dodger Stadium.

"Yo, service," called a guy sitting with some friends down the bar.

"Just a minute." The bartender looked at the passkey and then at Gwen, who blinked at him innocently. She casually folded her arms on the bar, resting the hand with her card key closest to Jerry's.

"Hey, buddy, can we get a coupla beers down here already?" The guy slapped the polished surface of the bar.

With obvious reluctance the bartender stepped a few

feet away to the taps and began drawing the beers. Any minute, she thought, any minute she'd get her chance. She took a quick glance at the security camera, which was panning away from her. Her pulse thudded in her temples.

The bartender gave Gwen a long stare before he turned to walk down the bar and deliver them.

As soon as his back was turned, she used her fingertips to slip her room key over Jerry's and slide his into her hand.

*Score!* Heart pounding, eye on the bartender, she dropped her hands back into her lap and put the key into her purse.

"Hey, babe."

Her vertical leap would have qualified her for the Olympic high jump.

"Edgy, huh?" Jerry made a clumsy attempt at pinching her butt, but she shifted out of his way.

Gwen gave a faltering laugh. "You were quick."

"Not quick at everythin'." He leered at her.

Gwen took a big swallow of her martini.

. The bartender reappeared. "You get your key all right, sir?"

"Right here." Jerry held it up and squinted at him. "Do I get another drink?"

"Not here, sir. Perhaps up in your room."

"Depends if I get company," he said archly.

Gwen shook her head. "You might have made it to round two, I'm still waiting for my heat. I've got to finish this and call it a night." She tipped up the last of her martini and rose. "Congratulations on moving up." She gave him a light thump on the shoulder and walked out.

SHE WALKED INTO THE ELEVATOR, a bubble of excitement swelling in her solar plexus. By the time she hit Del's floor, it was practically floating her off her feet. She hurried down the hall.

Del opened the door almost before she'd finished knocking and swept her inside. "'Bout time. I've been going nuts here. Are you all right? Did he touch you? What happened?"

"He was a little too hammered to paw anyone, let alone Nina." Because it felt too good not to, Gwen stepped closer and pressed a quick kiss on him. "You might ask me if I found out anything," she mentioned, twirling into the room.

Del's mouth was still ajar from the shock of the kiss. His gaze flicked over her from head to toe. "Did you find out anything?"

"I did, funny you should ask. Now ask me what I came away with."

"What did you come away with?"

She held up the passkey. "Ta da!"

"Your key?"

"Oh, no. This is not my key. This would be Jerry's key." She did a little dance step and turned in a circle.

Del whistled admiringly. "Nice. How'd you manage that?"

"Oh, alertness, timing and manual dexterity."

"If you tell me you picked his pocket, I'm going to be a little scared."

"Not that much manual dexterity. He put it down on the counter and went to the men's. I managed to swap it for mine under the eagle eye of the bartender, who seemed to think I was a woman of questionable virtue looking to take advantage of Jerry's condition."

He raised his eyebrows. "Well, you have to admit you did take advantage of Jerry's condition."

"But my virtue is hardly questionable."

"I can vouch for that. So, what do you plan to do with the key?"

"Wait for the right time and search his room, of course." She sat on the high bed and bounced a few times. "He's got no address that I can find. I figure he's got to have the stamps with him."

"What if he's got them locked up in the safe?"

She grinned, eyes merry. "Oh, no. I just happened to mention what a challenging time I was having with my safe, and he told me he never uses them since the time he locked his wallet up in one and forgot the combination."

"Well, isn't that convenient," he said admiringly.

"Isn't it just," Gwen agreed.

"So, when do you think the right time's going to crop up?"

She considered. "That part's going to be a bit tricky. Any ideas?"

"Yes, but it would mean sacrifice on my part."

"Sacrifice?"

"Vast sacrifice."

She leaned back on one elbow. "Do tell."

"Well, as you know, I had an interview with Jerry today for my series of articles. You know, to get the gritty reality of life in a poker tournament."

"I'm sure that was a fascinating experience."

"Oh, it was, it was. We shot some pool, drank some beer, talked about tournaments, making the big score, you name it."

"How's his pool playing?"

"He'd better not plan on making his score that way. To hear him tell it, though, he's already got two feet on easy street. Winning the tournament will just cement it."

"Did he tell you any more about his big score?"

"Just that smart guys figure out how to get ahead."

She snorted. "I'm sure."

Del stuck his tongue in his cheek. "Also that if he didn't get laid soon, he was going to find a pro."

"'Gritty reality,' I think you said?"

"He invited me to come out with him tomorrow night

after the tournament play ends to visit a gentlemen's club
and enjoy some fine exotic dancing."

"Is that how he put it?"

"No, I believe he said he wanted to go hit a titty bar and
get a load of some pussy."

"That's our Jerry, charming to the last."

His eyes glimmered with humor. "I told you it was a
guy-bonding experience."

"And did you take him up on his invitation?"

"I told him that to my everlasting regret I'd have to say no."

"I see. Not a big fan of gentlemen's clubs, are you?"

"I prefer private sessions with amateurs, thanks. But I'm
willing to sacrifice for the cause." He leaned against the armoire opposite the bed. "It occurs to me that if I go to the
gentlemen's club with Jerry, I'll be in a perfect position to
keep tabs on his whereabouts and call when he heads home
to warn anyone who might be taking part in a little breaking and entering."

"It's not breaking and entering if you've got a key," she
informed him smugly.

"Tell that to the hotel security."

"Or not."

"Anyway, I'll look him up before the tournament starts
tomorrow afternoon and take him up on his offer."

"Assuming your group reaches the magic number by a
decent hour."

"We're already down below one-fifty. I think we'll do
it by nine or ten."

"Leaving plenty of time for the gentlemen's club."

"Do I know how to have a good time?" He crossed over
to sit on the edge of the bed. "Anyway, I'll keep an eye on
him, you do your search and I'll call you when we head
home. Piece of cake."

"Very nice."

"We do make a good team." He kicked his shoes off. "So, if you swapped your key for his, I guess you can't get back into your room. What are you going to do?"

"Well, I figure Jerry's going to blunder downstairs, bitching about his key not working. They'll think it got demagnetized and recode it. It happened to me one time on a trip. They don't reset the door code unless you actually lose a key. It would probably look a little funny if I go down there tonight saying the same thing."

"Agreed."

"So I figured I'd wait until tomorrow morning and tell them I locked my keys in my room. I show ID, they give me new keys, no one is the wiser."

He stretched out facing her. "Of course, that does leave you with one problem." His eyes had become very dark.

"Which is?"

"Finding a place to sleep tonight." He ran a thumb along the line of her collarbone.

It shouldn't have made her pulse jump. After all, they'd already had sex. They'd slept together just holding each other the night before. There shouldn't have been any mystery to it. But when he leaned closer, her lungs took a breath of their own accord.

"Do you have any ideas about that?" It took her two tries to get the words out.

"Depends." He stroked his hand over her cheek and up into her hair.

"On what?"

"Whether you care about sleep." And his mouth was on hers.

# *13*

DEL SAT AT A TABLE IN THE conservatory café at the casino, waiting for Gwen to finish swimming laps and come meet him for breakfast. In the meantime he sucked down orange juice and reviewed his notes. Between hands the previous night he'd been scribbling madly and interviewing players. Now he pondered and framed his actual article.

Movement flickered in his peripheral vision and someone sat across the booth from him. It wasn't Gwen, though, but a dark-haired guy with a narrow face.

"Can I help you?"

"You're Del Redmond, right?"

Del blinked. Five hundred miles from his home, it was the last thing he'd have expected to hear. "And you are?"

"Pete Kellar, stringer for the *Globe*." The guy's speech was staccato. His chin punched the air assertively. "Greg Jessup asked me to look in on you." He squinted. "I gotta say, your head shot in the paper doesn't do you justice."

"So, what are you looking in on me for?" The kid didn't look old enough to be a stringer. He barely looked old enough to have graduated college. It didn't stop him from settling in as if he'd been invited, though. He'd apparently read all the books on getting ahead in journalism.

"I talked with Jessup yesterday about assignments. He said you were running down some kind of theft or con-spiracy story. I've got contacts with local law enforcement you might be able to use."

"Law enforcement's not involved."

"You don't know that," Kellar countered. His eyes were close-set and aggressive. Del imagined he practiced the look in the mirror. "They could be undercover. What's the deal with this anyway? Jessup couldn't tell me a whole lot."

And Kellar wasn't about to find out anything further from him, that was for sure. It was pretty obvious that the kid was a scrapper, Del thought, taking a drink of his juice. Kellar wanted to make points with the story, prove himself. "It's still too early to say what's going on. I'm just looking into things."

"Pass me a list of your sources, let me help."

*Fat chance, kid.* "I'm all set for now. Give me your card and I'll call you if I need anything," Del said pleasantly.

He held the card between his fingertips and looked at it. Stringer was an exaggeration. The card said freelancer, which explained Kellar's eagerness. He was probably looking for a means to shoehorn his way into the *Globe* organization. Jessup no doubt figured it couldn't hurt to have two people working on the same story. Or fighting over it—some editors believed in editorial Darwinism, and Jessup just might be one of them. Well, the story wasn't going to give Kellar a way in, that was for sure. If anyone was going to get mileage out of this story it was going to be Del.

He glanced across the room and saw Gwen walking in under a tree fern. "My breakfast date is here," Del said, "and you're in her seat."

"An interview?" Kellar's eyes lit avidly.

"No, just a date."

"Oh." Kellar rose. "Okay, I'm out of here. You'll call me?"

"I'll let you know if I need anything."

Kellar took a long look at Gwen and gave an appreciative nod. "You do that." He walked away.

Gwen arrived at the table and gave Del a kiss. "Who was that?"

"Just a guy I know."

She glanced at the business card on the table. "A freelance newswriter? Just a guy you know?" She stared at him a long moment, but he didn't say anything.

"Well, let's order some breakfast."

VEGAS WAS ALL ABOUT transporting reality: the Manhattan skyline of New York, New York, the gondolas of the Venetian, the scale-model Eiffel Tower of Paris. Restaurants like Nobu of Manhattan and Olives of Boston had established branches in the desert to cater to the more discerning palates of the visitors accustomed to luxury. She wasn't so surprised to see them, but she'd never in a million years have expected to discover an outpost of the Guggenheim there. The themes were still typically Vegas—the pursuit of pleasure—but the quality was surprising. Not only that, it was right off the gaming floor, so gamblers could take in art in between hands of cards.

"So, how do you want to do this?" Del asked her.

The polished wood underfoot rang as they walked through the open gallery. The blond maple ceiling soared overhead, above the copper-colored walls.

"You mean tonight?"

"Well, we could talk about your gallery strategy, but yeah, I think talking about tonight would be more practical."

Around them the space was mostly empty. Gwen guessed that the slots and gaming tables held more appeal for the guests than fine art. Most would duck in to see the exhibit just so they could say they had, so they could feel a little less dissolute after a week spent eating, drinking and gambling.

"What time are you meeting Jerry?" She stopped in

front of a painting of a group of peasants drinking in a tavern, a red-faced man playing a guitar and singing a no doubt ribald song, judging by the expressions on the faces of his audience.

"When play is done. Ten or so, I'm guessing. We'll grab bar food at the strip club."

"Lucky you. Is he planning on making a night of it?"

Del circled around a Rodin marble of Romeo and Juliet clasped together in a frozen desperation, passion in the touch of their hands, the lines of their bodies. "I'm guessing Jerry will get there, knock back some drinks, get a few lap dances. After that, who knows? He strikes me as the kind of guy who wouldn't blink at going looking for a pro."

"Class act all the way," she said with distaste.

He grinned. "Teach you to interview a little more thoroughly in future."

"Hey, he's a con man," Gwen protested. "Everything checked out on him initially. I got the impression from my sister, Joss, that he partied, but nothing too far out of control."

"So maybe he's making up for a month of clean living."

They walked onward to a tableau of lords lying about in a forest clearing. Above their heads a woman was swinging, skirts afroth, breasts nearly exposed in her low-cut gown.

"How long do you see him staying at the bar?"

Del considered. "I don't know, a couple of hours, maybe?"

"So I should watch for you to leave, add a half hour for safety and clock an hour for the search," she calculated. "That gives me slush time at both ends."

Del considered. "I don't like it. Too risky."

"What would you suggest?"

"You've got a cell phone, right?"

She pulled it out of her purse and held up the flat silver handset. "Don't leave home without it."

"Okay, so we exchange numbers. I call you when we get there, let you know we're in. That gives you the thumbs-up to go on up to Jerry's room and search. Try not to get too messy with any of it, though, nothing you can't straighten up in a hurry. We don't want him to know you've been there."

"Aye, aye, Captain."

He gave a faint smile. "Keep an eye on your watch. Call it ninety minutes from the time I call you, no more. When we leave the club, I'll call you again, give you plenty of warning."

"And Jerry's not going to notice you wandering away to make all these phone calls?"

"At the club? Trust me, he'll be preoccupied. I figure I'll just head up to the bar or something."

"How about after? It'll look suspicious if you wander away at both the beginning and the end."

"True." He thought a moment. "Okay—I'll check my messages when we leave the club, make like I've got to call someone back for work. Instead I'll call you. That'll be your signal to beat it."

"That could work. What would the code be?"

"Elvis has left the building?"

"Funny."

"The series on search engines is over?"

"You're a regular laugh riot."

"Okay, how about this?—I'll say 'I've filed my interview.' Jerry will like that because he's the interview."

Gwen studied the painting before her, an unholy excitement buzzing through her veins. Tonight could end it all. Tonight she could find the stamps and finish this business. "I like it."

"Good. You know how to search a place?"

"I've read my share of police novels," she told him. "I

know the procedure. Besides, it'll be easier because it's not his home, it's only a hotel room."

"True."

"And stamps aren't like gems or coins. There are only so many places you can hide them."

"Well, if you want to be sure, we can go upstairs and you can practice your searching techniques on me." He pulled her against him for a kiss.

Gwen laughed up at him, her hands on his shoulders. Then she sobered. "Thank you for doing this. I'm really not sure how I would have done it on my own."

"I think you would have figured it out. Nina's a pretty tough cookie."

And Gwen wasn't. She needed to remember that. Whatever chemistry was between them existed between Del and Nina, not Gwen and Del. She gave him a quick peck and made a move to separate.

"Hey." He scooped her closer. "I don't think we're finished yet."

Nina wouldn't be, Gwen reminded herself. Nina would take all she could get. And so should she—before it ended.

FLASHING LIGHTS AND ROCK music filled the club, the bass throbbing until it vibrated Del's bones. Chrome glittered on the rack above the bar, outlining the edge of the stage, on the vertical poles that the dancers swung and twirled around.

In this environment the naked bodies of the women dancing were just another part of the glossy show, the relentless spotlights above the stage picking out one pair of pneumatic breasts after another.

Del took a swallow of his overpriced bourbon and squinted down into the glass. Maybe he should just start downing them like Kool-Aid. It would be one way to make the evening less painful.

He worshipped the female body as much as the next guy. Especially certain female bodies, he thought, remembering Gwen's curves. But sitting in a club with a roomful of horny guys staring at a cavalcade of cartoonishly well-endowed, untouchable women twisting onstage was hardly his idea of a good time. He preferred a little quality one-on-one time with a woman he could connect with mentally as well as physically.

Still, he'd promised Gwen two hours, minimum, and that was what he was going to deliver.

Jerry nudged him. "How about that redhead, she hot or what?" The redhead grabbed the pole and did something Del would have sworn was anatomically impossible. "She comes offstage, she's going to be dancing right here, partner," Jerry boasted, slapping his thighs and signaling the waitress for another beer.

"Knock yourself out," Del said and took another swallow of bourbon. "Just don't expect to get your rocks off."

"Hey, man, it's all about the fantasy," Jerry said.

Sure it was about the fantasy—guys like Jerry had the fantasy that they were going to get off with the women dancing and the women had the fantasy that they were going to empty out the guys' wallets. He had a pretty good idea whose fantasy had the higher likelihood of coming true.

He thought of Gwen, hot and silky against him, and his cock stirred. Now that was his idea of a turn-on. Consoling himself with the knowledge that he'd end his night with Gwen, he checked his watch and eased back in his seat.

THE ELEVATOR STOPPED AT THE concierge level. Gwen wiped her damp palms on her denim miniskirt and waited for the doors to open. It would be okay, she told herself. Sure, the concierge level had an attendant at the lobby bar, but that person's job was to take care of the guests, not to police them. She had a key, after all, so who was going to stop her as long as she acted as if she belonged? It was just like playing Texas Hold 'em, she reminded herself—bluff, bluff, bluff.

When the doors opened, she squared her shoulders and walked out onto the floor.

A young, blond attendant stood behind the bar in a vest and bow tie. "Good evening."

Gwen gave him a brilliant smile. "Hi."

He smiled back at her, dazzled.

She walked by without stopping, trying to read the numbers on the doors without appearing to look too much. *Act like you belong here.*

She saw it on the right, just a couple of doors in from the lobby. Holding her breath, she slid the card key into the lock and pulled it out. With a little electronic peep and a smooth metallic snick the door unlocked. Relief made her weak. Telling herself the front-desk clerks hadn't recoded Jerry's lock the night before was one thing, being sure was another. She slipped inside and stood in the dark, waiting for her heart rate to level.

The light switches were by the door, just like every other hotel room. When the lights came on, though, it was clear that this room wasn't like any old hotel room. It wasn't a suite, it was a sybaritic palace. What seemed like half an acre of plush carpet covered the living room area, running from where she stood, past a built-in bar to a wall of windows. A glance into the bedroom showed her that it was just as large. How she was ever going to search it all in an hour, she had no idea.

Methodical. The thing to do was be methodical. She knew what she was looking for, knew that it couldn't be tucked into the bottom of a toothpaste tube. It had to be in an envelope or fold of cardboard and it had to be somewhere clean and dry. No matter how big the rooms were, there were only so many hiding places in them. It would be easier because she wouldn't have the kitchen area to go through. Or much of one, she amended, glancing at the built-in bar, with its glossy black marble counter and back-lit bottles of liquor.

She started in the living room, moving around the perimeter from the door, checking the back sides of the art, the mirrors, the undersides of the lamps and side tables, the back of the armoire that held the television. She pulled out every drawer she could find, checking the backs and undersides. The area behind the bar had a surprising number of them, not to mention bottles of liquor and boxes of snacks. None of them were opened up, though, so she figured she was okay.

She turned the couches and chairs on their sides, checking to see that the bottom fabric hadn't been cut or disturbed. She checked under cushions, along piping, between the springs in the back of the couch. Puffing a bit, she checked under and behind the television. She checked the corners of the carpet to see if it had been pulled loose.

No envelopes were to be found.

NIGHTS COOLED OFF QUICKLY IN the desert, Del thought, taking a deep breath of the chill air.

"Fucking dipshit bouncers," Jerry groused, brushing sidewalk grit from his hands. He picked up his cell phone from where it had fallen from his pocket onto the ground.

"Rules say no touching the lap dancers," Del said mildly.

"I didn't touch her."

"Jerry, you had your hands on her tits."

"She liked it."

"You figure that was when she was smacking you or when she was calling for the bouncer?"

"Assholes," Jerry mumbled. "Throw me out on the street. I was spending good money in there."

"And I'm sure they loved you for it."

"You coulda backed my play, y'know."

"Sorry, buddy." Del gave him a friendly pat on the shoulder. "I make it a habit to avoid fighting bouncers with scar tissue around their eyes. It's not a real healthy pursuit."

"Yeah." Jerry stumbled a bit on the sidewalk, though it was perfectly even.

"So, what now? Want to stop somewhere else?"

"Nah. We go into another bar and they'll just pull the same bullshit. Let's go back to the hotel."

Del pulled out his cell phone. "Gotta check my messages," he said briefly and dialed his voice mail. He listened a moment, then cursed for form. "Frigging editors think they own you," he muttered, skirting a man handing out handbills in front of an arcade. Dialing Gwen's cell phone number, he prepared to give her the code to flee.

And his phone beeped and flashed No Signal.

A shiver of alarm whisked down his spine.

# 14

GWEN STEPPED INTO THE BEDROOM and checked her watch.
The bathroom hadn't taken long. She'd used a little over
forty-five of her allotted ninety minutes. A half hour or less
for the bedroom and she'd be out. Systematically she began
checking under the mattress, under the box springs, on the
back of the headboard, searching for an envelope taped in
place. It wasn't underneath or behind the armoire, though
she wasted precious minutes wrestling the piece away from
the wall.

Did the fact that it was empty mean that he didn't have
the stamps with him or that he'd hidden them somewhere
else? It didn't pay to think the latter. She needed to search
everywhere she could to be sure.

So she opened up the doors of the armoire, pulling out
the first drawer with a sigh.

"WHY DON'T WE DUCK IN HERE and get a couple of bour-
bons?" Del nodded at a cocktail lounge as they walked
through the casino.

Jerry shook his head. "Hell, forget that. I got a suite with
a bar. We go up there, put some triple-X on the tube and
have our drinks there."

"Wouldn't you rather go see some live bodies?"

"Not if they're gonna toss me. Besides, I'm out of fives."

He pulled his key out of his billfold. "I'm gonna go on up. You coming?"

Del pressed redial on his phone, but he couldn't get a line out. He glanced at his watch. An hour and a half, they'd agreed. An hour and a half after the start, she'd be out. It hadn't been quite that long, though. Now, it was always possible that she'd been hyperquick. She could have finished already, be riding the elevator down or even safely back in her room with the stamps. She could be safely out of harm's way.

Or she could be knee-deep in Jerry's things.

They were coming back without warning, earlier than he'd promised. If she were in the room, there'd be no good excuse and no telling what might happen. At best, security and arrest. At worst?

With a sense of increasing desperation, he followed Jerry onto the elevator.

GWEN SLID THE LAST DRAWER back into the armoire. Carefully setting the swinging upper doors back where they'd been, she backed away and gave a final check to the room. She'd taken care to put everything back in its initial position. Not that Jerry would even know, given his obvious tendency to throw things around and generally make a mess.

She wouldn't give in to dejection. Just because she hadn't found it didn't mean it wasn't there to be found. She just hadn't looked in the right spot.

Gwen walked back into the living room, mentally ticking off all of the places she'd checked. She glanced at her watch. An hour and twenty minutes. She could afford five more and still have a margin for error. Time for a tour of the room to see if she'd forgotten anything.

She walked slowly and carefully, stopping occasionally to double-check a possible hiding place. Then she passed by the bar, with its glossy marble counter. She glanced behind it and stopped. The refrigerator. She'd checked behind the televisions and behind the safe, but she hadn't checked behind the refrigerator in the bar.

And time was rushing by.

She hurried back behind the polished peninsula. Quickly she crouched in front of the refrigerator, sliding her hands into the nook that held it. It was a close fit, impossible to fit both hands.

Swearing, she struggled to grip it in the narrow cabinet and shift it enough to check one side at a time. She moved it half an inch, then an inch, easing her hand back. She felt smooth metal and polished wood. She inched her fingers back a bit more—

And touched paper.

Adrenaline sprinted through her. It might be just a piece of paper that had wound up there. It probably was. But maybe, just maybe, it was an envelope.

She licked her lips and bent to push the refrigerator again.

And something knocked against the outer door.

Her heart leaped into her throat. Wildly she looked around for a hiding place, then realized the lights were still on. She could hear it now, the rustling of someone working to get a key into the slot. Her heart slammed into her ribs as she careened across to slap down the light switches, cringing at the sound of Jerry's loud and drunken voice outside. She ran back to the center of the living room and stood like a hunted creature at bay. Not the bathroom, not the closet.

Outside the card key snicked into the lock.

And she dived behind the counter of the bar.

"HERE WE GO," JERRY SAID drunkenly. "Is this a room or what? Just need a coupla chicks up here and we're in business."

Jerry'd become more hammered as his last drink from the club had hit, Del observed. Unfortunately he appeared to be one of those drunks who hit a certain level of inebriation and just stayed there, soused but alert to a point.

And focused on a goal.

Jerry stumbled to the couch and fumbled for the TV remote, staring at it blearily. "Hey, we need a coupla beers over here. I'll take care of the ennertainmen'." He managed to get the television on and squinted at the on-screen menu, trying to focus.

"I'll get the drinks." Del walked past the couch toward the bar, every atom of his being on alert. He couldn't see a sign that she'd been there, but he knew she had. He wondered if she was still in the room—there was a better-than-average chance that she was. He scanned the room, looking for likely spots.

And froze at the sight of a silver cell phone sitting on an end table.

"Scopin' out m'digs, huh?" Jerry said from behind him.

Del looked over his shoulder at Jerry on the couch as he walked toward the bar. "I thought you were working on the entertainment."

"Friggin' remote don' work." Jerry's voice was petulant and slurred.

Jerry's alcohol saturated vision didn't work, more like it. "Let me grab a couple of beers, I'll see what I can do," Del said over his shoulder. He deviated off course just enough to scoop up the phone, the back of his neck tingling as he waited to hear Jerry say something. Jerry was quiet, however, preoccupied with the remote.

She was still here, Del thought wildly, ticking off a list of possible hiding places—the shower, the closet, under the bed. He walked behind the bar.

And stumbled to a stop.

"Trouble walkin', thass it, y'cut off," Jerry mumbled.

"You better hope I can walk well enough to get your beer to you," Del threw back distractedly, staring at Gwen curled up in the furthest corner of the little U behind the bar. He pulled open the door to the little refrigerator mechanically, yanking out a couple of beers and setting them on the bar as his mind raced through his options.

One thing wasn't an option—getting Gwen out the door undetected.

"You growin' the hops back there?" Jerry looked blearily back from the couch.

Del turned to pick a bottle of Wild Turkey off the shelf behind him. The harder the liquor, the quicker he could put Jerry under, he calculated, mixing himself a weak bourbon and water and doubling Jerry's. "Beer's for wimps. How about some good old Kentucky bourbon?" He crossed to the couch and handed Jerry his drink. Grabbing the remote, he sat himself. "So, let's see, we want to check out some movies here?" He punched some buttons.

"Hey, turn on Beach Babes Gone Wild," Jerry directed him. "It's got that Misty Mancos in it. She's hot."

Del had an idea, but to carry it out he'd have to keep Jerry occupied. Porn and alcohol sounded like the ticket, and if Jerry passed out, so much the better. Del waited until the film was in full swing and half of Jerry's bourbon was gone before making his move. He rose. "Gotta hit the head."

He crossed to the guest bathroom, off a small hallway just before the door to the bedroom. Focus, he thought as he flipped on the light and fan. Every second counted. As soon as he closed the door, he began unspooling toilet paper, bunching it into a wad bigger than his fist. When he judged he had enough, he shoved it down into the toilet, packing it in the drain. It would work, he hoped, and pushed the flush handle.

"Shit." He didn't entirely have to fake his outburst as the water flowed up over the edge of the bowl and onto the floor. "Goddamn it," he complained, bursting out into the living room.

"What are you bitchin' about?" Jerry looked over from the television, where two stupefyingly endowed women were wrapped around one another.

"Your plumbing. The damned thing is pouring all over the floor. Get in here and look at this."

Jerry levered himself off the couch and stumbled over to the bathroom. "Ah, shit, what a mess."

"Hey, not my fault." Del stood at the door and glanced back to see Gwen peeking over the counter. He jerked his thumb toward the door and stepped back into the bathroom and closed the door. "Maybe if we flush it again."

"No, don't—" but Jerry didn't get a chance to finish the sentence as the water overflowed again. The noise effectively masked the faint click of the door, which Del was pretty sure he heard only because every fiber of his being was attentive for the sound.

The sound of Gwen getting to safety.

GWEN PACED AROUND HER ROOM, too amped on adrenaline to even sit down. Nearly an hour had passed since she'd stumbled through the door. Still, her system stubbornly refused to level. She'd tried to pour herself a drink but her hands had shaken too badly. Had Jerry heard anything? Was Del all right? It had all turned out to be a nightmare, especially since she'd walked away with nothing.

During the nerve-wracking walk from Jerry's room to the elevators, she'd fought to remain relaxed, taking her time even as every fiber of her screamed to run to the exit. A smile and nod to the concierge, as though she had all the time in the world. When the car came, she'd stepped on board, heart thudding, giving in enough to press the 'close door' button.

It had only been when she'd shut the door of her own room, safely inside, that she'd taken a full breath. And another, and another, until she still felt in danger of hyperventilating.

The sudden knock on the door made her jump. It was probably nothing, she told herself, but her imagination painted security standing outside the door instead, ready to lock her up for breaking into a guest room. She looked through the peephole.

It was Del.

He burst through the door when she opened it and pulled her to him, his arms coming around her hard. "God." He held her. "That scared the hell out of me." He pressed his face into her hair and inhaled.

Held close to him, Gwen finally began to shake, really shake, as though she could let loose because he was there. "It did a number on me, too, when—"

His mouth was on hers before she finished, hard and demanding. And that quickly the adrenaline residue of fear flashed over into passion. All she could register was need. She wanted his skin against hers, his body on hers. She wanted him inside her. And most of all she wanted it now.

It wasn't about romance. There wasn't a vestige of anything soft or tender about it. It was pure passion, hard and rough and uncontrolled. All the anxiety, all the tension, all the frustration of the past several hours poured into the heat of their fused mouths. Magnified by fear, desire became manifest.

Gwen gloried in the feel of Del's hands moving roughly over her body. She wanted it fast, she wanted it urgent. Every atom of her body seemed supernaturally sensitive. His teeth scraped against her lower lip and she moaned. His hands slid down to squeeze her breasts and she caught her breath. His fingers slid up under her skirt and she cried out. In that instant she felt supremely alive.

She tore blindly at his shirt, wanting it only off, not caring how. When he stripped her tank top off over her arms, she caught herself to him, nipping greedily at his shoulder, his throat. "I want you inside me," she murmured feverishly, leaning over to the bedside table for the condoms they'd left there. "I want your cock. Now."

With a noise of frustration Del turned her around and bent her over the couch, pushing her skirt up over her hips. When he saw and felt the warm curves of her framed by the red silk of a thong, it almost undid him. Gritting his teeth, he held on long enough to free his aching cock and roll the condom on even as Gwen reached back to touch him, stroking the lightly furred skin of his balls, the tops of his thighs.

And he thrust himself inside her.

Gwen cried out, her head arching back as she clutched at pillows, pushing herself back against him.

It was too fast, too hard, too rough, he thought in some sane part of his mind. But he'd stood by while she'd been in danger and now some primitive instinct drove him to mark her as his. Her tight, wet heat around him dragged him closer to the edge of control with every stroke. Her breasts filled his hands. She surrounded him, inflamed him. As he drove himself home, as he felt her shudder and contract around him, he pulled her hard against him and spilled his soul into her.

The silence was broken only by their breathing. When he thought he could stand without falling over, Del pushed himself upright. "Oh, man," he muttered. "Oh, man."

"You can say that again." Gwen stood shakily, one hand on the couch.

"Are you okay?"

"I'm not okay." His heart clutched as she turned to him. "I'm fabulous."

It took him a moment to catch up. "Yeah, that was…you were okay with that?"

"It was incredible." She sat on the arm of the couch and let herself fall back onto the cushions, stretching her arms out languorously. "Of course, if you wanted to give me some basis of comparison, I could give you a more accurate assessment."

He grinned. "Coming up, ma'am."


"WANT SOMETHING TO DRINK?" Wrapped in a terry cloth hotel bathrobe, Gwen stood at the minibar.

"Beer, please."

She handed Del one, grabbed a bottle of water for herself. He studied her. "So, you're okay?"

"Oh, yeah." She flopped on the couch beside him. "So, what happened with Jerry?"

"Everything's fine. He's passed out." Del twisted the top off the beer and took a long drink. "I don't think he figured out a thing. You got out at just the right time. Five seconds later he was in the living room calling housekeeping. God, I about flipped when I saw your cell phone lying there."

"I know. I realized I'd left it out when I was already behind the bar. Why didn't you call me?"

"I tried to. Couldn't get a signal." As though the tension had come back, he rose to pace across the room. "So, did you find them?" His eyes glowed green with excitement.

"I think so. I'd just found an envelope when you guys came in. It's wedged behind the refrigerator, I'm pretty sure, but I couldn't get it out."

"You're kidding."

"It's okay. Now I know where it is. Next time I'll get it."

"Next time." He turned to stare at her. "There isn't going to be a next time."

"Sure there will. We'll work out a better plan." Gwen opened her water and took a long pull.

"Oh, yeah? How do you figure?" He set the beer roughly aside. "We thought this plan was foolproof and it almost blew up in our faces."

"So? We'll figure out something else," she said impatiently. "Maybe I get a new phone, or you do."

"It's too dangerous. What do you think Jerry would do if he knew you were in his room sniffing around, particularly given what's at stake?"

"Probably try to get me into bed."

"Are you even listening?"

She'd underestimated the level of his agitation, Gwen realized. She'd underestimated the level of her own. She took a deep breath. "We're both tense over this. I think we should talk about this later once we've both calmed down."

"I don't want to calm down."

"Just because you volunteered to help doesn't mean that you're suddenly running the show," she exclaimed. "This is my hunt, Del. You're not going to stand there and tell me what I can and can't do."

"You're not going to do something that's going to put you at risk," he retorted.

Gwen took a deep breath. "Okay, we both need to take it easy. I'm not stupid, Del, I'm not going to take a ridiculous chance. But I do still have the key and I know where the stamps are."

"You think you know where the stamps are," he corrected.

"I'm going to get back in there and find out for sure. Not now, though," she placated. "For now we play wait and see. If the right opportunity presents itself, then we make a move. Agreed?"

"Maybe," he said reluctantly.

"Well, it's not like we can do anything else tonight." She reached for her sash. "Do you have any other ideas for ways to keep busy?"

# 15

EVERYTHING LOOKED DIFFERENT when you were the one at the tables, Gwen discovered. If she'd felt mild tension in the room the previous nights she'd been in the bleachers, now she felt an anxiety and strain so thick that it seemed to weigh her down.

Why had she thought entering the tournament was the way to go? She could monitor Jerry without the crushing pressure of knowing she could lose her place at the table and her ten-thousand-dollar stake in one night. She was in it now, though, obligated to play through to either win or lose. Cashing in her chips to get her money back wasn't an option. Chips now only meant points in the game.

"You okay?" Del asked as he stood beside her.

Gwen nodded. "Yeah, sure, no problem." She grimaced. "Except I feel a little sick."

"Don't worry, you're going to do fine. Just remember, you're only playing eight people at a time. Focus on them, not the big picture."

Gwen nodded. It helped to think of it that way. "I've been playing with the same people for years. Doing this feels a lot like jumping out of the plane without a parachute."

"You've learned from those guys, though. They might have their tells, but it's harder to bluff people who know you. Take what you've learned from them and go to the next level." He squeezed her hand.

"You do a nice line in pep talks."

He gave her a crooked smile. "I like to think of myself as multitalented."

"Oh, I can definitely verify that."

The MC began to call for players to go to their assigned seats.

Gwen looked at Del. "I guess that's me."

"Okay, relax and have fun." Del leaned over to press a kiss on her. "It's a little freaky at first. Don't do anything sudden, just take a couple of hands and let yourself get used to the feel of things. You're going to do great."

Fighting panic, Gwen took a deep breath. "Swear?"

"Damn," he said obediently and she grinned.

DEL SAT AT HIS HOTEL ROOM desk the next day, punching the keys of his laptop in a rapid tattoo. He knew plenty of guys on the paper who stuck with the two-finger hunt and peck. As far as he was concerned, you did the work and learned the drill. He'd done it when he'd been playing sports and he'd done it when he'd started on the paper and taught himself real typing.

His cell phone rang and he picked it up and flipped it open. "Redmond."

"At least you're answering on the first try today."

"Hello, Perry."

"What are you up to?"

"What does it sound like I'm up to?" Del rapidly finished typing his current sentence and hit the keyboard command to save the file. "Writing a story about how two women cleaned up in their first night of play yesterday."

"Ah, the sound of a column being finished. Warms an old editor's heart."

"Save the shtick, Perry. We both know you're not even fifty yet. What's up? The series okay?"

"Better than okay. I was reading the article today on the little hustler. Got any photos of this poseur?"

"He doesn't want any photos taken."

"Interesting."

"Kinda makes you wonder where he got his stake."

"Kinda does," Perry agreed. "I don't suppose it's got anything to do with a certain theft?"

Del closed his eyes briefly. "Jessup's been talking."

"He came and asked me if you were for real or if I thought you were putting him on about this story. I told him you were many things, including an occasional horse's ass—"

"Not often," Del put in.

"Not often," Perry agreed, "but that you were not the type to put anyone on."

"He believe you?"

"He seemed to take it okay. So, what's going on? What have you bumbled into out there, anyway?"

He'd opened Pandora's box, Del thought sinkingly, and putting the story back into it was going to be a job. He'd regretted his discussion with Jessup almost immediately. Now the more he discovered about Gwen, the more he was certain that doing a story on the stamp theft was the wrong move.

The question was, what would it do to his chances on the paper if he came back now and told Jessup to forget about it? Bye-bye, news job. Bye-bye, future. "It's not as big as I thought. I'm going to check it out a few more days and report in. I thought it would be a chance to show Jessup my stuff. Now I don't know."

"You know he's waiting for you to come up looking bad on this," Perry said impatiently.

"Yeah, I know."

"If you want this news job, I'd find a way to dig up a story."

"There's a complication."

"There always is with you. Let me guess, the hustler is actually a redhead with big blue eyes and enormous—"

"No, the hustler is a nervy little guy."

"But the redhead is somewhere in the picture."

"Well, actually she's a blonde," Del admitted.

"Del Do-Right."

He'd told Perry about it in a weak moment, after a few too many beers. "A classy guy wouldn't have brought that up."

"She throw her arms around your neck and beg you to save the family farm from the villains?"

"Actually no. She yelled at me and told me to mind my own business and that she could take care of herself."

"She should know."

"Maybe. The more I find out, the more I think maybe this story is a bad idea. I've been trying to think how to handle it with Jessup."

"Oh, just telling him that you're pulling your application will probably work," Perry said lightly. "Redmond, you *putz,* reporters aren't supposed to get involved. Rule number one. You know that. He finds out you've been suckered on your first story, you won't get near his precious news desk."

"I haven't been suckered."

"Well, I hope you haven't been suck—never mind," Perry said hastily. "Anyway, it might put him off you, but it won't put him off the story. If he likes it—and he does—he'll give it to someone else. Your best bet is to file something lukewarm but well written and tell him the story didn't pan out."

"Thus pulling my application."

"Yeah, but maybe keeping him off the story."

Del drummed his fingers on the desktop. He knew Perry was right, but that didn't mean he had to like it.

And he didn't. Not one bit.

Perry cleared his throat. "It's not my place to say, but you don't know this woman. She's probably not worth throwing this all away over. Can you even trust whatever it is she's telling you?"

"Yeah." He thought, anyway.

"You don't sound too sure."

"Don't push it, Perry."

Perry was silent for a little while. "This is the first one you've really gotten involved with since your divorce, isn't it?"

"Yeah."

"Hey, I've been there, too. Divorce sucks. It's hard to swallow failure and it's easy to go looking for something to erase that. But you've been in Vegas, what, a week?" He blew out a breath. "You just met her, Del. She's not going to be the one—they never are. Trust me on this."

Del pushed back from the desk and swung his chair around so he could look out into the pitiless sun of the Las Vegas day. "Don't worry, I'm not going off the deep end."

"I hope not. You've got the chance for a new career here. Something it sounds like you want. Don't throw it away on a Vegas squeeze."

Del hung up the phone and stared out the window at nothing for long minutes. Finally he came thoughtfully back to his computer and logged on to the Internet. *You don't know this woman.* Maybe it was time he started to. He brought up a search engine and plugged in her name.

THEY SAT IN ALIZÉ, ON TOP OF the Palms casino, staring out over the lights of Las Vegas. The gargantuan hotels along the Strip looked oddly graceful by night, reduced to streaks of color—the green of the MGM Grand, the red and purple of Rio, the lighted arc of the Wynn. The twinkling lights of the rest of the town looked diamond sharp in the dry desert air.

Despite the lateness of the hour, she was still buzzed from playing. She felt alert, energized and just a little bit wild. The lighting was dim, the heavy linen draped over the tables crisp. It gave her a decidedly Nina-like urge to do something just a bit outrageous.

Del raised his wineglass. "To making it to round three and to seeing us both at the final table."

"The final table? I'd just be happy to get through tomorrow night and make it into the money rounds."

"And I'm sure you will. You ran some pretty fearsome bluffs tonight."

It was probably the relief of surviving a second night and moving forward that was making her so giddy. "Speaking of bluffs, how did you get a table here tonight, anyway? Tell them you were Phil Hellmuth?"

"You don't get reservations at Alizé the night of," he told her. "I had confidence in you."

"Really?"

He nodded. "Just like I have confidence in you in other ways. You'll get those stamps back, I know it."

"I wish I were as sure," she sighed.

"I can see why the work fascinates you," Del said casually. "I was doing some research on stamps on the Internet today."

Her head came up like that of a doe scenting a predator. "Why were you doing that?"

"I figured I ought to know more about it. Anyway, I'm a journalist. Research is what I do. And the more I know, the better I can help. So Chastain Philatelic Investments is your family business, right? Is Hugh Chastain your uncle or your brother or something?"

"Grandfather," she said. "You've been busy."

"Not busy, just curious."

"Ah, you know what they say about curiosity and cats," she scolded and he felt something brush his leg.

He looked down. "What the...?"

"Maybe it's that cat," she said smoothly, and he felt it again, this time a satiny toe stroking up against his leg, under his pants.

It brought all of his nerves to awareness. "I think you're trying to distract me."

"Oh, no, if I were trying to distract you, I wouldn't do something like this," she said, stroking his leg with the side of her bare foot. "I'd do something like this." The stroke over his crotch was quick and soft and had his cock twitching under his napkin.

"Oh, goody, here comes the chocolate fondant cake," she said smoothly as the waiter walked up. Del just sat watching them go through the ritual pouring of the crème anglaise, grateful of the drape of linen in his lap.

And Gwen savored a bite of her cake, her tongue licking over the fork even as her toes stroked his balls.

"You're enjoying this, aren't you?" he asked tightly.

She took another nibble. "Yes, you want a bite? It's wonderful."

"I'm sure." He ground his teeth.

His jacket covered up his erection as they left the restaurant and made their way to the taxi line downstairs.

Gwen stretched against him in a movement that did nothing to ease the aching hard-on. "I can't believe it's after one in the morning and we're just leaving dinner," she murmured.

"Vegas is an all-night town."

"I guess."

There was something abandoned about her tonight, something loose and open. "I hope you were happy with yourself in there," he murmured.

"You liked it?" She gave him a naughty smile. "It's a little something I've been thinking about."

"It's not a little something now."

She wiggled against him. "I feel that. I've got a few more fantasies."

"And what would those be?"

"Well, I'm living one right now," she told him impishly and took his hand to rest it on her lower back. For a moment he just savored the smooth curve of her back into her haunches until he registered the fact that…

"You're not wearing any—"

The doorman turned to him. "Where to, sir?"

With a slow grin Del handed him a tip. "Versailles, please."

The doorman leaned down to tell the cab driver as Gwen slid across the seat. Carefully, he noticed, grinning broadly.

"Hey, kids," the cab driver said, "we having fun tonight?"

"Nothing but," Del said blandly.

The vinyl seat of the cab felt cooler to Gwen without her thong. Just her imagination, she told herself as the cab driver stopped at the light that led to the street. Del's hand stroked her leg. "You should be careful provoking people like that," he murmured in her ear. "They might retaliate."

And then his hand went higher. She jolted as his fingers slid up between her thighs to find her, nothing but her. To find where she was wet, already hot from teasing him during dinner, from imagining what came next.

Gwen stared at him but he looked steadfastly ahead. The first touch came when she didn't expect it, as the cabbie was checking for traffic to turn onto Flamingo Road. One minute a tease only, then the next those clever, clever fingers had plunged into her slick wetness to find her clitoris.

Gwen fought not to gasp.

"So, where you folks from?"

"San Francisco," Del said, stroking that hard nub, sliding against it in an irresistible tease that she couldn't react to. She wanted, oh, she wanted to pump her hips and moan. Instead she stayed stock-still, staring at the back of the cabbie's head while he chattered, oblivious.

"No kidding. I'm from the city, too. I moved here about a year and a half ago."

"You like it?" Del asked. He didn't flirt around with ways to tease her, just a slow, measured touch that was driving her insane, dragging her closer and closer to orgasm even as they waited at the light to turn onto the Strip.

"It's okay. I really miss the city, though, the arts community, you know. I hung out with a lot of creative types when I was there."

"Good arts scene," Del nodded, making conversation even as he was making her insensible with pleasure. He was relentless, driving her up with warm, wet strokes, each brush, each touch taking her closer to that zone where she just didn't care.

"I'm forgetting stuff already, though. I was trying to tell someone the other day about that café at the foot of Russian Hill—I can't remember the name of it."

The orgasm broke through her as Versailles came into view. Gwen made a strangled sound and tensed against the seat, trying not to shudder.

"What'd you say, ma'am?"

"I believe she said it's called Aah's," Del said helpfully as they pulled into the massive portico with its crenellated marble overhang.

"Aah's? Nope, that's not the one I'm thinking of."

Gwen took a minute to gather herself enough to get out of the cab, sliding carefully across the seat.

"That was evil," she told him as they walked into the hotel. The hour was late, and even in Vegas, there were few people around.

Del stopped and pulled her to him to press a hot, hard kiss on her. "That was hot is what it was. You have no idea what it does to me to feel you come like that, to get you that wet."

She slid her arms down his body. "You have no idea what it does to me." She moved her hips lightly against him.

"Upstairs," he said raggedly. "Now." They began to walk again. "So, tell me some more about these fantasies."

"I've been having these ideas about elevators," she whispered to him. "I keep finding myself in the car, waiting all that time to get to the top. I don't know, there's something about it that gets me thinking about the possibilities."

They stopped in front of the banks of elevators and Del unbuttoned his jacket. "Fast ride," he commented.

"But a hot one." She leaned in to take his earlobe between her teeth. "For a couple who's prepared."

"Did I ever tell you I used to be a Boy Scout when I was a kid?" he asked, pulling her close so that she could feel him hard against her. "You know their motto."

"Always prepared." His cock felt like granite to her.

"Always. Where's the damned elevator?"

Gwen rummaged in her purse to find a condom and tear open the package. "My question exactly. You're a rise-to-the-occasion kind of guy, aren't you?" she asked, kissing him with lips and teeth and tongue and pressing the condom into his palm.

"You kiss like that, you're going to get more than you bargained for sooner than you expect."

A chime rang and an elevator door opened up behind them. She stepped on and pressed the door-close button. "Oh, I hope so." She propped herself against the brass rail that ran around the car. "Top floor, cowboy."

The doors closed, the lights dimmed and control disappeared. In what seemed like a fraction of a second, Del had himself out and sheathed. When he slid into her, she cried out. It was crazy, insane to take the chance, and yet she laughed exultantly as she felt him slide gloriously home inside her.

Her legs were wrapped around him, her arms clawing his shoulders as she savored each savage stroke of his body into hers. He poured in the long temptation of the evening, making no attempt to slow his pace, no attempt to hold back. He was all surging, stroking and rock-hard deep inside her, where she craved him. Around them lights glittered on the Strip, but nothing like the show of seeing Del lose control, lose himself in her as she lost herself. And when he burst into groaning orgasm, she cried out at the sheer glory of being alive.

# 16

DAY OR NIGHT, THE CASINO looked the same, save only the number of people hunched at the slot machines. Now, for example, the fact that it was just shy of noon was revealed only in the ranks of empty gambling tables. Gwen shook her head to dispel the thought just as someone swooped down on her from behind.

She yelped even as she recognized the persuasive mouth and hands. "You scared me to death," she accused.

"Oh, I don't know, you feel pretty lively to me," Del countered, giving her a final squeeze before releasing her. "So, where do you want to go?"

She shrugged. "I don't care. Anywhere they've got lunch."

"I was thinking we could get outside the casino for a change. Celebrate both of us making it into the second round."

She gave him a bawdy wink. "I thought we did that last night."

"And memorably. But it's a big enough deal it deserves some extra treatment. Let's go. I'm stir crazy."

"Me, too," she confessed. "Getting out would be fabulous."

He kissed her. "Good." They walked out the front door, but instead of leading her onto the Strip he walked to the valet parking attendant and picked up a key.

"You've got a car?"

"I thought we both could use a break from the Strip. Unless you'd like to go back inside?"

She gave a giddy laugh and got into the spiffy red coupe that pulled up. "God, no."

It was easy to forget that there was life outside of the casinos. Las Vegas seemed to float in its own dislocated pocket of existence. It seemed that she'd always lived in the shadow world of recycled air and cigarette smoke, surrounded by people with the worn look of too many hours of gambling, too little sleep. The long hours spent in the casinos, the marching rows of the resorts banished all thought of the desert, except for the stupefying heat that slammed the senses the moment a person stepped outside.

Now it was all behind her, in another world, and her only reality was the open road.

As they drove along the freeway that paralleled the Strip, the line of casinos only looked more incongruous without the benefit of their elaborate facades. On the Strip it seemed as if the casinos dominated the known world. Now, from the outside, they seemed as absurd as moss flourishing in the desert.

Gwen stretched and let her right arm dangle out the window, surfing the slipstream of air as the last of the casinos gave way to the suburbs. "This is great. I forgot what this was like, the out-of-doors."

"It's a nice reminder, isn't it."

"Of course, you know we should be at Versailles watching Jerry."

"Knowing Jerry, he's probably still in bed with a hangover. We'll be back by afternoon, when he gets up. You can't watch him every minute, you know."

"I just keep thinking I'm going to miss something and so much for my chance to get the stamps back."

"Let it go. He told you he was expecting his big score

next week. We've got time. Give yourself a break." Del headed toward the hills that formed an arc on the horizon.

It was an artificial world out here, vivid green lawns shockingly incongruous against the sere desert landscape. The housing tracts seemed to stretch for miles.

"So, where are we going?"

"Hoover Dam."

Gwen blinked. "You big on public-works projects?"

"Seemed worth seeing. Besides, one of the guys I met at the tournament told me about a barbecue joint in Boulder City. I thought it would be a nice break from resort food."

"I'll buy that."

The subdivisions finally gave way to the open desert and Gwen caught a breath of pleasure. "Now this is more like it."

Away from the artificial constructs of suburbia, the desert emerged in all its subtle beauty. Pink terrain, gray-green sage, golden-brown mesquite and pale blue sky all blended together in a pastel fantasy. The serried ranks of ruddy hills rose sharply in the distance, stark and clear in the dry desert air.

Gwen took an exultant breath, savoring the spicy scent of the air. "This is wonderful," she said, buoyed by the sense of light and openness and space.

Del gave her a sidelong glance. "I thought you might like it, Gwendolyn."

"It's not Gwendolyn." She flushed.

"Really?" he asked with interest. "What is it short for? Gwendy? Gwenda?"

"Stop it."

"Come on, fess up. It can't be that weird."

She sighed. "Guinevere."

"So, what's wrong with that?"

"Oh, don't be nice. It's ridiculous, I know it. It was my mother's idea."

"A romantic."

Gwen watched the landscape roll by a few moments before answering. "My mother's something of a free spirit, you might say. She and my dad are doctors working in Africa."

"Takes more than a free spirit to be an M.D."

"Oh, I know that. She's brilliant. She works unimaginably hard and she's very passionate about making a difference. I guess what I was trying to say is that she marches to her own drummer." Gwen could admire it, be often puzzled by it, but never really understand. "I was five when she convinced my dad to join Physicians Without Frontiers. My sister Joss was six. They scooped us off to Zimbabwe."

"You went to Zimbabwe?"

"And Botswana and Tanzania. I got out when I was fourteen. Joss stayed until she was grown. My mom thought it was a good cultural experience for us."

"She was probably right."

"I suppose." Gwen turned to study him. "Where did you grow up?"

"Huntington Beach."

"Surf's up?" she asked dryly.

"Some of the time. We didn't live in luxury or anything. I was just a normal kid."

"That was all I ever wanted to be. Just a normal kid."

Del reached over and took her hand, lacing his fingers with hers. "And you weren't?"

"It's hard to be normal when you're a blond white kid in Zaire," she said simply. "We'd come back to the U.S. for a month every year, stay with my grandparents. I just wanted to eat hamburgers and watch TV like everybody else. My mom had other ideas."

"Which were?"

Gwen stared out at the deep red rocks surrounding them. "Making us the poster children for a global society."

"Heavy load for a kid," Del commented, slowing down a bit to take a curve. The freeways had given way to a narrow highway that dived between ranges of hills.

"We'd go give talks at schools and stuff. The way they'd look at us…" She sighed. "Joss loved it, but she always liked being the center of attention. I've always been more comfortable on the sidelines."

"Must be harder now."

She could feel herself tense, she thought in annoyance, wishing she'd never started this line of discussion. He didn't want to hear about Gwen. He was a guy. Nina would be his thing. *I have a soft spot for Nina.* Ordinary Gwen wouldn't even register on him.

"Does it feel awkward, being dressed up?"

"Not as much as you'd think. It's Nina they're looking at, not me. It's not so bad." Now that she thought about it, she'd stopped feeling awkward and conspicuous as the days had passed. It had become kind of fun. Maybe there was more Nina in her than she'd realized.

"So, you said you stayed in Zimbabwe or wherever until you were fourteen. Why did you leave?"

"We'd come back to visit my grandparents like we did every year. It was so great I just hated going back. I was evil for a good two months after that, the way only an adolescent can be. My parents finally broke and let me move in with my grandparents. I said it was so I could get into a good college, but I think they knew."

"And loved you enough to let you go."

"Yes. And my grandparents loved me enough to give me a home."

"The grandfather who taught you to play poker."

She laughed. "You remembered."

"He must be loving the fact that you're here playing."

"Well, he doesn't know," she said, suddenly uneasy.

"He and my grandmother are off on a long trip to the South Pacific."

"My grandparents did that when they retired."

"Well, he's not quite there yet. They call this their practice retirement. I was supposed to be minding the store until they came back."

"The stamps?"

"Yes, I—oh," she broke off as they rounded a curve and the deep blue of Lake Mead swung into view. Framed by the serrated lines of the pastel hills, it stretched away from them, cool and sapphire-dark. There were houses here, but they blended pueblo-style into the desert, colored in warm ochers and rose tones, topped with ruddy terra-cotta roofs.

The road curved around through the hills now, first rising steadily, then dropping in great loops toward the dam. When the tangle of high-voltage towers materialized, it was a shock after the open landscape. Then the dam itself appeared, its smooth, warm curve blending seamlessly with the hills around it.

"Do you want to drive across?" Del asked. "We can."

Gwen shook her head. "Can't we ditch the car and walk?"

"Whatever you'd like."

The heat was there, ever present, but she was too preoccupied with the sight ahead of her to really notice. They passed a monument to the workers, a pair of almost unearthly winged figures seated with arms pointing to the heavens. Beyond them the dam stretched around.

"Do you ever get the urge to step up on a railing like this and just jump out into space?" Gwen asked idly as they stopped to lean over the waist-high concrete wall and stare down at the dam. It was like looking into a giant funnel, the broad curve tapering down to the narrow bottom, where the Colorado River flowed away in a gleaming ribbon.

He cocked an eyebrow at her. "This isn't the part where you start talking about your suicidal thoughts, is it?"

"Good god, no. It just always seems like you could just jump out and soar away like a bird, you know? Part of my mind whispers 'Go ahead and do it, you could fly.'" She wrinkled her nose at him. "See if I ever share my innermost thoughts with you again." They stepped back from the rail and began ambling slowly along the dam. "So, tell me more about life as a surfer boy."

"Life as a surfer boy? Not exactly. We lived inland, not on the water." When he slipped his arm around her, it was the most natural thing in the world.

"Did you surf?"

"Some. Skied, went rock climbing in the desert."

"You've got that look." She stopped in front of the bronze dedication plaque.

"You think so? Mostly I played sports."

"Yikes. A jock? You weren't one of those football guys who dated the cheerleaders, were you?"

"Not football, baseball."

"And the cheerleaders?"

He grimaced and the fun faded briefly from his eyes. "Married one."

"Married?"

"Divorced," he elaborated, holding up his ringless left hand. "You can't always trust everything you see with the golden girls."

Something about the way he said it discouraged her from asking more. She turned to a safer topic instead. "So, you played in high school?"

"College, too. It covered my tuition."

"You didn't go pro, did you?"

He shook his head. "I was good in high school and okay

in college, but I was nowhere near good enough for the pros. I found that out pretty quickly."

She stopped and leaned against the concrete wall to look at him. "That must have been tough to give up your dream."

Del shrugged. "It wasn't my dream so much as what was easy. Just like marrying Krista. Just like sportswriting. I was good in English and it seemed like a good way to take what I knew and parlay it into something."

"You don't seem thrilled."

"I don't know." Seeming suddenly uncomfortable, he began walking. "I've just always taken the easy way out. I'd like to do something because I made it happen for a change, not because I was good at it and it fell into my lap."

"So, what do you want to do?"

"I don't know, something meatier than sports, I guess. Tell stories that really matter. I think I'm ready to make a change."

They'd reached the other side of the dam, Gwen realized in surprise. Del leaned on the railings to look out at Lake Mead, cradled between the walls of the canyon bridged by the dam. He looked back at her. "You getting the urge to climb up on the rail and jump off here?"

She shook her head. "Here it'd just be like jumping into a pool."

"That's the difference between us, I guess. I want to dive in and you want to fly."

THE SUN WAS SETTING BY THE time they got back to the hotel. Del turned the car back over to the valet and they trailed into the hotel, sunburned and spent.

"What are you doing tonight?"

"I thought I'd take a nice cool bath to wash off all the dust." Gwen gave him a thoroughly naughty look as she got off the elevator. "Care to join me?"

"I'm your man." He followed her to her door, where she fumbled her key out of her purse. She opened the door, took two steps and stopped abruptly.

"Oh, my god."

# 17

THE ROOM HAD BEEN TOSSED thoroughly and by someone who didn't much care how much of a mess they made. Del followed Gwen through the haphazardly thrown-around clothing and personal items. "Careful," he said, catching her before she walked over broken glass. "See if anything's missing."

Gwen walked through the room in a daze, picking things up and setting them down, her breath hitching unsteadily. Del swept some papers off the sofa and pulled her down to sit on it. "It's okay," he said softly, catching her hands between his, but they were ice-cold.

"Someone's been in here," she whispered, shivering. "They've been through everything."

It was a violation, at least as much as her attack. That they'd searched Jerry's room just days before didn't make it easier. This didn't have the look of a purposeful search, Del realized. It had the look of maliciousness. "Make any enemies at the tournament?"

Gwen turned to him and it was as though they arrived at the same point at the same time. "The stamps."

"But why would someone break in here looking for the stamps?" she asked.

"Maybe they knew you were at Jerry's. Maybe they've noticed all the time you've spent with him and they figure he handed off something to you. Maybe it's a warning."

For the first time she registered the torn drapes, the split pillows. "We're going to have to report this, aren't we?"

"Don't see how we can avoid it."

Her face paled. "I don't want the police in on it."

"Why the big hush job?"

"I don't want them in on it," she repeated.

"That'll be up to hotel security."

"They can't know about the stamps. They can't report it." She rose and began to walk agitatedly through the mess.

"Is anything missing?" He had to ask her three times before she could answer.

"I can't tell. Everything is such a mess. There wasn't much of anything to take. My computer and jewelry are in the safe. Nothing else..." she spread out her hands.

"You should open it just in case, but the safe doesn't look touched."

It hadn't been, near as he could tell. Perhaps whoever had tossed the room had been disturbed.

Or perhaps they just wanted to send a message. *We're watching you.*

ONE THING WAS CERTAIN—THE head of hotel security was watching her. Tall and gaunt-cheeked, Howard Ahmanson had disillusioned-cop eyes that surveyed the world with a cynical stare. Currently he'd turned the cynical stare on her. "Know any reason someone would have broken in here? Anyone got a grudge against you? Old boyfriend? Someone you beat at the tables?"

Gwen shook her head. "Nothing like that. Anyway, I'd hope it wouldn't be that easy to break the locks."

"You trying to say it was an inside job?"

"Not at all. I have no idea what kind of job it is. I just know I haven't made any enemies and I don't have any jilted lovers running around."

"And nothing's missing, you say."

"The only valuables I had were in the safe, and that held."

"Whoever got into your room was a pro. We could call the cops and get them to look for prints, but the perp probably used gloves. Anyway, if nothing's missing, the only thing you could charge them with would be destruction of property."

Gwen sat on the couch and massaged her temples. "Do I have to file a report to get the property damage waived?"

"Eventually. Not tonight, though. You can change rooms when you're ready. Just go down to the front desk."

She nodded.

"You know," he said casually, "seems funny that someone would go to that much trouble to make a mess in the place of someone who doesn't have an enemy in the world. Looks to me like someone's maybe trying to tell you something." He gave her a long look, then walked to the door. Just before he reached it, he turned. "You think of anyone or change your mind, you let me know, okay?"

"Okay."

"And put on the dead bolt when you're in here."

The door closed behind Ahmanson. Del walked back toward Gwen. "He's right, you know, you should file a police report. You should call the cops, period, blow the whistle on things."

"No," she said abruptly. She huddled on the couch, the shakes just starting. "I can't."

"Gwen, we don't know what's going on here. Someone tried to hurt you four days ago—"

"You don't know that that was connected," she said hotly.

"And you don't know that it wasn't. And now we come back and find your room torn apart. Nothing's gone but everything's a mess and it looks a whole lot like it might be connected to Jerry and to the guy that grabbed you the other night."

The shakes got stronger. "I can't get the police involved."

"You've got hundreds of dollars in damage to the furnishings here. Unless you win the poker tournament, you're going to damned well have to."

"It's my problem, Del." Nina wouldn't be shaking. Nina wouldn't be on the edge of tears. She'd take it in the gut, hold up her head and go on. Gwen took a breath.

"God, you're doing it again," he said disgustedly.

"What?"

"Channeling."

"What do you mean?"

"You think I don't see it? You think I don't know when it's going on? One minute you're you and then the screens go down and someone else is looking out of your eyes. All of a sudden you're being Nina."

He saw a whole lot more than she'd given him credit for. A whole lot more than she wanted him to. "What's wrong with Nina?"

"She's not real. She's not a person, she's just a construct, someone you use to give yourself guts. Well you've got guts already, so why don't you have the guts to be yourself?"

"Maybe I don't want to be just Gwen. Maybe I like being Nina."

"Well, being Nina has you taking stupid chances, thinking you're some sort of superwoman who can go up against the bad guys. Maybe you can't, and being Nina is just going to get you into a dangerous situation you can't get out of. You've got this thing about being Nina and it's going to get you into some very bad trouble if you don't watch out."

"What about you? Who were you talking with that first night at the blackjack table, anyway? If I'd been Gwen, I'd never have come up to you and you'd never have given me the time of day. You probably still wouldn't. I might be

Gwen inside, but I'm Nina on the outside and Nina's your golden-girl fantasy. So don't go lecturing me, Del," she snapped and turned to the windows. She pressed her forehead to the glass, feeling the warmth left over from the Las Vegas day.

Outside the sun had set in the time between their discovery of the room and meeting with security. Lights glittered and flashed in the dusk. People flocked down the Strip to the casinos. Life went on as usual.

Del walked over to her, watching her shoulders, knowing the strength that was in them, seeing the fragility. "Look, I don't always say the right thing. You'd think I would. I work with words for a living. Sometimes, though, when I'm angry or scared, it comes out wrong. And I'm scared for you right now and angry that someone's doing this to you. So I screwed up and I'm sorry."

Gwen raised her head and turned to look at him.

"The thing is, I don't think I'm wrong," he continued. "I think you're taking some risks with an unknown quantity. I think you think you can carry it off, and it worries me that something might happen to you." He jammed his hands into his pockets. "I don't think Jerry tossed your room. This is bigger than him. You've got to bring in the cops."

Gwen was silent for a long time. Finally she spoke. "I told you my grandfather's in the process of retiring. I didn't tell you everything. You figured out my grandfather owns the stamp store, the one Jerry stole from. Jerry didn't just take stamps from the store inventory, though. He stole the best of the stamps that my grandfather is depending on for his retirement."

"Your grandfather doesn't know?"

Gwen shook her head, walking over to sink down on the bed. "If I'd told him, he'd come back home the next day and he's in less of a position to get them back than I am."

"Insurance?"

She shook her head and laid back, staring at the ceiling. "He was planning to start selling them over the next two years. Four and a half million out the door and into Jerry's pocket."

It was still hard to accept that little chips of paper could be worth so much. A testament to human acquisitiveness, Del supposed, or to obsession. He sank down on the bed beside her and gathered her against him, kissing her hair and saying nothing.

"There's more to it than just the money, though. It would still leave him with a million or so in holdings, but he's an investment philatelist."

"Meaning?"

"He advises people on investment stamps. And because of the way his contracts with them are written, word getting out about the stamp theft could take everything that's left." She turned to face him. "I can't bail on this, even if someone's trying to intimidate me. Even if they're watching me. I don't care who they are, I've got to find a way to get those stamps back from Jerry without word getting out."

Del brushed a hand over her hair and pressed a gentle kiss on her lips. "You will. We'll do it together."

But long after her eyes had closed, he lay staring at the ceiling.

# *18*

DEL STOOD AT HIS WINDOW, looking out at the Strip, wishing he could do anything but make the call he was about to make. Then again, unpleasant things were best done quickly, he thought and punched the numbers on his cell phone.

"Jessup."

"Greg, it's Del Redmond here."

"How's that story going, Redmond?"

"That's why I'm calling." He was calling because it was, quite simply, the right thing to do. "The story's evaporated."

"Evaporated?"

"It's not as big a story as I anticipated."

"Four and a half million in rare stamps isn't a story? What, did they show up? Did the owners miss seeing them the first time around?" The sarcasm was ripe in Jessup's voice.

"No," Del said evenly. "The more I investigated, the more it became clear that it's not a straightforward, clean story."

"Those are usually the best kind."

"Not this one. It's not going to come together and it's not going to be timely." That was always the card to play with a newshound. Late was as good as never as far as a good editor was concerned.

"Doesn't help us much, does it?"

"Would you rather I turned in twenty column inches of useless crap?" Del countered.

Jessup gave a bark of laughter. "Balls, Redmond. I like

that in a reporter. All these kids that I'm interviewing are afraid to stand up for themselves. Don't want to take a chance on irritating me."

"I've already got a job, Jessup. I was thinking I'd like a chance to work news for you, but I might be revising that opinion."

Jessup snorted. "I might be revising my opinion, too. That story would have helped you, you know that?"

"Only if it were solid. If I'd sent you twenty column inches that stank to high heaven, I don't think it would have done a whole hell of a lot for my case."

"I suppose not."

"And by the way, you can tell your little terrier Kellar to back off."

"Kellar?"

"Yeah. Calls himself your stringer? He hunted me down the other day."

"Oh, right. I thought he might be able to help you with some local contacts."

"Well, be sure to tell him the story's been spiked. I don't want him nosing around anymore."

"Uh-huh." There was a short silence. "You seem awfully anxious to have this story killed, Redmond."

"That's because it's the right thing to do." Del's fingers clenched the phone just a bit tighter.

"Well, I suppose I have to trust the instincts of my reporters."

"I'm not your reporter," Del reminded him.

"Well, you're still in the pool, anyway. I'm interviewing through the end of next week. You come up with anything I can use out there, send it along. If not, well, we'll be in touch."

THERE WAS SOMETHING ABSOLUTELY intoxicating about winning, Gwen thought as she grinned into the mirror over the sink in the ladies' room halfway through the day's play. Every two hours the tournament ran, they got fifteen minutes to stand up, move around and take a break. She dried her hands and looked over to where Roxy was slicking on a new layer of lipstick.

"You doing all right?" Gwen asked.

"Sweetie, I am doing fabulously. They're all like soft little bunnies and I'm the saber-toothed tiger."

"Now there's an image."

"I caught the guy in the number seven seat at my table staring at my knockers."

"Nice," Gwen said with a grimace.

"Hell, I don't care. If he's busy looking at my chest, he's not thinking about poker."

"On the other hand, it's going to be harder to pick out a bluff if the vein beating on the side of his head is throbbing for another reason."

"Nope, the vein that's throbbing because of that is a whole lot lower." She winked. "So, where are you at?"

"In a really weird spot. I feel like I can see what they've got and I know which way to push them. The cards just keep falling my way."

"Sounds like you're in the zone."

"I hope so." Gwen walked toward the door.

"So, are we going to go out and celebrate after?" Roxy followed her out into the lobby area where drinks and snacks were laid out. "What about going over to the vodka bar at Mandalay Bay?"

"Forget that. I'm having a party for all the winners up at my suite." It was Jerry coming up behind them to hang his arms over their shoulders.

Roxy made a face and did a little sidestep to get out from under him. "Watch out," she suggested, "or you might be missing a hand for the last go-round."

Gwen moved aside.

"Oh, come on, guys, it's going to be party time."

"We have to make the cut first," Gwen reminded him.

He snorted. "We all know it's just a matter of time."

"For someone," Roxy said.

"Hey, you gonna come or not?"

"We all win, sure, we'll stop by for a drink," Gwen said. "Won't we, Roxy?"

Roxy looked at her as if she'd lost her mind but gave a grudging nod. "Sure, for starters." The bell rang to summon them back to the tables. "Right now, though, we'd better go in and finish the job."

FORGET ABOUT LIQUOR—THE PURE, hard rush of making the cut beat it all. The field had been narrowed. Only a total of thirty-six players had survived round two, each of whom would walk away with at least eighteen thousand dollars. Those who stayed in longer, well, the sky was the limit— or as much of it as you could buy with two million.

Roxy came up and hooked an arm over her shoulders. "We're in the money," she singsonged. "Let's go get your main squeeze and a man for me and celebrate." She whooped and gave a little shimmy.

"The party, remember?"

Roxy made a face. "And we have to do that why?"

"You don't have to do it, but I do."

"He's an idiot," she said with a frown. "He was at my table the last part of the night and I had to put up with his poker-brat routine. What do you want to hang around with him for?"

"Hang around with who?" Del came up behind them. 

"Jerry's having a party," Gwen explained. "I figured we could stop by and have a drink."

"Oh, if Jerry's buying, I think the least we can do is stop

by," he said. "But first I need to do some congratulating. To you." He leaned over to give Roxy a hug. "And to you." He gathered Gwen against him and pressed his mouth on hers, hard.

"And to you," Gwen said back to him. The heat from the brief contact surprised her. The promise made her want. Jerry's party didn't matter, she thought dizzily. The only thing that mattered was getting Del alone. Now.

"Hey, how do I get me some of that," Jerry said behind them.

Del shot him a frown. "I think the supply is all out, buddy. You're going to have to settle for a poker groupie."

"Don't listen to him." Gwen forced flirtatiousness into her voice. "Congratulations. We'll see you upstairs at the party," she told him, making herself lean in to peck him on the cheek before turning back to Del and Roxy.

"So," Del said, "party first, then I need to take you two poker superstars out to celebrate a little."

"Man after my own heart," Roxy said, ruffling his hair affectionately. "You don't happen to have a brother, do you?"

"Yep, but he's married with three kids."

"Rats. You'll tell me if anything changes?"

"You'll be the first," he promised.

THE PARTY MIGHT HAVE BEEN IN Jerry's suite, but it had spilled out into the concierge bar and lounge area. Guests milled about, only a fraction of whom he probably knew, Gwen was betting. Behind the bar a hotel staffer mixed drinks. Appetizers tempted the hungry from tables covered in snowy-white linen.

"Quite the host, our Jerry is," Del murmured in her ear.

"Just as long as he's not planning to pay for it in cash," she responded. "You might want to skip the me-Tarzan-you-Jane routine, by the way," she added in a low voice.

"As long as Jerry thinks he has a chance, he might tell me something."

"He'll tell you more if he's trying to impress you into dumping me and taking up with him."

She slanted a look at him. "Which would be the only reason you did it, of course."

"Of course," he said blandly. "And now I'll wander over and talk with Roxy, leaving you wide open for Jerry."

"You are devious." She gave him an admiring look.

"That's why you love me." He walked off, leaving her staring after him.

Just a joke, Gwen decided, blinking away her shock. Definitely nothing she should take seriously. It wasn't as though she could possibly be foolish enough to let herself have feelings for Del, anyway. It was just a fling while they were working together. What happened in Vegas stayed in Vegas, she reminded herself.

"Hey, you made it!" Jerry came up to her. "How you doing, babe? Ready to mow 'em down in the next round?"

"Careful. You might just wind up at my table."

"Hey, the other night showed us who was hot."

She tilted her head. "You mean the night I took you to the cleaners?"

He frowned, the memory coming clearer. "Yeah, but I'm on a roll now. I'm hot and the cards are loving me."

"We're all hot."

"I've got a license to print money," he told her.

A weedy-looking blonde with a deep tan and the carved lines of a longtime smoker walked up to them carrying a highball glass of what looked like whiskey. "Well, if it isn't the hotshot kid himself," she said and took a swallow of her drink. "I guess you're the host of this little do."

"Hey," Jerry crowed and gave her a sloppy kiss. "Rennie, I want you to meet Nina. Nina, this is Adrienne—or Rennie, as we call her."

Every atom of Gwen's being went on alert. It was Rennie—the Rennie listed in the matchbook, the Rennie who'd begun the whole chase.

The Rennie who might know something about where the stamps were.

Staying relaxed took work, but Gwen managed to put out her hand. "Nice to meet you. So, what do you think of our boy making it into the money round?"

"Oh, Jerry's always done well for himself," Rennie said in a not-entirely-pleasant tone. "I should know it. I've watched him for a long time."

"Rennie and I go way back," Jerry put in. "We met up in Reno. Used to joke about starting a radio show. 'And now,'" he announced, "'it's Jerry and Rennie from Reno.'"

"The way I remember it, it was Rennie and Jerry from Reno." She took another gulp of her drink. "It's that memory of yours, Jerry, always gets you in trouble."

There was definitely something simmering here, Gwen thought. If she could coax it to the boil, who knew what might bubble up? "Jerry, sweetie, can you go get us drinks?" Gwen asked, channeling a bit of Nina, a bit of Roxy.

"Drinks?"

She nodded. "A martini for me and what, whiskey?" She looked at Rennie inquiringly.

"Jack Daniel's," Rennie supplied and took a last swallow of what was in her glass.

"Okay, a martini and a Jack Daniel's." He went off a bit unwillingly, but he went, allowing her to concentrate on Rennie. "So, nice party, huh? Has to be costing a bundle. Of course, I'm just a guest, so I guess I shouldn't worry about it." *Poke the sore spot, see what happens,* Gwen thought.

"He always was a dipshit when it came to money." Rennie looked after Jerry with a scowl.

"So, you from here in Vegas or still living in Reno?"

"I'm a dealer here at the hotel. He wouldn't even have known about the tournament if it weren't for me."

And another puzzle piece clicked into place. "Wow. He's lucky he's got a friend like you. I just found out by accident. So, what did you guys do up in Reno?"

"Who, me?" Rennie took another look at Jerry. "I was dealing blackjack and passing odd jobs to the hotshot kid. 'Course, it don't look like he needs the work anymore," she added, turning to survey the concierge area. "Fancy place, his own bartender—looks like he's got all the money he needs." She bit off the words and stood staring moodily until Jerry returned.

"Here we go, a martini for you and a J.D. for you. Let's toast to the big payoff at the final table," he said, holding up his glass.

"Let's toast to payoffs, period," Rennie returned in a hard voice. "And promises. Remember promises, Jerry? You ain't too good on them." The bourbon was hitting her bloodstream; it showed in her eyes and the increased volume of her voice.

Jerry's eyes narrowed. "Maybe you ought to quiet down," he suggested.

"Don't tell me what I oughta do." Her voice rose.

"We're gonna talk about this in private," he hissed and half led, half pulled her into the hallway that led to the bedroom.

Del drifted over to Gwen. "That looked interesting."

"That was Rennie," she said.

"So maybe we need to go lean against the wall over there and canoodle a bit?"

"You read my mind."

The bedroom door closed, but Gwen and Del were able to get close enough to hear faint voices behind it.

"What's your problem?" Jerry demanded.

"What's my problem? You gotta ask? You owe me money, you asshole. You're here having a great old time with big bucks from a job that *I* threw your way. Meanwhile I'm spending eight hours a day on my feet dealing cards, waiting on that big lump of cash I was supposed to get from you. 'It'll pay off big, Rennie,'" she mocked savagely. "'Take a couple months off.' Pissed off? Damned right I'm pissed off."

"You'll get your money." Her response must have been a rude look because Jerry's voice roughened. "I'm working the deal as fast as I can."

"Keep talking, you're breaking my heart here. You look like you're workin' real hard, playin' poker, sucking down liquor, acting like the big man."

"There's been a holdup."

"Always is with you."

"Look, you brought me the guy. If he's a screwup, then it's partly your fault. If that means you got to sweat a little more, well, it ain't gonna keep me up at night."

"Asshole," she spat.

"Yeah? Right back atcha. He's the one who ain't paying. Until he coughs up the cash, I don't get it, which means you don't get it. Unnerstand?"

"Tell me you didn't make some idiot move like giving him the goods already."

"The stuff's in a safe place. It's cool. Everything's cool, or it would be if you'd stop being such a psycho bitch."

"I'll back off for now, but I'm warning you, I'd better see something soon."

"Saturday night is gonna be the handover, babe. I'll get you the dough, you can put in your notice. Maybe we'll take a nice trip or something."

"I'll show you a nice trip if you're feeding me a line."

"Hey, Ren, would I do that?"

"You always did have a habit of asking stupid questions," she returned.

GWEN LAY ON THE SHEETS, waiting for her breath to return to normal.

"Are you trying to give me heart failure so I'll forfeit my seat at the table?" Del croaked.

She grinned. "I just wanted to help you release your post-tournament tension."

"You helped me release my tension, all right."

"Mmm." She moved so that her head lay across his belly. "So, based on that conversation we overheard, it sounds like Jerry's planning the handoff on Saturday, which means we've got to get our act in gear."

"Yep."

"So, I think I've figured out a way to do it."

"How?"

"Well, it depends on Jerry making the final table. If he does, then we'll know without a doubt where he is during the last night of play."

"Of course, you might be there also."

"I suppose, but just because I start the game doesn't mean I'll be the last one standing."

"What's that supposed to mean?"

"Everybody but the champ has to lose sometime. If I'm the first one out, I'll be free to roam while Jerry's stuck there."

"Too chancy."

"Not at all," she argued, rolling over to prop her arms on his chest. "They'll be showing the play on the closed-circuit television system throughout the hotel. All I need to do is put it on and I can monitor Jerry the whole time. I know where they are, Del," she reminded him. "It won't take long."

"And what do you think he's going to do when he finds them gone?"

"What can he do? They were stolen to begin with."

"What about fingerprints, assuming he does go to the cops?"

She dismissed it. "We were just in his suite. My fingerprints are going to be all over the place anyway."

"You made sure of it, didn't you?"

She grinned at him. "Nina's no dummy."

"It still feels risky to me. What if someone catches you up there?"

"It'll work out fine. You can put money on it."

"That's what I'm worried about."

# 19

DEL LEANED AGAINST ONE OF the marble pillars of one of the casino bars—the Sun King Court—and watched Gwen being interviewed for the tournament video. It was one of the fifteen-minute segments the filmmakers were doing with all the front-runners. He'd done his only the day before. Somehow, though, Gwen's segment had stretched to nearly an hour. Not that he blamed them. She made a fetching subject and it wasn't just him being biased.

Behind him, on the stage in the bar, the singer of the house band warbled a version of Madonna's "Holiday." That was what this whole week felt like, a holiday from the real world.

He pulled out his cell phone to check his voice mail while he waited. It might feel as if he was on vacation, but there was still work to think about.

He punched in the number and then navigated his way through the voice-mail menus, punching the key to play his first message. "Hey, Redmond—" the voice jumped out of the phone "—it's Kellar." A casino waitress hustled past, her tray of drinks held high. "Jessup put me full-time on that stamp story you dropped. I need to get a list of your sources and where you left things, so give me a call or shoot me an e-mail, okay?"

Del jabbed at the key that deleted the message and stood, quietly steaming. Maybe Jessup hadn't been ready to let the story go so easily and had asked Kellar to follow up. More likely it was Kellar getting industrious, Del figured, hoping that a little sniffing around would net him a story and a clip. *Dream on, buddy.* No journalist who wanted to remain competitive coughed up his sources. Anyway, it wasn't as if he owed Jessup anything. The thing to do was sit tight and let Kellar cool his heels. With nothing to go on, the kid couldn't possibly get an angle on the story.

Del hoped.

Someone bumped him on the hip and he turned to see Gwen. "Hey, you," she said, giving him a quick kiss. "Sorry that took so long. Did I miss anything important?"

"Not a thing," he told her and hoped like hell he was right.

"WELCOME TO THE THIRD ROUND of the Tournament of Champions." The MC's voice came across the PA system as the players and audience milled around the tournament room. The mood had become even more focused, even more intense as the tournament had progressed. The good news was that everybody was in the money. The bad news was that the sooner a player went out, the less of a payoff they got. By the end of play that day, the field would be winnowed from thirty-six to the final table of nine.

And someone at that final table would walk away with a cool two million.

On the surface, players behaved just about the same, only more so. The loquacious ones coffeehoused just as much as they always had, perhaps out of nerves or as a calculated attempt to distract their cohorts. Punks like Jerry grated ever more on the nerves.

And the cool, focused players like Del just kept coming. The power balances had changed at the tables. The chip leaders, some of them sitting on several hundred thousand dollars' worth of chips, bet relentlessly, raising and reraising, trying to break their poorer competition.

Much to her own surprise, Gwen had worked her way up to over two hundred thousand dollars in chips by the time she was reseated at a shorthanded table with Jerry.

A chance for a little revenge.

She didn't want to knock him out of the tournament. She needed him there where she could keep an eye on him. The more of his chips she could steal away, though, the higher up the ladder she would move and the more of her grandfather's property she could buy back.

And she began to seriously play.

THE NIGHT AIR WAS COOL AS Gwen pushed through the doors that led out of the casino and onto the long, covered arcade that looked down on the front entrance. The hint of coolness in the air helped ease the stress headache that beat in her temples. After ten hours at the tables, the players had winnowed their numbers from thirty-six to thirteen, and the pressure rose every time someone dropped out.

Four more and they'd be down to the final table. Four more and she'd be guaranteed enough money to buy back all of the low-value stamps that Jerry had sold and then some. She'd taken a few chips from Jerry, but she'd left him with enough to survive and he'd built back from there. If luck were with him, he'd get to the final table.

If luck were with them both.

The message light on her cell phone flashed a peremptory red. *A minute,* Gwen thought, leaning down to rest her forehead briefly against the cold marble of the railing. She'd give herself just one precious moment before she hit redial.

When she did, Joss answered. "Hello?"

"What's going on?"

"It's Grampa. You need to call him."

"Come on, Joss, it's eleven o'clock at night."

"So? It's the middle of the morning there and he just called again. I'm out of excuses and he's starting to get suspicious. You've got to call him."

Gwen squeezed her eyes shut. "I can't now, Joss. We're down to the final thirteen. I've got to go back inside in, like, ten minutes."

"I told him you've been really busy. Just five minutes?" she wheedled. "He just needs to hear your voice."

The headache felt as though someone was merrily thumping Gwen's brain with a meat tenderizer. "All right."

Gwen repeated her grandfather's phone number as Joss read it out to her, repeated it again before she said goodbye, then recited the number out loud as she punched the keys. The clicking in the electronic circuits and the ring sounded farther away somehow. *Half a world away,* she thought suddenly. Half a world and a dozen time zones.

"Good morning."

It might have been coming from half a world away, but when she heard her grandfather's voice, it was as though he were right beside her. "Grampa. It's Gwen."

"Gwennie!" The pleasure in his voice warmed her, easing her headache. "I was about ready to come looking for you. What have you been up to? All Joss can ever tell me is that you're off somewhere busy."

"Oh, just working hard," she said vaguely. "I only have a few minutes to talk but I wanted to say hi. How's Australia?"

"Tasmania today," he corrected her. "And we leave for Papua New Guinea day after tomorrow."

His voice sounded richer, she thought, more thrummingly full of bass, as though a tightness none of them had been aware of had eased. "You sound happy, Grampa."

"We're having the time of our lives. Your grandmother learned how to use a boomerang a couple of days ago."

"A boomerang?" The image of her quiet, buttoned-down grandmother hucking around a boomerang made her laugh.

"Almost took my head off with it, but she had fun. Oh, we've been having a blast. I don't know why we didn't do this before."

"You were married to your business?" she speculated.

"No longer," he assured her. "That's someone else's job now. Speaking of the business, how'd that new kid you hired work out?"

The headache returned with a vengeance. "Oh, all right," Gwen said briefly, hating the fact that she wasn't being straight with him. But how could she tell him and chase away all the joy and pleasure she heard?

"How'd the Chicago estate sale go?"

"Great. Made a couple of surprise finds and already unloaded some of the issues."

"Nice work. But I know you haven't told me everything."

For an instant her heart stopped. "What do you mean?"

"About the business."

"Have you heard something is wrong?" How could he have found out, she wondered wildly.

"No, of course not. I'm sure it's all fine and dandy with you at the helm. But that's what I'm talking about. I know you've been unhappy about closing the store down," he told her. "You haven't said anything about it, but you didn't have to—I know."

Gwen breathed a silent sigh of relief. "I'll miss it," she told him, "but I'll find something else I like. Maybe go to work for Stewart."

"It's not the same as running your own shop, though, is it?"

Her throat tightened.

"There's something I want to toss out to you, just food for thought. Your grandmother and I have been talking."

"In between throwing boomerangs?"

"In between," he agreed. "We've talked it over and the business is yours if you want it."

Gwen's jaw dropped. "You mean you want me to run the store?"

"No, we want to turn the whole business over to you, lock, stock and barrel. If you want it."

It was as though the world had been dropped in her lap. "Grampa. I—I don't know what to say."

"Don't answer right away," he returned. "Think about it and we can talk next month once we're all home. Oh, we can't give it to you outright, there are the other kids to consider. But if you'd like it, we'll find a way to make it happen."

"Like it?" Gwen spluttered, "I'd love it."

"Well, take some time and think it over. Owning your own business is a big job, remember."

"It's exactly the right job," she told him. The door opened behind her.

"Gwen." She heard Del's voice. "They're calling us back to the tables."

"Be right there," she told him. She'd get the stamps back, she thought with renewed purpose. She'd take care of her grandparents and she'd start into business right.

"You have to run?" her grandfather asked.

"I have to get back to the game," she said without thinking. "You're wonderful, Grampa. Give Grandma a big hug for me."

"Oh, yeah, I guess it is Thursday night back there," he

said, clearly thinking she was at the weekly home game. "You going to come out ahead tonight?"

"I'm going to come out ahead on everything," she promised him.

A ROUND OF APPLAUSE BEGAN IN the bleachers and spread throughout the room. Gwen looked up, blinking. That was it, she realized, stunned. A player at the other table had just gone out and now they were nine. The long night was over. She caught Del's eye and suddenly the excitement surged through her. They'd made the cut. They were in the serious money.

Without thinking, she rose and ran the few steps over to his table. He grabbed her in a huge bear hug and swung her around. "We did it," she laughed. "We're in."

And then his mouth was on hers, all heat and promise, and the room and people around them faded away. Everything faded away except the immediacy of him, the taste of his mouth, the feel of his body.

"God, I want you," he murmured in her ear.

It was intoxicating. Being in the running to win two million dollars was nothing compared to the way he made her feel.

"Are you two going to come up for air long enough to accept congratulations?"

Gwen opened her eyes to see Roxy watching them.

"Sorry." She could feel the heat of a blush on her face.

"Don't worry about me. The news cameras are having fun, though." She pointed to the black circles of the lenses pointed their way.

"Settle up your chips, folks," the tournament manager reminded them, walking through the tables. They all straggled back to their seats to count up their chips and sign and staple the colorful clay disks in Ziploc bags.

The final day of play in the tournament would begin the next afternoon and run until only one of them was left.

"So, where should we go to celebrate?" Roxy asked, her arms around both of their shoulders. "The Ghost Bar over at the Palms?"

"I'd settle for dinner," Gwen said.

"Dinner was only a couple of hours ago."

"For those of us who could eat."

"Nerves, huh?" Roxy winked at her. "Okay, let's go over to the Hard Rock and hit Nobu. I adore the tuna on miso chips. Meet in the lobby in, say, five minutes?" She waved and peeled off to the ladies' room.

Gwen and Del headed down the escalator into the casino and headed toward the elevators.

"Hey, Redmond, made the final table," came a voice from behind him. "Congratulations."

Del turned to look at the source of the voice.

It was Kellar. "Hey, I been leaving messages for you, you know?"

"I'll talk with you later, Kellar," he said and continued toward the elevators.

"No." Kellar's voice became more insistent. "You're a hard guy to track down." He followed them into the marble-lined elevator lobby.

"Kellar, let it go," Del snapped, punching the call button. "Later, okay? This is not the place."

"That's what you said before and it's later now. I'm not going to hold you up, I just need a list of your sources on the stamp story." Behind them one of the elevators chimed.

"The stamp story?" Gwen asked.

"Yeah. For the paper." He gave her a pugnacious glance. "I'm taking over."

"Really."

Del felt Gwen's hand drop away from his as she turned

to stare at him. Without saying a word she turned and got on the elevator. Del followed.

Kellar blinked. "Hey, Redmond, you can't do that," he protested.

"Watch me."

The atmosphere was glacial as the door closed. Gwen didn't say anything, just punched the button for her floor. When the doors opened, she got out without a word or a backward glance. Del followed her.

She did turn then. "Get away from me."

"Gwen, don't."

"Don't what?"

"Shut me out. Let me tell you what's going on."

"Why?" She glared at him. "So you can pump me for more information for your article, you and your buddy?" She headed toward her room. "When you talked about changing your career, you never told me that my family was going to be the means to your end."

"I didn't mean it to happen like that."

"Oh, yeah? Exactly how did you mean it?" She slammed her passkey into the lock and shoved the door open.

"Look," he said, following her into the room. "I proposed that story before I knew about your grandfather, before I knew about much of anything except that stamps worth a lot of money were missing and someone had stolen them. I wasn't even sure that they weren't stolen property to start with."

She threw down her key and turned to face him. "I told you they were ours. I told you I had proof."

"And you'd told me your name was Nina. I barely knew you at the time."

"I thought maybe you'd believe me."

"You'd just told me you'd been jerking me around for days, when you'd been swearing the whole time that there was nothing going on. What was I supposed to believe? Everything I knew about you in the beginning I found out on the Internet. You didn't give me any information."

"Obviously you had enough to pitch a story, though, didn't you?"

"It was stupid, okay? I admit it. I did it without thinking during a phone interview with the city editor."

"A phone interview?"

"For a news job I thought I wanted."

Her gaze was filled with disgust. "Of course. That's what really matters, right? Whether you get the job, no matter who else pays. So you pitched the story."

"And I unpitched it."

"What's that supposed to mean?"

"Yesterday morning I told the editor that I wasn't going to do it, that there wasn't enough meat to it. Why do you think Kellar's sniffing around now? He's hungry and he wants to dig something up."

Her eyes blazed. "So it doesn't really matter that you've gotten off the story—thanks to your little discussion with them, it'll still be in the paper."

"It would have been in the paper anyway, the minute you turned Jerry over to the cops."

"What is this, a way to make yourself feel better? I keep telling you I want to keep the police out of it."

"You mean, as long as you got back the stamps, you were planning to let Jerry walk?"

"I don't know," she burst out. "I thought I'd get the stamps first and then I'd figure it out. Of course, that was before you blew the whole thing out of the water. Goddammit," she said furiously, rounding on him, "I *trusted* you."

"Did you, now," he said, equally angry. "When was that? When you were telling me you were Nina? When you wouldn't tell me why you didn't want to call the cops?

When you wouldn't show me proof of ownership or even tell me where the stamps came from? You wouldn't even tell me who they were stolen from. Just when did you start opening up to me?" His voice dripped with frustration. "You've been playing a game with me from the beginning, pretending to be someone you weren't, telling me whatever was convenient at the time. You've been showing me the flop but holding on to your pocket cards. Well, this isn't poker, Gwen, this is life. It's supposed to be real."

"I haven't been pretending to be someone else."

"Oh, no? You think I haven't noticed every time you've put on your game face, every time you were doing Nina for me?"

"Doing Nina for you? Nina's the one you wanted. Nina's the one you're hung up on."

"I'm the one who's hung up on Nina? Sorry, that would be you."

"What are you talking about?" she demanded, two spots of color burning high on her cheeks.

"You're the one who's in love with Nina because she lets you do the things Gwen doesn't have the nerve to do. You don't trust Gwen for the important stuff. I see little flashes of her come through when you're not acting, and she's pretty gutsy. I like her. A lot. But you don't let her out often. You keep her inside, give all the flashy stuff to Nina when Gwen's the one who really gets it done."

"Maybe Nina's not just some role I'm playing. Maybe Nina's a part of who I am."

"I don't know who you are, do you? I'm not into hidden pictures, Gwen. That was what happened with my ex-wife. I don't want that. I can't do that again. I don't want to always be wondering who you really are."

"Then I guess you don't want me," she said softly.

# 20

IT WAS THE NIGHT HOURS THAT were the hardest. Gwen tossed restlessly, searching for oblivion that never came. Instead the awful scene with Del played itself over and over in her head. Her dreams, when she dozed, were dark and chaotic, full of faceless threats chasing her down shadowy passages. And in that dawn moment when the veil of sleep thinned to consciousness, loss crouched there waiting for her.

There was no point in searching again for the sleep that would not come. Lying in bed only gave her more time to think. Instead she rose, beaten with exhaustion yet unbearably present. In the shower she turned up the heat as high as she could tolerate, standing under the pulsating spray. After she got out, she concentrated on the little things: drying her hair, rubbing lotion into her skin, applying her makeup. She wished she had Roxy's skill with makeup; then again, it was unlikely that any cosmetics would entirely disguise what she'd been through in the previous twenty-four hours.

*Activity,* she told herself, doggedly getting out her computer and working. Finally it was late enough that she could legitimately call Stewart. It took tracking him down by his cell phone, but eventually she reached him. "Stewart, Gwen." She wasted no time on pleasantries. She had none.

"Gwennie?" Concern sharpened his voice. "What's going on?"

"You said for me to call if I needed your help."

"You've got it. What's up?"

"Can you get out to Vegas by this afternoon?"

He answered without hesitation. "Of course."

"It's not strictly legal," she warned him. "In fact, I don't think it's legal at all."

"Does it have to do with getting Hugh's stamps back?"

"Yes."

"Then I don't think it matters."

"Two wrongs don't make a right." The reminder was as much to herself as to him.

"I don't really give a damn," he said pleasantly. "You need help, I'm there. It's seven o'clock right now? I'll see you at one."

"Good."

"What do you need me to do?"

"Watch my back."

LIKE THE SHOWER, THE POOL drew her with the lure of oblivion. The water sluiced over her in a mind-numbing rush. As though she were a machine, she scythed her arms through the water in a rhythmic stroke, pulling herself along, concentrating on the feel of the water in her hands, the slide of it against her body, the number of laps.

Concentrating on anything but Del.

How painfully ironic that she'd feared he cared only for Nina, when apparently just the opposite had been happening. Only when he'd walked out had she realized just how much she'd let him into her heart.

Only then had she realized she was in love with him.

She'd been so preoccupied with the stamps, the tournament, the chase, that Del had snuck up on her blind side. In a terrifyingly short time he'd become necessary to her.

And he'd betrayed her. The things he'd said about how

concerned he was, how frightened for her, how much she'd meant to him, had been so much talk. Maybe she meant something to him, but his career meant more, obviously. He'd backed off on the story? Maybe. And maybe not. She had only his word to go by and right now his word didn't mean very much.

But that wasn't what tore at her deep down. What tore at her was that he couldn't accept her for who she was, couldn't understand that she could be both Gwen and Nina, that she didn't have to be one or the other. He'd fallen for Nina, he'd wanted Nina, he'd seen Nina and yet he'd castigated her for being Nina. *You're the one who's in love with Nina.* It wasn't true. She wasn't turning into Nina. She'd realized, perhaps, that Nina was one part of her—a part she'd always denied. Did that make it wrong? And why, when Nina was the one who'd attracted him, was he now using Nina as his excuse to walk away from her?

She couldn't bear it, Gwen thought.

She had to.

Suddenly she noticed the legs of a person standing directly in her lane. To avoid running over them, Gwen stopped abruptly. Treading water, she popped her head above the surface and blinked.

It was Roxy. "Hey, enough already. You know you've been swimming for almost an hour and a half? You're going to kill yourself."

An hour and a half? Had it been that long? Now that she'd stopped, Gwen felt almost dizzy. "I was just...I was..." Her arms and legs suddenly leaden, she gave up, wading the last few steps to the side of the pool through chest-high water. It was all she could do to get out of the pool and collapse on her chaise.

"So, what's going on?" Roxy settled on the chaise next

to her. "You suddenly decide to start training for the Olympics? You were like maniac woman there."

"I was just thinking."

"That must have been some thinking," Roxy said flippantly. "What's on your mind, the final?"

"What?"

"*What,* she says. You know, the final? That pesky game that could win you a couple million dollars?"

Gwen shook her head wanly. "Aw, hell, Roxy, I don't care about the tournament," she said, folding her arms over her face. It seemed like the least important thing in her life just then. It seemed like a part of another life. And she'd have to see Del again at the final.

She'd have to face Del.

"You know," Roxy said conversationally, "if I didn't know better, I'd say this smelled like man trouble. Of course, you being smart enough to not get involved, it probably couldn't be that."

"I broke things off with Del last night," Gwen said in a small voice, staring very hard at the brilliant, cloudless blue of the sky overhead.

"Aw, hell, hon." There was a wealth of sympathy in the three words. "Was he an asshole? They usually are, you know. Kind of goes with the DNA. 'Course, he didn't really seem like the type," she added thoughtfully.

An asshole? No, Gwen couldn't say that. He'd betrayed her, though by his lights what he was doing was right. The problem was that he didn't want her. It didn't make him an asshole. It just made everything impossible.

"Why don't you tell me about it? You'll feel better."

She wanted to, more than anything she wanted to just spill it out. And yet, hadn't she had a very clear object lesson what happened when she let information go? "I can't."

Gwen could feel Roxy staring at her. "What do you mean, you can't?"

"It's complicated. There's…something going on."

"Obviously."

"I'd tell you if I could. It's just that I told Del and now everything's a mess."

Roxy looked at her for a moment. "Yeah, sure," she said finally. "I understand." But Gwen swore she saw a spark of hurt in her eyes. "Well, if we can't do talking therapy, we'll have to do therapy of another kind."

"What do you mean?"

"Retail therapy," she said briskly. "Come on."

HER CHARGE CARDS—AND POSSIBLY her feet—would never be the same. Gwen walked into the lobby of the Versailles with her hands loaded with shopping bags. Shoes, makeup, resort wear, lingerie—they'd done it all. Somewhere in the mad shuffle of going from store to store, stopping for drinks and coffee, listening to Roxy's jokes, Gwen had actually found her mood lifting just a bit. She didn't need Del Redmond. She didn't need any man who could worm his way into her life that easily, who could abuse her trust, using what she'd told him in privacy to damage those close to her. She didn't need Del Redmond at all.

Except with every breath she took.

The man ahead of her walked along slowly, bent over slightly. She started to skirt her way around him and head to the elevators, then she caught sight of his face. "Stewart?"

"Gwennie?" He stared at her, incredulous.

"You're here." She wrapped her arms around him, bags and all. When he grunted, she stepped back. "Is something wrong?"

He winced. "I tripped on the trails while I was running this weekend and dinged up my ribs."

"Are you okay?"

"Sure. It's nothing serious, just a few bruises. Takes a little while to get over. I'm just not as young as I used to be, you know."

It was true, she saw. The two years that he'd been gone from San Francisco had added a lot more gray to his hair and a network of lines to his face. A subtle tension hung around him, or maybe it was just the stiffness, she couldn't tell. "Jeez, be more careful when you're running. Being too healthy can kill you, you know."

"I'll keep that in mind." He studied her. "So, is this the new you?"

She shrugged. "It's the me for now."

"It suits you." He hesitated. "I wish I could say that you look a hundred percent great, but you're looking a little rough around the edges. This whole stamp thing getting to you?"

She shrugged. "I've had better weeks. Where's your stuff?"

"I checked in already. Figured I'd come on up. So what's the deal?"

"The good news is that I think I know where the stamps are. The problem is getting into Jerry's room when he's not around. He's up on the concierge level, so it's a little tricky."

"I'd say the problem is getting in, period."

"Not exactly." She held up the key.

"How'd you get your hands on that?"

"I have my ways. Now, the only place I can guarantee he'll be will be the final round of the tournament tonight."

"You want me to search while you're playing?"

She shook her head. "I'm going to bail out of the tournament as early as I can without making it obvious. I'll meet you up here. The passkey will get the elevator up to the concierge level and get us into the room."

"They won't notice anything?"

"I'm Jerry's buddy. I was just upstairs partying with him after the last round. They won't think a thing."

"Remind me never to get in your way," he said admiringly.

"Save it until we've got the stamps back. They're showing the tournament on the closed-circuit TV system, so we can keep an eye on him at all times, make sure he's at the table where he belongs."

"It could work."

She fought back nerves. "I'm pretty sure I know where the stamps are, but it's not easy to get to. I'll need your help."

"You've got it."

"Great." She took a long breath. "Well, play starts in half an hour. I'm just going to drop this stuff in my room and I'll be back down to meet you."

"I'll be waiting."

# 21

A WEEK BEFORE, GWEN HAD watched the tournament start with no expectation of success. Now she stood with Roxy in the players' lounge waiting to be introduced as a finalist. Waiting to find out whether she was going to walk away with a hundred and fifty thousand dollars or two million. She should have been thrilled.

She couldn't muster up a modicum of excitement.

Roxy gave her a narrow-eyed stare and took her by the arm. "Come on."

"What?"

"In here." She dragged Gwen into the ladies' lounge. "Where's your head?" she demanded. "You're sitting down with the barracudas in about five minutes and you've got to be focused."

"I am focused," Gwen protested feebly.

"No, you're not. You space out tonight, you're letting him win. No matter what happened between you—and I'm not asking about it—you've got to get past it and play this round."

Roxy was right, Gwen realized, but not in the way she thought. Gwen had to get it together in order to exit the tournament without raising suspicion and get into Jerry's room to find the stamps. The previous Saturday she had tried and failed. This time, she had to make it work. She had to get her mind off Del.

She bent over and took several deep breaths and then stood quickly upright. "Okay," she said. "Let's do it."

"You've got every reason to be confident," Roxy told her as they walked out the door. "You're in the final round, so you're in the money. No matter what happens, you're pulling down some serious bucks. And we're seated side by side, so we're coming in with big advantages."

"Which are?"

"Hooters. Show me a man who can think straight when staring one pair of breasts in the eye, let alone two." She grinned. "Not even professional gamblers are that good. The money gets serious for the top seven finishers, so all we need to do is jettison a couple of these jokers and we're in there."

"After which, of course, it's every woman for herself."

"Of course."

"Don't expect your secret weapons to dazzle me," Gwen warned her, feeling her fog of depression lift a bit.

"I knew you wouldn't be so easy," Roxy sighed. "Oops, they're starting."

The room had undergone another transformation. Gone was the bustle, the explosion of tables everywhere you looked. Now only a single spotlit green oval sat before the bleachers in the darkened room, a strip of white illumination circling its base. Blue drapes around the walls dotted with pin lights added drama. Behind the table, on the dealer's side, a large projection screen showed an image of the empty table, the green baize with the brown leather padded rim. It looked innocuous, but over the next few hours it would be the site of something extraordinary, a pile of two million in bricks of hundred-dollar bills.

Seat by seat, the MC began introducing the players. Before, the tournament had been something of a cattle call, populated by hordes of nameless, faceless competitors. As the field had narrowed, the reporters had clustered around the well-known players and the crowd had begun following favorites, cheering them on by name. Now the MC was working the room, hyping the crowd more with each introduction.

Gwen watched Del walk to his seat to the accompaniment of whoops from some of the women in the audience. In a way she ought to have thanked him. If she hadn't been so numb, Gwen would have been nervous. Instead her emotions felt so deadened, it was hard to worry about anything too much, except maybe getting into Jerry's room.

The only thing left that mattered.

"In seat number six, placing seventh in last year's World Series of Poker and the winner of last year's Tournament of Champions, Roxanne Steele."

"Oops, that's me." Roxy gave Gwen a quick hug and broke away to sashay through the gauntlet of flashbulbs, waving her arms, the shiny tournament bracelet on her wrist winking.

Gwen swallowed and took a breath. "In position seven, competing in her first tournament, San Franciscan Nina Chatham."

Gwen walked across to the table, staring at Del. It felt as if someone were sitting on her chest, making it hard to breathe. Del sat there, his sunglasses reflecting her form as she approached. In a way it paralleled their relationship, neither one of them able to get past the wall between them. Whether that wall was mirrored sunglasses or the persona of Nina or something else, it was there. Maybe she never had gotten any deeper than the surface with him. Maybe she never had gotten through to what was behind.

Tucking her skirt under, Gwen sat. *Look away,* she told herself, but she couldn't. Was it the distortion of the lenses or did her cheeks really look that drawn, did her eyes really look so smudged with exhaustion? How was it that Del seemed just the same when her entire life had changed in a day?

The pain suddenly sliced through her and Gwen took a ragged breath.

Someone grabbed her hand and squeezed. It was Roxy. "Look at me," she commanded.

Gwen tore her gaze from Del and turned to stare into Roxy's gray eyes.

"Don't lose it, hon," Roxy whispered. "Hold on. Remember, walking away with the most chips is the best revenge."

The dealer shuffled and the dance began.

DEL STARED AT THE TABLE, trying to concentrate on the play and failing miserably. He should have been focusing on the nearby faces, some of whom were new to him. He should have been following their choices, logging them mentally so that when a crucial hand arose, he'd know how to handle it.

Instead behind his sunglasses he watched Gwen. He could see that the night had been no easier on her than it had been on him, but it was scant comfort. He'd never meant to hurt her. What he'd wanted was trust, honesty. What he'd looked for was some assurance that his feelings were valid, that the person he'd realized he'd fallen in love with was real.

Instead she'd thrown up a wall before him, a wall between them. And maybe that was for the best. Maybe they didn't have a future together. If so, better to know it now.

"Your bet, sir?" Not only the dealer but the entire table was looking at him, Del realized. Quickly he assessed and saw that nearly everyone at the table had folded save him and Gwen. She'd just raised and sat staring at him, eyes defiant, challenging him to take her on.

He took a quick glance at his pocket cards. Ace and king of hearts. There was a determined set to her shoulders that told him she had something. Queens? Jacks? He raised. It was worth it to him to hold on and find out.

Gwen called to stay with him and the flop brought a jack of diamonds and a ten and a two of hearts. There were hearts everywhere, it seemed, he thought as he raised. So why did his own chest feel so hollow?

Gwen called and they both nodded to the dealer.

The turn brought a four of spades. *Call a spade a spade, Del, old boy, and admit that you're not going to walk away from this one without leaving a piece of yourself behind.* Whether he'd intended to or not, he'd screwed up by telling Jessup about the story. He'd broken Gwen's confidence. Even if they managed to get past that, the fundamental problem of who she was and who she was pretending to be remained. He'd fallen for a pretty face and deception once already in his life. He couldn't do it again.

Gwen curved her fingers around her stacks of chips. For a few seconds she didn't move, as though she were steeling her nerve. She stared at the table and then raised her head and stared directly at Del. She moistened her lips. "All in," she whispered.

All in was a challenge, it was a confrontation. So why did it feel like a reproach? The seconds ticked by. He could see the pulse beating in her neck; he couldn't tell if her reaction was fear or excitement. *Stop making it personal and start playing the game.*

He called her.

All in meant showing everything. Gwen turned up her hole cards to reveal a jack and a seven. He turned up his king ace. The silence was deafening. The lights felt hot. He stifled the impulse to take Gwen's hand. For an instant he had the ridiculous thought that whatever they had to face, they could face together. And he knew he was wrong, because they were facing it apart.

The dealer laid the river card on the baize facedown and set his fingertips on it. The seconds crawled by. Then he turned it over.

And a cheer erupted from his supporters in the stands. Jack of hearts. His heart was on the table, Del thought aridly. He'd won the pot, his flush beating Gwen's three of a kind. He should have been overjoyed.

He wasn't.

GWEN SWALLOWED. EVEN THOUGH her goal had been to knock herself out of the tournament to go search Jerry's room, it had taken so much to push all of her chips forward. Watching Del rake them in was easy. He'd taken her heart already. What was a few hundred thousand in chips? He'd won the hand just as he'd won whatever had passed between them. And now her part in the game was over, just as her part in his life.

The humming silence within her matched the silence around the table. She rose, gave Roxy a hug and walked away.

And at the edge of the crowd she saw Stewart.

JERRY'S ROOM LOOKED THE worse for wear when they walked in, with clothing strewn around and empty bottles set out. As soon as they closed the door, Gwen crossed to the television and turned it on to the poker game, muting the sound.

And, of course, the camera was focused on Del's face as he stared down at the table. Was it her imagination or was there regret in the set of his mouth? *Foolish,* she chided herself, seeing what she wanted to see. It wasn't there. He was perfectly happy with the way things had worked out between them. There was no point in thinking differently.

Just as there was no point repeating her search. She knew where the envelope was. The challenge was to get it. "Over here," she told Stewart and walked into the minibar area. The refrigerator was just as difficult to get to as it had been before. With his thicker hands, Stewart had less luck than she had had.

Her hand on the refrigerator, Gwen looked around vainly for something long and skinny to use to draw the envelope out with. Why hadn't she come prepared?

"Let's just pull it out of there," Stewart said, edging past her.

He managed to get his fingers on the top and bottom of the refrigerator to pull it out enough that Gwen could get her hand underneath. So close, so close. "Can you pull it out a little more?" she asked.

"Can't. The cord's too short."

She edged her hand in just a bit farther, gritting her teeth against the discomfort. *Almost there,* she thought, brushing it with her fingertips. Almost… "I've got it," she cried out jubilantly and slid the envelope out.

It was stiffened with cardboard, still warm from its contact with the refrigerator. Finally, at last, it was in her hands. Now all she had to do was look. It was like taking the first peek at her pocket cards. She pulled up the flap of the envelope. And disappointment filled her, dry and bitter like ashes in her mouth.

The envelope was empty.

Stewart read it all in her face. "Gone?"

She nodded numbly, trying to comprehend the enormity of the disaster. "Gone."

"He couldn't possibly have sold them."

"It doesn't matter. They're not here."

"We need to search the rest of the place." There was a note of desperation in his voice.

"I've looked everywhere else."

"But that was almost a week ago, right? He could have moved them." Stewart went to the bedroom.

Gwen started to follow and froze. "Stewart." She gestured to the television. It was panning over the whole final table.

And Jerry was nowhere to be seen.

Stewart cursed. "How long's he been out?"

"I don't know," she snapped. "I wasn't watching. Come on, get the refrigerator back in place, quick. We can go down the stairs to the next floor, take the elevator from there."

"All right. I—"

Before he could finish, there was a click at the door. It opened to reveal Jerry.

"What the—" He stepped through the door. "What the hell are you doing in my room?" he demanded, taking two swift steps inside.

Gwen opened her mouth, trying wildly to think of an explanation that would work. "It's not how it looks. I—"

"You've been a bad boy, Jerry."

The words came from behind her. Gwen whipped around to see Stewart staring ahead of her, staring at Jerry.

And in Stewart's hand, a gun.

# 22

DEL SAT AT THE TABLE, splitting a stack of chips with one hand and riffling them together as if they were playing cards. Outside he appeared calm. Inside his thoughts were buzzing.

Both Gwen and Jerry were out, within maybe twenty minutes of one another. Both of them had been high in the chip count. Both of them had gone out on a limb with only so-so cards—Gwen on a jack seven, Jerry on a jack two.

He didn't like it. He didn't like it a bit.

Her plan had been to bail out of the tournament and use the time to finish her search of Jerry's room. If she'd gone through with it, she'd be in Jerry's room right now. Del tensed. As soon as Jerry had cashed out, he'd left the table. For where? Maybe the bar, maybe a strip club.

Or maybe his room.

She'd told him it wasn't his problem. She'd told him she didn't want him involved. He should just sit here then and let her deal with it, right?

Bullshit.

Del looked around trying to spot someone from security. He needed to dig up Ahmanson and he needed him now. The last thing he needed to do was sit here flipping chips in a card game.

"Your bet, sir," the dealer said.

*Just do it,* Del told himself. So he'd played his way to

number six. He was an amateur. He'd probably be out legitimately any hand anyway. It wouldn't hurt. Not much.

He pushed his chips forward. "All in."

"STEWART, WHAT IN GOD'S NAME are you doing?"

"Please, Gwen, no more interference," Stewart replied in a strained voice.

She stepped toward him. "But, Stewart..."

Stewart moved the gun slightly in her direction, freezing her. "I mean it, Gwen. Please."

Jerry's face clouded. "Gwen? I thought your name was Nina," he said.

"Come now, Jerry," Stewart said mockingly. "Surely you ought to have recognized Gwen Chastain, even if she does look a little different these days. Gwen's been very helpful in all this. She was the one who tracked you down. Stealing the Ben Franklins was an idiotic, greedy thing to do."

Jerry glowered at them both.

"What's this all about?" Gwen demanded.

"Later. Mr. Messner and I have business to discuss."

"You got no business with me unless you got money," Jerry snarled.

"Well, yes, it's true—money has been a problem. That's why I brought this." Stewart tilted the gun slightly. "Changes the negotiating strategy, don't you think?"

"Oh, come on, Stewie. You been watching gangster movies lately, learning how to act like you've got balls?"

Stewart almost smiled. "I don't need balls. I have a gun."

"You don't scare me with that. You don't have what it takes to pull the trigger. Besides, you shoot me, you're going to bring a crowd of people running in here."

"Well, I guess that will be my problem, won't it? Since you'll be dead."

"You wouldn't," Jerry repeated, though suddenly a little more subdued.

"Not if I don't have to." Stewart turned to Gwen. "Gwen, search him. Pay close attention to his pockets. Shoes and socks off, Messner. Pretend you're at the airport."

Gwen obeyed him automatically, her mind trying to process the situation. Stewart and Jerry knew each other. Stewart was holding a gun. Her mind couldn't accept the obvious conclusion that the man her grandfather had trusted for over twenty years had betrayed him, betrayed them all. There had to be an explanation, she told herself. It was like having a suited king queen in her pocket. The flop and the turn and the river ought to come and convert them to a straight, into something that made sense.

Only the turn was already here, standing in front of her. And she had nothing.

She ran her fingers through Jerry's pockets, pulling out keys, a lighter, a pack of cigarettes, his cell phone—hating to touch him and wanting to get through it as quickly as possible. She put the collection on the coffee table.

"Smart enough not to have the stamps on you, not smart enough to protect yourself, huh, Jerry?" Stewart coughed and winced, holding his side.

"You're the one's going to need protection, Oakes," Jerry replied, suddenly more confident. "That ain't a cold you've got, is it? You've had visitors. What, your Swedish buddy getting impatient? Or are you running behind on the vig again?"

"Oh, Stewart," Gwen said as understanding began to dawn. "You said you had stopped."

"Yeah, old Stewie's gotten his nuts in a vise, haven't you, Stewie?" Jerry taunted. "Mr. High Roller here can't play poker for shit and he doesn't know when to say enough. So you can't kill me, can you? You can't afford not to have those stamps." The cockiness was back in full force. "So why don't we just cut the crap and talk about when I'm going to see my money."

Stewart looked at the pile of objects on the coffee table.

"Keep going, Gwen," he said quietly. "The jacket."

Jerry stiffened.

As soon as Gwen patted his breast pocket, she knew. The envelope felt stiff and just thick enough. She slid it out and stepped away from Jerry. Hardly daring to breathe, she opened up the flap—

And stared at the upside down airplanes of the inverted Jennys, rising and falling across the block. And in front, shimmering in glassine, was the rich blue of the two-penny Post Office Mauritius, the white profile of the monarch looking imperious and just a bit amused.

After all that had passed, here they were in her hands. She began to flip through to check the contents of the envelope. The Ben Franklins and the Columbians were gone, she knew that. She frowned.

"The red-orange Post Office Mauritius won't be there," Stewart told her matter-of-factly, "and whatever this idiot fenced from the store inventory. But the rest should be there."

"What do you mean, the red-orange Mauritius will be gone?"

"He means I gave it to him before I realized he was trying to stiff me and he's sent it off to his friend," Jerry put in.

"Not now, Jerry."

"Why not?" Jerry glared at Stewart. "You gonna shoot me?" He turned back to Gwen. "Old Stewie here got himself in a hole in Vegas, the kind of hole that takes a loan to get out of. I see it happen to losers like him all the time. You get a little bit of money and it costs a whole lot—and it costs more all the time. And once they own you, you stay owned. Unless they sell you. Is that what happened with your Swedish friend?"

Stewart's face looked gray and sweaty, tight with strain. "That was a legitimate business deal."

"Legitimate, my ass. These guys are connected and they sell information. Anyone got a paper on Stewie Oakes? And they flick the right lever and you dance."

"It would all have worked out if Hugh had sold," Stewart said, looking at Gwen. "Everything would have been fine. The commission I was going to make on the sale was enough. It would have taken care of…my problems." His jaw tensed. "But no, he's just so damned stubborn."

"He wasn't ready to sell yet, Stewart. And he wants to go to auction."

"Poor Stewie, no deal," Jerry said sardonically. "Too bad you already spent the finder's fee on keeping your knees intact." Stewart looked sharply at him. "Come on, don't be surprised—I know people in this town, I check jobs out before I take 'em. I'd be careful if you're thinking about taking your Swedish friend for a ride, though. I got a feeling he might take care of you good if you try. He sounds like the kind of guy who'll make sure you don't even notice your knees anymore. And it'll serve you right, chiseling me out of my cut," he finished bitterly.

"So you blew your commission on a gambling debt so you didn't have it to refund when Grampa wouldn't sell," Gwen said, putting the pieces together. "And then you went to Jerry."

"If Hugh had been insured, no one would have gotten hurt." Stewart's voice was barely audible. "I never meant it to work out this way. You have to believe me."

"We're all crying for you, Stew," Jerry sneered.

Stewart glared at Jerry. His eyes hardened. "Yes, well, since I have the stamps and you don't have the money, I guess some crying is in order." He turned his eyes to Gwen. "Gwen, bring me the envelope."

"Don't do it," Jerry snapped.

Stewart's voice was flat and cold. "Gwen…"

It all happened so quickly. She took a step toward Stewart, then Jerry's hand gripped her arm like a tourniquet as he spun her around. "Don't you give 'em to that rat bastard!" he yelled.

And then his voice was drowned out by the loudest sound Gwen had ever heard.

When she recovered her senses, Jerry was lying on the floor, his shoulder a mass of raw red.

Gwen stared at Stewart in horror. His eyes blinked rapidly.

"Oh, my god," he said faintly. "Oh, my god."

It was as though time had stopped. She couldn't blink, couldn't stop seeing Jerry, the torn flesh, the blood. She could hear him groaning softly. Then she looked back at Stewart, the man who had been her bridge to civilization, the man who had betrayed her grandfather.

The man who had just shot a person.

"He's still alive," she said, her voice sounding very far away to her own ears. "We've got to get him to a hospital."

Stewart looked down at Jerry, then back to her. "I still need the stamps," he said in a quiet, breathless voice.

"Stewart, he's going to die if we don't get him to a doctor!"

"You don't understand," Stewart continued. "It's so much money, more money than I could ever hope to pay."

"Stewart…"

"No," he said, the strength returning to his voice. "Bring me the stamps."

Gwen's heart was beating like a trip-hammer. Her gaze shifted wildly around the room—to the door beyond Stewart that might as well have been a million miles away, to the bar she'd hidden behind a few nights before.

The bar that couldn't protect her now.

On the television behind the coffee table the game went on. How inconsequential it seemed now. When she'd been sitting at the table, everything had been so simple, she thought, watching the dealer lay down the flop on the green baize. Watch the cards, watch Jerry. Get the stamps back. Now, in minutes, everything had all changed.

"Gwen, bring me the envelope," Stewart repeated.

The dealer laid down the turn. The camera panned up to show the players at the table, to reveal that their number had been reduced yet again.

Del was gone.

Hope vaulted through her.

"Gwen." There was a warning in Stewart's voice.

"I can't do that, Stewart." If she could stall for time, maybe she'd have a chance. "I can't do that to my grandfather. You know he loves you like a son? He wanted to pass on his business to you."

"No, he didn't." Stewart's faced screwed up in disgust. "I left because it was clear he was going to pass it on to you. All the years I spent working with him and suddenly I didn't count. Blood is thicker than water."

"Then you know why I can't give you these stamps—even though you were almost like family." Gwen did her best to force a smile onto her face. "You know how much it meant to me for you to teach me all those things about life in America, to help me to become a normal person here?"

Stewart's face softened. "Gwennie, don't…"

"It's true," she continued as soothingly as she could. "In many ways I owe my happiness to you."

"But you don't understand," Stewart said, almost pleading. "I have to have those stamps."

"I can't give them to you."

"Then I'll have to take them." Beads of sweat sprang out on his forehead. "I'm sorry, Gwen. You have no idea how sorry. I tried to scare you away. But you're like a pit bull, you just wouldn't give up."

"The guy who jumped me, the room search—you were behind that?"

"I hoped it would push you away, but you just stuck with it. And now I don't have a choice."

"Of course you do."

"No, I don't." Stewart raised the gun and pointed it squarely at Gwen's chest. "Now give me those stamps."

And for the second time a loud sound boomed through the room.

"Security!" someone shouted and pounded on the door again. Stewart's attention flickered.

And Gwen saw her moment.

It happened in a fraction of a second that seemed to last forever. Her leap toward him, the feel of his arm as she thrust up the gun, the shot that shattered the window.

And the form of Del leaping through the opened door.

Suddenly they were all on the floor as the gun went skittering across the carpet, coming to rest under the bed. Stewart scrambled after it on all fours and Gwen grasped desperately at his arm while Del jumped on him, slamming his fist into the back of Stewart's head. Then there was another body on top of them and she was trapped in a maelstrom of flailing arms and legs. Gwen rolled away to see Stewart fighting wildly with Del and the security man Ahmanson. She crawled quickly to the bed.

With a strength born of panic, Stewart broke loose and swung at Del, catching his jaw. His arms surged toward Del's neck and gripped.

"Stop right there." Gwen's voice shook a bit, but the hand that held the gun on him was steady. "Give it up, Stewart, it's over."

"AND THEN DEL AND AHMANSON came in," Gwen finished, looking at the young police officer who was taking her statement. Stewart had already been cuffed and hauled off; Jerry was in an ambulance on the way to the hospital. Del was giving a statement elsewhere. In the end she'd told them about the stamps, partly because the envelope was there in the middle of the room and partly because she hadn't a clue how to go about tracking down the one-penny Post Office Mauritius. This time she really did need professional help.

"We're booking him down at the station, but you're going to need to come down to the security area in the casino to press charges, ma'am," a young officer with eyes far too old for his face told her.

Gwen nodded. "Just give me a couple minutes and I'll be there," she promised. She was exhausted enough to fall over. Instead she walked out into the concierge area by the elevators.

And saw Del waiting for her on a couch.

She crossed to him and sat. "How are you doing?" he asked.

She nodded. "Fine. They're going to charge Stewart with attempted murder, assault with a deadly weapon and anything else they can think of. I'm sure Jerry will be eager to hang it all on Stewart, but I doubt he'll be looking forward to leaving the hospital himself."

"Do they know where the other stamp is?"

"They mentioned some Swedish guy—a collector, I think. Stewart's clammed up about it. From what they said before you came, it sounds like Stewart owed money to some leg breakers and just about the time they were getting serious about hurting him, the collector came asking if he could get my grandfather to sell the Post Office Mauritius pair."

"Those stamps are hard to find, I take it?"

"Almost impossible. All but two or three are in museums. Stewart figured it was a slam dunk because my grandfather was retiring, so he got ahead of himself and used the down payment to pay off the leg breakers. Then my grandfather said no."

"Oops."

"Exactly. Stewart knew Rennie from when he used to go to Reno and when he saw her in Vegas one weekend, he figured she might help him out. Enter Jerry." She shrugged. "You know the rest."

"All but who the collector is."

"I've got some guesses, but I want to wait and see if Stewart says anything." But why were they talking about what didn't matter now? What she needed to say was how she'd felt when she'd known he was coming, when she'd seen him hurtle through the door and she'd felt not only relief but a rush of recognition, connection, rightness.

He stared ahead a moment, a muscle jumping in his jaw. "You don't know what it did to me to come through that door and see him with the gun," he said at last.

"There aren't any words to thank you for today. You saved my life." And it made her tremble a bit to know the words were true. "If you hadn't been there, I don't know what would have happened."

"When I watched Jerry walk away from the table, it scared the hell out of me. All I could think was that you might be up in the room and he might hurt you."

"And you walked away from the tournament. God, Del, two million dollars."

He brushed it off as he might an annoying fly. "Gwen,

you could have been hurt, killed. Who cares about the tournament? You were all that mattered," he said softly. "You still are."

She swallowed. "Last night—"

"Last night we both said a lot of things. But not the really important stuff."

"I love you, Del. I know this isn't the time or place to say it, but I do and you should know that."

He stared at her. "God, Gwen, I don't—"

The elevator doors opened to arguing. Pete Kellar walked into the lobby, arguing with an officer. "Hey, I got a press pass. I'm coming through to meet with a colleague." He walked up to Del. "Hey, Redmond. Brother, you look like shit. The guy caught you with one, huh?"

Del's eyes iced over. "What are you doing here, Kellar?"

"Hey, gotta get the story. I heard it on the police band. I figure with an exclusive interview with you, this is going to be killer." He shoved his pocket recorder in front of Gwen. "So, you part of this? You the one with the stamps or you just helping him out?"

"Kellar." Something flinty and cold and absolutely dangerous looked out of Del's eyes. "You've got exactly one second to put that thing away before I put your nose through the back of your skull."

Kellar backpedaled. "Hey, you got no call to talk like that. I'm just doing my job. I've only got a coupla hours to get the story done."

Del stared at him.

"Hey, this could be front page in the Vegas paper, maybe even make the *Globe* or get picked up on the AP." He gave Del a look of disdain. "Come on, buddy, you're a reporter. You can't stand in the way of a story, particularly not one like this."

Del stared at him, then nodded slowly. "Okay. Five minutes, then we talk."

"Yeah? Cool." Kellar bounced a little on his toes. "Okay, I'll just wait for you out here." He gave a little wave and left.

IT WAS LIKE CLIFF DIVING HE'D done in high school from the bluffs of La Jolla—knowing what he had to do, scared as hell of what it meant, but still making himself take that step. And then flying through space, hoping to god that he'd do it right.

Gwen stared at him, her face paper-white, her eyes enormous. "What are you thinking?" she whispered.

Watching her, he felt as though he'd been gut-punched himself. "I have to work with him, Gwen."

"What, because of some fraternal secret-handshake thing? The Loyal Order of Reporters? I tell you I love you and you want to violate me in the papers with that guy?" Her words dripped with loathing.

"It's not like that," he told her steadily.

"Then what's it like?"

"Gwen, I have to do this story." He took her hands in his. "I don't have a choice. *We* don't."

She yanked them away. "Funny, that's exactly what Stewart said when he was holding a gun on me."

That one got to him. "Gwen, this story is going to happen no matter what. If I work with Kellar, I can spin it in the way that hurts you least. If I'm not a part of it, he's going to dig deep, because he's young, he's ambitious and he wants to move onto the main paper."

"And, of course, you don't have any ambitions at all, right? Nothing that a story like this would help?" Gwen rose and walked blindly toward the elevators.

"Gwen, wait."

"I don't need to hear any more, Del. You want to do this, fine, but don't sit there trying to justify it and make it all right, because it's not."

"Just listen to me."

"No!" She spun to face him, eyes burning with fury and betrayal. "I won't. You said just trust me before and I did and then I found out that you sold me out the first time. And then, dummy me, I fall for your line again. 'Gwen, you're all that matters,'" she mocked. "How *dare* you?"

He looked at her helplessly. She wasn't playing a role this time. This wasn't Nina doing the dirty work. This was Gwen in full righteous fury and there was no way to reach her. "Gwen, think about this for a second," he said softly. "I don't want this to be the end."

For a moment something utterly vulnerable looked out of her eyes and then was gone, supplanted by anger. "Just stay the hell away from me, Redmond. Stay the hell away."

# 23

GWEN SAT AT HER DESK IN THE familiar confines of her office and lifted up a bright vermillion stamp with a pair of tongs. She didn't inspect it, though. Mostly she stared into space.

She'd been doing that a lot since she'd come back from Las Vegas. Ever since Kellar's story had appeared in the metro section of the *Globe*. If it hadn't been as detailed as she'd feared, it still reported the basics of the theft.

It was missing a lot of the details of the case that would have gotten the media excited.

And it was missing Del's byline.

It had been picked up by the AP wire and, she'd heard, the *Los Angeles Times*. Then again, Stewart's fall was the talk of the stamp world. She'd fielded phone calls for a while, but not as many as she'd anticipated, and her grandfather hadn't found out. Without the sensational splash, the run she'd feared hadn't materialized. So far, so good.

If waking every morning feeling as if she'd had her heart cut out could be called good.

If she focused on the details, things were infinitely better than they'd been before she went to Vegas. All but one of the issues were back in their appropriate slots, the burgundy albums safely tucked away in a bank vault. Insurance now protected the store inventory. No more would they be vulnerable to theft. She was back in familiar surroundings, back in her own clothes, back in her old life.

So why couldn't she relax and be comfortable with plain old Gwen again?

So why couldn't she forget?

The phone rang. It was the San Francisco police inspector assigned to her case. "I just wanted to let you know, we're going to have to drop the investigation into the Swede."

"But he's still got one of the stamps."

"We think that, but we don't know it. If he does, it goes under international jurisdiction."

"But he's got something worth more than a million dollars," she said a little desperately.

"Or someone does. This whole Swedish thing may be an invention, something Oakes cooked up to tell Messner. Maybe he just wanted them to sell himself."

"He wouldn't have done that to my grandfather."

A world of disillusionment went into his sigh. "You'd be surprised what people will do for money."

Maybe he was right. Gwen wanted to think that Stewart had been desperate and frightened and grasping at the only out he could find. She didn't want to think the theft was calculated purely for his gain.

Just as she hadn't wanted to think that Del had calculatedly given her up for a news story. And how gullible did that make her, since she had proof of both of their treachery?

"What does Stewart say?"

"He says he never met or saw the guy, just dealt with an intermediary, and he had no fixed contact information for him. We've got no trail. We couldn't follow it even if we had the jurisdiction."

"So you don't do anything?"

"On the missing stamp, no. Let Interpol look into it. Maybe they'll take it on. On Oakes, you bet. Las Vegas has got him cold on the assault and we've got him on the con-spiracy charges—Messner's so ticked at being double-crossed and shot that he hasn't stopped talking yet. Oakes will definitely do time."

"How about Jerry?"

"There, I'm not so sure. His shoulder will heal. He's got a deal with the D.A., probably to plead to a lesser charge, es-pecially since nearly all of the property has been recovered."

"Except for the million dollars," she said, discouraged.

"Except that," he agreed. "I understand your frustration, but it's more important to put away the guys who wave guns around than the small-timers like Messner. You can always file a civil suit against them both to try to recover damages. See if you can get some of Messner's tournament winnings."

Yeah, right. Good luck. She didn't even want to think about lawyers and lawsuits just yet. "So it's in our laps."

"For a lawsuit, yes." His voice hardened. "Don't even think about trying to pull your detective stunt again to get the other one, though. You got lucky this time, but you could have wound up with a bullet in your brain."

If it hadn't been for Del, she probably would have. Did she regret taking the chances—with Jerry, with Stewart? With Del? *No,* she thought. It was the living with it that was the hard part. "You're right, Inspector," she sighed. "I ap-preciate everything you've done. Thanks for filling me in."

Some things were easily cleaned up, she thought as she hung up the phone.

And some things weren't.

She was doing better these days. She managed rou-tinely to go as much as thirty seconds at a time without thinking about Del. It would get longer as time went by, and maybe someday she'd get over this hollow feeling.

Maybe someday she'd get over him.

It was just the contrast, she told herself, all that excitement, then going back to her quiet life. She wasn't comfortable anymore as just Gwen, but she wasn't Nina, either. She didn't know who she was. She hung Nina's clothes in her closet and found herself sprinkling the garments into her normal wardrobe. Joss did a double take the first time but didn't say anything.

It was the glamour, the adrenaline rush. Del was just part of what she associated with it all, that was why she couldn't stop thinking about him. It had only been two weeks, after all. Sooner or later she'd forget.

In the meantime it helped to be busy.

Joss walked into the room. "I've closed everything up."

Gwen nodded, concentrating on her stamp.

"That means it's the end of the day," Joss told her. "You know, as in quitting time? When normal people go home and have dinner and relax?"

"I'm going to stay and finish some things up. You go along."

Instead Joss plunked down into a chair. "Earth to Gwen. Working yourself to death isn't going to make it go away."

"What do you mean?" Gwen asked with forced casualness.

"You've been at it until nine or ten at night since you got back from Vegas. It's not like this is brain surgery. There isn't that much work to do here." She looked at Gwen sympathetically. "But then, it's not about work, is it?"

Gwen blinked. "I miss him, Joss. I shouldn't. I know it's stupid and I know he screwed me over, but I can't get him out of my head." Her eyes filled and she blinked furiously.

"It's okay to be upset."

"No, it's not." She wiped her eyes. "I figured being back here would help. You know, same old, same old." Settle back into her familiar routines, pretend that whirlwind of Vegas had happened to someone else.

She'd been wrong.

She missed it. She missed the tournament. She missed Roxy, who she'd never even congratulated on her second tournament win.

And she missed Del most of all.

"I keep thinking I'm going to run into him somewhere. It makes me afraid to go out." And it made her wonder, every street she walked down, every restaurant and store she entered, whether she'd see him, whether he'd been there. He haunted her everywhere she went.

He was going to for a long time.

DEL WALKED INTO THE UNION Square station of the Muni Metro, working his way around the rush-hour crowd. He walked up to the newsstand, scanning the magazines. There was a time he'd have read the *Globe* during his commute, but no more. All the paper was for him now was a reminder of all that had gone wrong.

He hadn't worked on the story after all, pleading involvement. Talking to Jessup hadn't gotten the story spiked, but it had pushed it to a small item on an inside page. He'd done what he could.

He didn't know when or if Gwen would understand. And he couldn't really blame her. Circumstances didn't matter. If he hadn't brought the original story idea to Jessup, none of this would have been put in motion. The gunshot might have wound up as a small item in the Las Vegas paper, if even that.

No matter how you stacked it up, he was at fault.

In the end he'd turned down the news job that Jessup had offered him. The cost, quite simply, had been too high. But it was more than that. Maybe he wasn't cut out for hard

news. He liked investigating, but he couldn't maintain quite
the remove from his subjects, he didn't think.

Certainly he hadn't when it had come to Gwen.

Regret twisted viciously in his gut. To have lost her was
impossible, but to have lost her over a job that he now knew
he didn't want was worse.

He now stared at the bright colors of the magazine covers. *Vanity Fair, Esquire, Harper's*—those magazines carried the kinds of stories that interested him. News but with
depth. He wanted to get to know his subjects, not to be pre-
cluded from identifying with them. He wanted his insights
to be a part of the story. He picked up *Vanity Fair* and
flipped to an article on a lynching in the 1960s South.
Then he stopped.

If these were the kinds of stories he wanted to do, why not
pursue the magazines? It was all here before him, he realized,
a chance to pursue the deeper, edgier stories that interested
him with the depth he craved. He could keep writing for the
newspaper and develop the magazine writing as a side career.

He handed the magazine to the cashier. Time to go home
and start making some phone calls. It wouldn't be easy, he
knew that, but with his track record he was confident he
could get his foot in the door. Once he had a clip with one
magazine, he could nudge his way into others. It wouldn't
be easy, but it would be his, it would be something he'd
made happen on his own.

Now if only he could make things right with Gwen as
easily.

SUNDAYS WERE ABOUT ROUTINE, blessed routine. A long,
lazy brunch at her little local café on Russian Hill that put
tables outside when the weather was nice. The Sunday
crossword with her orange juice. There was some small
comfort in sameness, even if leisure time had become

something to avoid. She'd stick grimly to her tradition and trust that eventually the pleasure would return.

"Pass me the comics, would you?" Joss asked, a piece of toast in her hand.

The morning sun was surprisingly warm on Gwen's shoulders—at least, by San Francisco standards. It was nothing compared to the baking heat of Las Vegas, though. She blocked the thought almost as soon as she had it. Las Vegas meant the tournament, and the tournament meant Del.

Gwen picked through the paper for the funnies, avoiding the sports page as she had ever since she returned from Vegas. She was having a reasonably good morning. The last thing she needed to do was see Del's picture above his column. These were the little tricks she'd found to help her get through the day. Avoid Las Vegas, avoid the *Globe,* but she was damned if she was going to give up the Sunday paper.

Joss took the comics from her with a sigh. "I missed this so much in Africa, the funnies every week."

"Me, too."

"Mom says it was the crossword puzzle for her."

Gwen fished out the *Globe* magazine that carried the puzzle. "That's my favorite part."

"See, you're more like her than you thought. You're more like me than you thought, too."

Gwen looked at Joss in surprise. "How do you figure?"

"Looks like a little of your alter ego rubbed off on you when you were out in Vegas. You're different since you came back."

"I am not," Gwen protested, but she knew it was true.

"I always wondered if you were really as quiet as you've always acted. About time you let that side of you out."

But what had been the cost, Gwen wondered as she flipped through the magazine, looking for the crossword. And found instead a photo that dragged her back to the final table at the tournament. It was a picture during play, a picture of all of them—Jerry sulking in his best poker-brat style, Roxy peeking at her hole cards, Gwen tossing forward a stack of chips. And Del.

And Del.

All In, read the headline. Life, Love and Tournament Play in Vegas. The author was Del Redmond.

His jaw was set, his face sober. His hair poked up in spiky disorder. And the silver lenses of his sunglasses reflected Gwen's face.

"She said her name was Nina," the article began. Palms damp, Gwen read on. When she reached the end, she blinked. The article had not, as she'd feared, been about the stamps. It hadn't even identified her, only mentioned Nina.

In the end poker is a little like life and a lot like love. You never know what's in the pocket cards of the person you're facing. Not unless you go all in. And when you do that, you hope to god you haven't totally misjudged the situation and lost everything. Because it can happen. I'm here to tell you it can happen. But sometimes, sometimes, you get it just right and the big risk gets you the big win.

The ones that haunt you, though, are the big losses. Those are the hands you play over and over in your head in the wee, wee hours when everything around you is still. Those are the hands you'd do anything in the world to have a chance to play again.

She said her name was Nina. I never got a chance to tell her I was sorry.

Gwen laid the magazine down on the table. "My god," she said faintly. "I've got to find him."

"SPORTS SECTION," ANSWERED A clipped man's voice.

"I'm looking for Del Redmond," Gwen said.

"He doesn't work on Sundays."

"Do you happen to know where I might find him? This is a friend of his from the tournament."

"Who from the tournament?" the guy asked suspiciously.

"Nina."

"Well." The voice was freighted with speculation. "I wish I could give you his number, but I can't."

"Could you call him and give him mine?"

The guy thought a moment. "Tell you what. He's doing his weekend radio show today. You could go down to the studio, maybe catch him afterward."

It was all she needed. Just a chance and a chance now. She couldn't wait.

GWEN SAT IN THE LOBBY OF THE radio station, watching the receptionist file her nails and listening to the current host trading badinage with a caller. Del's show was long over. Now she just waited patiently and tried not to scream.

The studio door opened and Del came out, laughing with another guy. There was that grin that had first stolen her heart, that devilment in his eyes. For a minute her heart just swelled. Then he caught sight of her and stopped. For a moment all he did was look, hope flickering over his face. He turned to his companion. "Hey, I'll see you later, man." They shook and he walked toward Gwen.

She rose. "Hello," she said stiffly. Now that she was here, all the words had dried up in her throat. When she'd been reading the article, she'd known what came next. Now she hadn't a clue.

"Hey." There was an awkward pause. "Big fan of sports radio?"

"I knew you were here. I saw the article in the Sunday magazine," she blurted. "I had to talk with you."

He nodded at that. "Talk works." As though remembering they had an audience, he looked around. "How 'bout we get out of here, then grab a cup of coffee?"

Outside on the street she felt as if she could breathe again.

Del sighed and thrust his hands in his pockets. "So, Kellar's article wasn't bad enough, you wanted to know why I wrote another one?"

"No, that's not it," she replied. "It was a nice article."

He looked at her, eyes direct. "I screwed up, Gwen, plain and simple. I know apologies don't mean much, but I wish there was some way to let you truly understand how sorry I am about the way things worked out."

"I'm sorry about the way I acted, too. I'm sorry about how all of it came out."

"I didn't work with Kellar on the story."

She nodded. "I saw."

"I tried to get them not to do it, but the best I could manage was convincing the editor it wasn't worth the full treatment."

"It wasn't as bad as I thought it might be. I think I have you to thank for that."

"It wasn't enough, but it was all I could do."

"It was more than I deserved." She paused. "Did you get the job?"

"I told Jessup I didn't want it."

*"What?"*

He shrugged. "I'm looking for magazine work. I think that's going to be a better fit for me."

She couldn't stop the smile from coming. "After reading your article, I bet you'll do a great job."

"Look." He stared into her eyes. "I meant what I said about the mistakes that keep me up at night. I fell in love with you in Las Vegas, Gwen." She caught her breath, but he pushed on. "I screwed it up and it's all I've been able to think about. I should never have said all those things to you about Nina. You're perfect just the way you are and I have missed you so much."

She moistened her lips. "I changed in Las Vegas."

"Maybe we both did." He reached out and brushed his fingers along her jaw. "I'm just sorry. And I'm sorry about the news story. It was a bad hand. I should have just gone out rather than play it the way I did."

"Well—" she gave an awkward laugh "—that game's over."

"Maybe we should open another," he said, watching her closely. "Start with a fresh deck, deal out a new hand."

"Okay, let's do that." Gwen stepped in and put her arms around his neck. "I'm all in."

His eyes came alive. "You mean it?"

"Weren't you the one who said that going all in was the only way to win big?"

"Only if you can get someone to match you."

"And are you going to?"

He pulled her to him and fused his mouth to hers. Then he raised his head and laughed. "You bet."

\* \* \* \* \*

*Turn the page for a sneak peek*
*at Joss's story...*
*Coming in Blaze August 2005!*

# 1

"HEY, GWEN, I'M GOING TO HAVE wild sex on a jetliner today." Joss Chastain sprawled on one of the chairs in the back office of her grandfather's stamp store, coffee in one hand and the newspaper in the other.

Her sister, Gwen, blond and poised behind her desk, merely raised an eyebrow as she sat on hold. "And here I didn't know you were going on a trip."

"It says so right here," Joss said, pointing to her horoscope. "'Love and romance are in the air. Travel likely. Big dreams will come true if you leap for the stars.' And yours says, let's see…oh, yeah, 'hunky, adoring sportswriter will sweep you out for dinner and wild sex in his marina condo afterward.'"

"You don't say. Horoscopes have gotten a lot more interesting lately."

"So has your life," Joss observed, pointing to the head shot of Gwen's new boyfriend smiling out at them from the sports page of the newspaper.

Gwen grinned, then snapped to attention as someone apparently came on the line. "Yes, Agent Lechere, this is Gwen Chastain of Chastain Philatelic Investments. I'd like to talk with you about the theft of my grandfather's stamp." She gave him the case number.

Joss listened for a few minutes, then abandoned the effort. Better to wait until all was said and done and Gwen could fill her in. In the meantime she took a sip of latte and stared at the print on the paper.

*Big dreams will come true if you leap for the stars.*

Or maybe not. After seven years of leaping for the stars in her music career, she'd finally fallen to earth with a resounding thud. Four bands, four breakups, a résumé dotted with gigs at bars and small clubs around the Pacific northwest. Along with the magic shows, it had paid the bills, but not much more than that. At twenty-six, she wasn't one step closer than she'd been at nineteen. At twenty-six, she didn't have a cent to her name. Maybe it was time to admit that she wasn't going to find the lucky confluence of circumstances that was going to let her perform for a living.

At twenty-six, maybe it was time to look for something else.

All things considered, she was probably lucky that the most recent band implosion had taken place in San Francisco, home of her sister, her grandparents and her grandfather's investment stamp business. After all, it was a place to stay and a place to work while her grandparents went on their three-month tour of the South Pacific. For a few weeks she'd fought the inevitable restlessness and worked to get on her feet.

And then everything had gone to hell in a handbasket.

"Dammit."

Joss jumped at the sound of Gwen slamming down the receiver in the cradle. "You've gotten louder since you came back from Vegas, that's for sure. What's up?"

"Interpol," Gwen said, investing the word with an immense amount of disgust. "They're dropping the investigation of the one-penny Mauritius." Her voice rose in anger. "A million-dollar stamp, one of the rarest in the world, and they're just giving up the investigation."

"How can they drop the case? I thought you knew who had the stamp."

"I have a theory, even a name, but apparently that's not enough."

"They're investigators, aren't they? Can't they figure it out?"

Gwen dragged her hands through her hair. "They don't believe the story. Jerry was the one who mentioned the Swedish collector when Stewart was holding a gun on us in Vegas."

Joss closed her eyes against the image of her little sister trying to regain the stolen stamps, going up against a thief and the mastermind of the theft at the same time. "Of course, Jerry could have just cooked up the story to make Stewart look bad."

"That's what Interpol's saying. It doesn't make sense to me, not the way they were talking that night in the hotel room. I mean, Jerry says he stole the stamps for Stewart because Stewart had a client who wanted them—the collector. It makes sense that Stewart might have slipped and said too much to him. They were buddies."

Joss gave her a wry look. "Is that why they're testifying against one another?"

"I think Jerry took it kind of personally that Stewart shot him."

"Sensitive. So Interpol doesn't believe that Jerry's Swedish collector is the same guy who tried to buy the two Mauritius stamps from Grampa?"

Gwen nodded.

"But Jerry stole a lot of stamps from Grampa's collection and the store inventory."

"The store inventory he was doing on his own. The stamps from Grampa's collection were for Stewart, who was supplying them to the collector."

"The one you think you know and the police don't believe you about."

"Karl Silverhielm. He's got a reputation for being obsessive and he's been after the Post Office Mauritius pair for the last five years."

It mystified her that anyone could be that hung up on little squares of colored paper. "What's the big deal about these stamps, anyway?"

"There are two of them—the one-penny and the two-penny Mauritius. Only the two-penny stamp is blue—the Blue Mauritius. The one-penny is a kind of a red-orange. I keep forgetting you never saw them."

"So why does anyone care?"

"They're over a hundred and sixty years old, for one thing, and they're the result of an error. They've got a story. They were printed by an island printer when the local post office ran out of stamps. The postmaster asked him to print *Post Paid* on them, but when he got around to printing he couldn't remember what the postmaster had said, so he put *Post Office* on them instead."

"And that's what all the fuss is about?" Joss shook her head in amazement. "You collector types."

"Not me, Silverhielm—who's been after a Post Office Mauritius pair for years. He pushed Grampa hard to sell them, but Grampa didn't like his offer. The thing is, they're worth more as a pair than separately. Grampa might have gotten as much as three million dollars for them when he was ready to start auctioning them off."

"Nice little chunk for retirement."

Gwen shrugged. "He might love stamps, but he's also a savvy investor. Why invest in something like stocks that he knows nothing about when he could invest in top-quality stamps instead?"

"Except that it's not so easy to stick stocks in your

pocket and walk away with them the way Jerry did with the stamps."

"Our bad luck," Gwen told her.

Joss stared moodily into her coffee cup. "My screwup, more like it. It kills me to think about Grampa and Grandma coming back from their South Pacific trip to news like that."

"Hey, we retrieved almost every one, remember?"

"*You* retrieved almost every one." Joss picked a quarter up off the desk and began rolling it in her fingers. "So why is Interpol dropping it? Did you tell them about Silverhielm?"

Gwen nodded. "They say they've done some investigation and can't find out anything about it. They don't have anything further to follow up on. They can't just search his house."

"I suppose not, but have they interviewed Stewart?"

"He doesn't know anything."

"Or won't say." Joss tipped her head consideringly. "Why don't you try talking to him? He might tell you."

"I don't think he knows anything. And even if he did, what am I going to do—fly to Stockholm and camp out on Silverhielm's front porch?"

"Isn't that international stamp expo in Stockholm next week?"

"Yes, but I've got the court dates with Jerry and Stewart. I can't go."

"No, but I could. Remember? *Travel is likely.*"

"Don't be ridiculous, Joss."

"Why is that ridiculous? You did it." A chance, she thought, a chance to make things right.

"I went to Las Vegas. This is Stockholm. You don't even speak the language," Gwen said in exasperation.

"I'll find someone who does. Hell, I'll hire a translator. Look, Gwen, all of this was my fault."

"It was both of our faults."

Joss shook her head. "If I hadn't left Jerry in the store with access to the safe, he'd never have taken all of Grampa's stamps and we wouldn't be in this pickle to begin with."

"I should never have hired him."

"Which you did because of me." In an instant it had gone from a passing thought to something Joss wanted passionately. Needed passionately.

"Even if we lose the stamp, it's not a complete loss. We got most of them back."

"*You* got most of them back. I just sat around doing nothing." And it had rankled at her every minute. "I want my chance to make it right, Gwen. You already had yours."

"And I almost got killed for it, remember? It's too risky, Joss."

"So I'll get some help," she said impatiently.

"Like who?"

"I don't know," she snapped. "I'll call my friend Richard, the promoter at Avalon."

"A music promoter's going to be able to go with you to Stockholm and get stolen property back from a criminal?"

"Why not? A sportswriter helped you. Look, Richard knows this town pretty well. He might be able to point me to someone who could work with me."

Gwen gave her a skeptical look. "This isn't just about having sex on an airplane, is it?"

Joss laughed. "Who am I to look a gift horse in the mouth?"

# Blaze

## HARLEQUIN® Blaze™

### Where were you when the lights went out?

Shane Walker was seducing his best friend in:

## #194 NIGHT MOVES
### by Julie Kenner  July 2005

Adam and Mallory were rekindling
the flames of first love in:

## #200 WHY NOT TONIGHT?
### by Jacquie D'Alessandro  August 2005

Simon Thackery was professing his love...
to his best friend's fiancée in:

## #206 DARING IN THE DARK
### by Jennifer LaBrecque  September 2005

### 24 Hours:
### BLACKOUT

If you enjoyed what you just read,
then we've got an offer you can't resist!

# Take 2 bestselling love stories FREE!

# Plus get a FREE surprise gift!

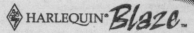

# *Blaze*

**HARLEQUIN® *Blaze*™**

*New York Times* bestselling author

# Elizabeth Bevarly

answers the question

## Can men and women have sex and still be friends?

with

# INDECENT SUGGESTION
### Blaze #189

Best friends Becca and Turner try hypnosis
to kick their smoking habit...instead, they get
the uncontrollable urge to burn up the sheets!
Doesn't that make them more than friends?

**Be sure to catch this funny,
sexy story available in July 2005!**

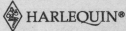

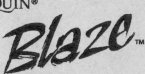

## COMING NEXT MONTH

### #189 INDECENT SUGGESTION Elizabeth Bevarly
It's supposed to help them stop smoking. But the hypnosis session Turner McCloud and Becca Mercer attend hasn't worked. They're lighting up even more. What a waste! Or is it? Since then, the just-friends couple has become a bed-buddy couple—they can't keep their hands off each other. In fact, it's so hot between them, why didn't they do this years ago? It's almost as if they've had some subliminal persuasion....

### #190 SEXY ALL OVER Jamie Sobrato
She's going to dress up this bad boy in sheep's clothing. Naomi Tyler is the image consultant hired to tone down reporter Zane Underwood's rebel—and sexy—style. Too bad Zane is unwilling to change. Since her career depends on making him over, she's prepared to do whatever it takes…even if it means some sensual persuading from her!

### #191 TEXAS FEVER Kimberly Raye
Holly Faraday, owner of Sweet & Sinful gourmet desserts, is thrilled to learn she's inherited her grandmother's place in small Romeo, Texas. That is, until she learns that her grandmother was the local madam—and the townspeople are hoping she'll continue the family business. And once she meets her neighbor, sexy Josh McGraw, she's tempted....

### #192 THE FAVOR Cara Summers
*Risking It All*
Professor Sierra Gibbs didn't realize a speed date could lead to a thrilling adventure. Was it that earth-shattering kiss from sexy Ryder Kane that set her heart pumping? Or the fact that somebody's trying to kill her? Either way, Sierra's feeling free for the first time in her life… and she's going to enjoy every minute of it. She's going to make sure Ryder enjoys it, too....

### #193 ALMOST NAKED, INC. Karen Anders
Scientist Matt Fox perfects the silkiest, sexiest material ever invented, but he knows nothing about business, even less about fashion. Yet childhood friend Bridget Cole sure does—she's a hot model with all the right contacts. Soon she's got a plan to get his material into the right hands, though first she'd like to get her hands on Matt....

### #194 NIGHT MOVES Julie Kenner
*24 Hours: Blackout Bk. 1*
*When lust and love are simmering right beneath the surface, sometimes it takes only a single day to bring everything to a boil....* Shane Walker is in love with his best friend, Ella. But no matter what he does, he can't make Ella see their relationship any other way. It looks hopeless—until a city-wide blackout gives him twenty-four hours to change her mind....